THE SWISS FAMILY
ROBINSON

Johann Wyss

OTHER TITLES IN THIS SERIES

The Swiss Family Robinson

Published by Peter Haddock Ltd.
Bridlington, England. ©

Printed in Russia.

The writer to whom we are chiefly indebted for *The Swiss Family Robinson* was born at Berne in Switzerland in 1781, and eventually became professor of philosophy in his native town, where he died in 1830. The notion of the story was his father's, who, it seems, had no idea of publication; and various anonymous minds probably contributed to the story as we know it.

CONTENTS

THE
SWISS FAMILY ROBINSON

CHAPTER I

A SHIPWRECK, AND PREPARATIONS FOR DELIVERANCE

Already the tempest had continued six terrible days, and far from subsiding on the seventh, its fury seemed to increase. We had wandered so materially from the right track that not a creature on board knew where we were. The ship's company were exhausted and the courage which had hitherto sustained them now began to fail. The masts had been shivered and cast into the sea; several leaks appeared, and the ship began to fill. "My children," said I to my four boys, who clung to me in terrible alarm, "God can save us; but if He sees fit that we should not be saved, we must but rely that what He does is most for our good."

My excellent wife wiped her tears and became more tranquil and encouraged the youngest children, who were leaning on her knees.

At this moment a cry of "Land! land!" was heard through the roaring of the waves, and instantly the vessel struck; a tremendous cracking succeeded, as if the ship was going to pieces; the sea rushed in; we perceived that the vessel had grounded and could not long hold together. The captain bade the men lose not a moment in putting out the boats. The sounds fell on my heart like a blow from a dagger. " We are lost!" I exclaimed, and the children broke out into piercing cries. I then recollected myself; and addressing them again I exhorted them to courage, by observing that the water had not yet reached us, that the ship was near land, and that Providence would assist the brave. " Keep where you are," added I, " while I go and examine what is best to be done."

I left my family and went on the deck. A wave instantly threw me down and wetted me to the skin; another followed, and then another. I steadied myself as well as I could, and when I could look around a scene of terrific and complete disaster met my eyes: the ship was split in two. The ship's company crowded into the boats till they could contain not one man more, and the last who entered were now cutting the ropes to move off. I called to them to stop and receive us also, but in vain; for the roaring of the sea prevented my being heard, and the waves would have made it impossible for a boat to return. My best consolation now was to observe that the sea could not enter the ship above a certain height. The stern, under which was the cabin that enclosed all that was dear to me on earth, had been driven to a considerable height between two rocks, where it appeared fixed; at the same time, in the distance southward, I descried, through clouds and rain, several nooks of land.

Sunk and desolate from the loss of every chance for human aid, it was yet my duty to appear serene before my family. " Courage, dear ones," cried I on entering their cabin, " all is not yet lost! I will not conceal from you that the ship is aground, but we are at least in greater safety than we should be if she were beating upon the rocks: our cabin is above water, and we may yet find means to reach the land in safety."

What I had just said appeased the fears of all, for they had the habit of confiding in my assurances. My wife, however more accustomed than the children to read my inmost thoughts, perceived the anxiety which devoured me. I made her a sign which conveyed an idea of the hopelessness of our situation, and I had the consolation to see that she was resolved to support the trial with resignation.

" Let us take some nourishment," said she, " our courage will strengthen with our bodies."

Soon after the evening set in: the tempest and the waves continued their fury; the planks and beams of the vessel separated in many parts with a horrible crash. It seemed impossible for the boats to escape the raging of the storm.

In the meanwhile my dear wife had prepared our meal, and the four boys partook of it with an appetite to which their parents were strangers. They afterwards went to bed, and in a short time, were snoring soundly. Fritz, the eldest, sat up with us.

" I have been thinking," said he after a long silence, " how it may be possible to save ourselves. If we had only some bladders or cork-jackets for my mother and my brothers, you and I, Father, would soon contrive to swim to land."

" That is a good thought," said I; " we will see if we can bring it to bear this very night, for fear of the worst."

Fritz and I immediately looked about for some small empty tubs or casks, or tin canisters, large enough to float one of our children. These we fastened two and two together with handkerchiefs or towels, leaving about a foot distance between them, attaching this sort of swimming-jacket under the arms of each child, my wife at the same time preparing one for herself. We all provided ourselves with knives, some string, and other necessaries which could be put into the pocket.

Fritz, who had been up the whole of the preceding night, and was fatigued with laborious occupation, now lay down near his brothers and was soon asleep; but their mother and I, too full of anxiety to close our eyes, kept watch, listening to every sound that seemed to threaten a further change in our situation. We passed this terrible night in prayer, in agonizing apprehensions, and in forming various resolutions as to what we should next attempt. We hailed with joy the first gleam of light which shot through a small opening of the window. The raging of the winds had begun to abate, the sky was serene, and with hope swelling in my bosom I beheld the sun already tinging the horizon. Thus revived in spirit, I hastily summoned my wife and the boys to the deck.

" Now let us consider," said I, " what we had best do."

Fritz advised that we should all throw ourselves into the sea while it was calm, and swim to land. " Ah! that may be well enough for you," said Ernest, " for you can swim; but we others should soon be drowned. Would it not be better to make a float of rafts, and get to land all together upon it?"

" Very good," answered I, " if we had the means for contriving such a float, and if, after all, it were not a dangerous sort of conveyance. Come along, my boys, let each go a different way about the ship, and see what he can do to be useful, and what he can find to enable us to get away."

They now all sprang from me with eager looks to

do what I had desired. I, on my part, lost no time in examining what we had to depend upon in regard to provisions and fresh water, the principles of life. My wife and the youngest boy visited all the animals, whom they found in a pitiable condition, and nearly perishing with hunger and thirst. Fritz repaired to the ammunition chamber, Ernest to the carpenter's cabin, and Jack to the apartment of the captain. Scarcely had Jack opened the door, when two large dogs sprang joyfully upon him, and nearly suffocated the boy with their affectionate licking of his face and hands in their delight at seeing a human being once more.

By and by my little company were again assembled round me, each proud of what he had to contribute. Fritz had two fowling-pieces, some powder, and some small shot contained in horn flasks, and balls in bags. Ernest produced his hat filled with nails, and held in his hands a hatchet and a hammer; in addition, a pair of pincers, a pair of large scissors, and an auger peeped out of his pocket. Even the little six-year-old Francis carried under his arm a large box of fish-hooks.

" I, for my part," said my wife, " have brought nothing; but I have some tidings to communicate which I hope will secure my welcome. What I have to tell is, that I have found on board the ship a cow and an ass, two goats, six sheep, and a sow, all of whom I have just supplied with food and water, and I reckon on being able to preserve their lives."

" All this is admirable," said I to my little labourers, " and there is only Master Jack, who, instead of thinking of something that might be useful, has done us the favour to present us two personages, who no doubt will be principally distinguished by being willing to eat more than we shall have to give them."

" Ah !" replied Jack, " but I know that if we get to land, you will see that they will assist us in hunting and shooting."

" True enough," said I, " but be so good as to tell us how we are to get to land, and whether you have contrived the means."

" I am sure it cannot be very difficult," said Jack, with an arch motion of his head. " Look here at these large tubs. Why cannot each of us get into one of them, and float to the land? I remember I succeeded very well in this manner on the water when I was visiting Grandfather last summer."

Every hint is good for something, and I began to think that what Jack had suggested was worth a trial.

" Quick, then, Jack. Give me the saw, the auger, and some nails, and we will see what is to be done."

I recollected having seen some empty casks in the hold. We went down, and found them floating about in the water, which almost filled the vessel. It cost us but little trouble to hoist them up and place them on the lower deck, which was at this time scarcely above water. We saw with delight that they were all made of excellent wood, well guarded by iron hoops, and in sound condition. They were exactly suited for our purpose, and with the assistance of my sons I instantly began to saw them in two. In a certain time I had produced eight tubs of equal size and of suitable height, which I contemplated with perfect satisfaction. My wife, however, sighed deeply as she looked at them.

" Never, never," cried she, " can I venture to get into one of these."

" Do not decide so hastily, my dear," said I. " My plan is not yet complete, and you will soon see that it is more worthy of our confidence than at present may appear."

I then sought for a long plank capable of being a little curved at the ends. I fastened my eight tubs together, and then fixed on the plank by way of a keel. The tubs were nailed to each other, and, to make them the firmer, two other planks of the same length as the first were fixed on each side of the tubs. When all this was finished, we found we had produced a kind of boat divided into eight compartments, which I had no doubt would be able to perform a short course in calm water.

But, unfortunately, our marvellous craft proved so heavy, that with the strength of all united we were not able to move it an inch from its place. I bade Fritz fetch me a crowbar, who soon returned with it. I sawed a thick round pole into several pieces for rollers, and easily raised the foremost part of our boat with the crowbar, while Fritz placed one of the rollers under it.

I tied a long cord to its stern, and the other end of it to one of the timbers of the ship which appeared to be still firm, so that the cord, being left loose, would serve to guide and restrain the craft when launched. We now put a second and a third roller under, and, applying the crowbar, to our great joy our contrivance descended into the water with such a velocity, that if the rope had not been well fastened it would have gone far out to sea. But now a new misfortune presented itself: it leaned so much on one side that my boys all exclaimed they could not venture to get into it. I was for some moments in the most painful perplexity, but it suddenly occurred to me that ballast only was wanting to set it straight. I threw everything I could find that was weighty and of small size into the tubs, and at length our quaint home-made boat floated quite straight and firm in the water, and seemed to invite us to take refuge in its protection.

All now would have thrown themselves at once into it, and the boys began to push each other, and dispute which should get in first. I, however, drew them back, plainly perceiving that at best the voyage would be hazardous, and that the least motion of even one of these boisterous children might upset it and cause us to be all drowned. In seeking for a remedy for this difficulty, I recollected that some savage nations make use of a paddle fore and aft to help balance their canoes. With this thought I once more set to work to make a paddle of a kind.

I took two of the smaller yards, upon which the sails of the ship had been stretched, and fixed one of them at the bow and the other at the stern of my floating machine in such a manner as to enable us to turn them at pleasure to right or left, as should best answer the purpose of steadying and guiding our craft.

There remained nothing more for me to do but to find out in what way I could get clear from the wreckage that lay around us. I got into the first tub, and steered the head of our craft so as to make it enter the breach in the ship's side. I then got on board the ship again, and with saw and hatchet cleared away everything that could obstruct our passage. That being effected, we next secured some oars for our voyage.

We had spent the day in laborious exertions; it was already late, and as it would not have been possible to reach the land that evening, we were obliged to pass a second night in the wrecked vessel, which at every instant threatened to fall to pieces. We now refreshed ourselves by a regular meal, for during the day's work we had scarcely allowed ourselves to take a bit of bread or a glass of water. Being in a more tranquil frame of mind than on the preceding day, we all abandoned ourselves to sleep; not, however, till

I had used the precaution of tying the swimming belts round my three youngest boys and my wife, as a means of safety if the storm should again come on and should put the finishing stroke to the destruction of the vessel. Our arrangements being now as complete as our united foresight could make them, we one and all crept into our separate hammocks, where a delicious repose prepared us for the renewal of our labours.

CHAPTER II

A LANDING, AND CONSEQUENT OCCUPATIONS

By break of day we were all awake and alert, for hope as well as grief is unfriendly to lengthened slumbers. When we had finished our morning prayer, I said:

" We now, with the assistance of Heaven, must enter upon the work of our deliverance. The first thing to be done is to give to each poor animal on board, before we leave them, a hearty meal; we will then put food enough before them to last for several days. We cannot take them with us, but we will hope it may be possible, if our voyage succeeds, to return and fetch them. Are you now all ready? Bring together whatever we mean to take, whatever is absolutely necessary for our wants."

I decided that our first cargo should consist of a barrel of gunpowder, three fowling-pieces, and three carbines, with as much small shot and lead and as many bullets as our boat would bear; two pair of pocket pistols and one of large ones, not forgetting a mould to cast balls in. I told each of the boys and their mother also to take a game-bag. We added a chest containing cakes of portable soup, another full of hard biscuits, an iron pot, a fishing-rod, a chest of nails and another of different tools, such as hammers, saws, pincers, hatchets, augers, &c., and lastly some sail-cloth to make a tent. In short, the boys brought so many things that we were obliged to reject some of them, though I had already exchanged the worthless ballast for articles of use for our subsistence.

When all was ready, we stepped bravely each into a tub. At the moment of our departure we heard all the cocks and hens begin to crow, as if they were conscious that we had deserted them, yet willing to bid us a sorrowful adieu. This suggested to me the idea of taking the geese, ducks, fowls, and pigeons with us, observing to my wife that if we could not find means to feed them, at least they would feed us.

We accordingly executed this plan. We put ten hens and an old and a young cock into one of the tubs, and covered it with planks. We set the rest of the poultry at liberty, in the hope that instinct would direct them towards the land—the geese and the ducks by water, and the pigeons by the air.

We were waiting for my wife, who had the care of this last part of our embarkation, when she joined us loaded with a large bag, which she threw into the tub which already contained her youngest son. I imagined that she intended it for him to sit upon, and also to confine him so as to prevent his being tossed from side to side. I therefore asked no questions concerning it. The order of our departure was as follows:

In the first tub, at the boat's head, my wife;

In the second, our little Francis, a lovely boy, six years old, full of the happiest dispositions;

In the third, Fritz, our eldest boy, between fourteen and

fifteen years of age, a handsome, curl-pated youth, full of intelligence and vivacity;

In the fourth was the barrel of gunpowder, with the cocks and hens and the sail-cloth;

In the fifth, the provisions for the support of life;

In the sixth, my son Jack, a light-hearted, enterprising, audacious, generous lad, about ten years old;

In the seventh, my son Ernest, a boy of twelve years old, of a rational, reflecting temper, well informed, but somewhat disposed to indolence;

In the eighth, a father, to whose paternal care the task of guiding the craft for the safety of his beloved family was entrusted.

Each of us had useful implements within reach; the hand of each held an oar, and near each was a swimming belt in readiness for what might happen. The tide was already at half its height when we left the ship, and I had counted on this circumstance as favourable to our want of strength. We held the two paddles longways, and thus we passed without accident through the breach in the ship. The boys devoured with their eyes the blue land they saw at a distance (for to us it appeared to be of this colour). We rowed with all our strength, but long in vain, to reach it; the boat only turned round and round. At length, however, I had the good fortune to steer in such a way that she proceeded in a straight line. The two dogs we had left on board, perceiving that we had abandoned them, plunged immediately into the sea and swam to the boat. They were too large for us to think of giving them admittance, and I dreaded lest they should jump in and upset us. Turk was an English dog, and Ponto of the Danish breed. I was in great uneasiness on their account, for I feared it would not be possible for them to swim so far. The dogs, however, managed the affair with perfect intelligence. When they found themselves fatigued they rested their fore-paws on the paddles, which were now turned crossways.

Our voyage proceeded securely, though slowly; but the nearer we approached the land the more gloomy and unpromising we thought its aspect appeared. The coast was occupied by barren rocks, which seemed to offer nothing but hunger and distress. The sea was calm; the waves, gently agitated, washed the shore, and the sky was serene. In every direction we per-ceived casks, bales, chests, and other vestiges of ship-wrecks floating round us. In the hope of obtaining some good provisions, I determined on endeavouring to secure two of the casks. I bade Fritz have a rope, a hammer, and some nails ready, and to try to seize them as we passed. He succeeded in laying hold of two of them, and in such a way that we found it easy to draw them after us to the shore. Now that we were close on land, its hideous aspect was considerably softened; the rocks no longer appeared one undivided chain. Fritz with his hawk's eyes already descried some trees, and exclaimed that they were palm-trees. Ernest expressed his joy that he should now get much larger and better coco-nuts than those to be had in Europe. I for my part was venting audibly my regret that I had not thought of bringing with us a telescope that I knew was in the captain's cabin, when Jack drew a small spy-glass from his pocket, and, with a look of triumph that he was able to compensate this neglect, instantly presented it to me.

In reality the glass was of great service, for with its aid I was able to see which was the best route to take. I remarked that the shore before us had a savage aspect, but that towards the left the scene was more agreeable. But when I attempted to steer in that direction a current carried me towards the coast that was rocky and barren. By and by we perceived a little opening between the rocks, near the mouth of a creek, towards which all our geese and ducks betook themselves; and I followed in the same course. This opening formed a little bay, the water of which was calm, and neither too deep nor too shallow to receive our boat. I entered it, and cautiously put on shore on a spot where the coast was about the same height above the water as our tubs, and where at the same time there was a quantity sufficient to keep us afloat. The shore extended inland in a shelving declivity in the form of a triangle, the upper angle of which terminated among the rocks, while the margin of the sea formed the base.

All that had life in the boat jumped eagerly on land. Even little Francis, who had been wedged in his tub like a potted herring, now got up and sprang forward; but, with all his efforts, he could not succeed without his mother's help. The dogs, who had swum on shore, received us as if they were appointed to do the honours of the place; the geese kept up a loud continual cackling, to which the ducks with their broad yellow beaks contributed a perpetual thorough bass; the cocks and hens, which we had already set at liberty, clucked; the boys chattering all at once, produced altogether an overpowering confusion of sounds. To this was added the disagreeable scream of some penguins and flamingoes, which we now perceived, some flying over our heads, others sitting on the points of the rocks. By and by the notes of the latter had the ascendant from the superiority of their numbers; and their society became the more unpleasant, from a comparison we could not avoid making between the sounds they uttered with the harmony of the feathered musicians of our own country. I had, however, one advantage in prospect; it was that these very birds might serve for our subsistence.

The first thing we did on finding ourselves safe on terra firma, was to fall on our knees, and return thanks to the Supreme Being who had preserved our lives, and to recommend ourselves with entire resignation to the care of His paternal kindness.

We next employed our whole attention in unloading the boat. Oh, how rich we thought ourselves in the little we had been able to rescue from the merciless waters! We looked everywhere for a convenient place to erect a tent under the shade of the rocks; and having agreed upon a place, we set to work. We drove one of our poles firmly into a fissure of the rock—this formed the ridge of our tent. We rested upon it another pole, and thus formed a frame. We next threw some sail-cloth over the ridge, and stretching it to a convenient distance on each side, fastened its extremities to the ground with stakes. By way of precaution we left the chests of provisions and other heavy things on the shore, and fixed some tenter-hooks near the edge of the sail-cloth in front, that we might be able to close the entrance during night. I next desired my sons to collect grass and moss, and spread it to dry in the sun, as it would then serve us for beds. During this occupation, in which even the little Francis could take a share, I erected at a small distance from the tent, and near a river, a kind of little kitchen. A few flat stones that I found in the bed of the river served for a fire-place. I got a quantity of dry branches: with the largest I made a small enclosure round it; and with the little twigs, added to some of our turf, I made a brisk, cheering fire. We put some of the soup-cakes, with water, into our iron pot, and placed it over the fire; and my wife, with her little Francis for a scullion,

took charge of preparing the dinner. Francis, from
their colour, had mistaken the soup-cakes for glue.

" Why, Mother," said he, " what are you going to
use glue for?"

" I am going to make some soup of it," said his
mother, laughing.

" That is droll enough," answered he; " for how
shall we get any meat to put into it here, where there
is nothing like a shop?"

" My boy," said I, " what you have been thinking
was glue is in reality excellent meat, reduced to a jelly
by the process of cookery, and which, being dried, is
in no danger of becoming stale. In this state it will
bear long voyages, where it would be difficult to take
sufficient animals for the use of the ship's company,
who would otherwise be kept constantly on a less
wholesome soup made from salted meat; but ours,
I assure you, Francis, will be excellent."

In the meanwhile Fritz had been reloading the guns,
with one of which he had wandered along the side of
the river. He had proposed to Ernest to accompany
him, but Ernest replied that he did not like a rough
and stony walk, and that he should go alone to the
sea-shore. Jack took the road towards a chain of
rocks which jutted out into the sea, with the intention
of gathering some of the mussels which grew upon
them. My own occupation was now an endeavour to
draw the two floating casks on shore. But I did not
succeed, for our place of landing, though convenient
enough for our craft, was too steep for the casks. While
I was looking about to find a more favourable spot,
I heard loud cries proceeding from a short distance,
and recognized the voice of Jack. I snatched my
hatchet, and ran to his assistance. I soon perceived
him up to his knees in water, and that a large sea-

lobster had fastened his claws in his leg. The poor boy screamed pitiably, and made useless efforts to disengage himself. I jumped instantly into the water, and the enemy was no sooner sensible of my approach than he let go his hold, and would have scampered out to sea, but that I indulged the fancy of a little malice against him. I turned quickly upon him, and took him up by the body and carried him off, followed by Jack, who shouted our triumph all the way. He begged me at last to let him hold the animal in his own hand, that he might himself present so fine a booty to his mother. Accordingly, having observed how I held it to avoid the gripe, he laid his own hand upon it in exactly the same manner; but scarcely had he grasped it than he received a violent blow on the face from the lobster's tail, which made him lose his hold, and the animal fell to the ground. Jack again began to bawl out, while I could not refrain from laughing heartily. I picked up the lobster, and on Jack's entreaty let him carry it to the kitchen, which he entered, triumphantly exclaiming:

"Mamma, Mamma, a sea-lobster! Ernest, a sea-lobster! Where is Fritz? Where is Fritz? Take care, Francis, he will bite you!"

Ernest, ever eager about his meals, now bawled out that the lobster had better be put into the soup, which would give it an excellent flavour; but this his mother opposed, observing that we must be more economical of our provisions than that, for the lobster of itself would furnish a dinner for the whole family. I now left them, and walked again to the scene of this adventure and examined the shallow. I then made another attempt upon my two casks, and at length succeeded in getting them into the shallow, and in fixing them there securely on their ends.

On my return I complimented Jack on his being the first to have procured us an animal that might serve for our subsistence.

" Ah! but *I* have seen something too that is good to eat," said Ernest; " and I should have got it if it had not been in the water, so that I must have wetted my feet——"

" Oh, that is a famous story!" said Jack. " I can tell you what he saw—some nasty mussels. Why, I would not eat one of them for the world. Think of my lobster!"

" That is not true, Jack; it was oysters and not mussels that I saw," said Ernest. " I am sure of it, for they stuck against the foot of the rock, and I know they must be oysters."

" Fortunate enough, my dainty gentleman!" cried I, addressing myself to Ernest; " and since you are so well acquainted with the place where these shell-fish can be found, you will be so obliging as to dismiss your fears about wetting your feet, and to return and procure us some. In such a situation as ours, every member of the family must be actively employed for the common good."

" I will do my best with all my heart," answered Ernest; " and at the same time I will bring home some salt, of which I have seen immense quantities in the holes of the rocks, where I suppose it is dried by the sun. I tasted some of it, and it was excellent. Papa, is it not left there by the sea?"

" No doubt it is, Mr. Reasoner, for where else do you think it could come from? You would have done more wisely if you had brought us a bag of it, besides spending your time in such profound reflections; and if you do not wish to dine upon a soup without flavour, you had better run and fetch us a little immediately."

He set off, and soon returned. What he brought back was so mixed with sand that I was on the point of throwing it away. My wife, however, prevented me; and by dissolving and filtering it through a piece of muslin, we found it admirably fit for use.

After adding the salt, my wife tasted the soup, and pronounced that it was all the better for the salt, and now quite ready.

" But," said she, " Fritz is not come in. And then, how shall we manage to eat our soup without spoons or dishes? Why did we not remember to bring some from the ship?"

" Why did we not think of them? Because, my dear, one cannot think of everything. We shall be lucky if we do not discover that we have forgotten even more important things."

" But indeed," said she, " this is a matter which cannot easily be set to rights. How will it be possible for each of us to raise this large boiling pot to our lips?"

A moment's further reflection convinced me my wife was right. We all cast our eyes upon the pot with perplexity, and we looked a little like the fox in the fable, when the stork desires him to help himself from a vessel with a long neck. Silence was at length broken by all bursting into a laugh at our want of every kind of utensil, and at our own folly in not recollecting that spoons and forks were things of absolute necessity.

Ernest observed that if we could but get some coco-nuts, we might use the pieces of the shells for spoons.

" Yes, yes, that is true enough," replied I, " but we have them not."

" But at least," said the boy, " we can use some oyster-shells."

" Why, this is well, Ernest," said I, " and is what

I call a useful thought. Run, then, quickly and get us some of them. But no one of you must give himself airs because his spoon is without a handle, or if he should chance to grease his fingers in the soup."

Jack ran the first, and was up to his knees in the water before Ernest could reach the place. Jack tore off the shell-fish and threw them to the slothful Ernest, who put them into his handkerchief, having first secured in his pocket one shell he had met with of a large size. The boys came back together with their booty.

Fritz not having yet returned, his mother was beginning to be uneasy, when we heard him shouting to us from no great distance, and shouted in reply. In a few minutes he was among us; his two hands behind him, and with a sort of would-be melancholy air, which none of us could well understand.

" What have you brought?" asked his brothers.

" Nothing at all," said he.

But now, on fixing my eye upon him, I perceived a smile through his assumed dissatisfaction. At the same instant Jack, having stolen behind him, exclaimed, " A little pig! A little pig!" Fritz, finding his trick discovered, now proudly displayed his prize, which I immediately perceived, from the description I had read in different books of travels, was an agouti, and not a pig, as the boys had supposed.

" Where did you find him? How did you get at him? Did he make you run a great way?" asked all at once the young brothers.

I for my part assumed a serious tone. " I should have preferred," said I, " that you had in reality brought us nothing rather than to have heard you assert a falsehood. Never allow yourself, even in jest, my dear boy, to assert an untruth. By such trifles as these, a habit of lying, the most disgusting and frightful of vices, may be induced. Now, then, that I have given you this caution, let us look at the animal. Where did you find it?"

Fritz related that he had passed over to the other side of the river. "Ah!" continued he, "it is quite another thing from this place; the shore is low, and you can have no notion of the quantity of casks, chests, and planks, and different sort of things washed there by the sea. Ought we not to go and try to obtain some of these treasures?"

"Certainly we must do so," said I. "And we ought also to make a voyage back to the vessel and fetch away our animals; at least you will all agree that of the cow we are pretty much in want."

"If our biscuit were soaked in milk it would not be so hard, but much improved," said our greedy Ernest.

"I must tell you too," said Fritz, "that over on the other side there is as much grass for pasturage as we can desire, and, besides, a pretty wood, in the shade of which we could shelter. Why then should we remain on this barren desert side?"

"Patience, patience!" replied I. "There is a time for everything, friend Fritz; we shall not be without something to undertake to-morrow. But, above all, I am eager to know if you discovered any traces of our ship companions."

"Not the smallest trace of man; but I have seen some other animals that more resembled pigs than the one I have brought you, but with paws more like those of the hare. The animal I am speaking of leaps from place to place on the grass, now sitting on his hind legs rubbing his face with his front feet, and then seeking for roots and gnawing them like the squirrel.

If I had not been afraid of his escaping me, I should have tried to catch him with my hands, for he appeared almost tame."

Ernest now turned the agouti backwards and forwards to examine him on all sides. After a long silence, he said with importance: " I cannot be sure that this animal, as you all believe, is a pig. His hair and his snout pretty much resemble, it is true, those of a pig; but look at his teeth, he has but four incisors in front similar to the genus Voracious animals. In general he has a greater resemblance to the rabbit than to the hare. I have seen an engraving of him in our book of natural history; if I am not mistaken he is the *agouti*."

" Ah ha !" said Fritz, " here is a learned professor !"

" And who this once is not mistaken !" cried I. " Spare your raillery, Fritz, for it is really an agouti. I have never myself seen the animal, and only know him by his description in books and from engravings, with which your supposed piggie perfectly corresponds. He is a native of America, lives underground on the roots of trees, and is, as travellers report, excellent food. But of this we will judge for ourselves."

While we were speaking, Jack was trying with all his might to open one of the oysters with his knife, but he could not succeed. I laughed heartily at his disappointment, and put a few of them on the fire, where they soon opened of themselves. Each then proceeded to dip his shell into the pot to get out a little soup; but, as I had foreseen, each drew out a scalded finger. Ernest was the only one who had been too cautious to expose himself to this misfortune; he quietly took his mussel-shell, as large and deep as a plate, from his pocket, and carefully dipping it into the pot, drew it out filled with as much soup as was his fair share, and casting a look of exultation on his brothers, he set it down to wait till it should be cold enough to eat.

" You have taken excellent care of yourself, I perceive," said I. " But now answer me, dear boy, is the advantage worth the pains you take to be better off than your companions? Yet this is the constant failing of your character. As your best friend, I feel it to be my duty to balk you. I therefore adjudge your dish of delicious soup to our followers, Turk and Ponto. For ourselves, we will all fare alike, you as well as the rest—we will simply dip our oyster-shells into the pot till hunger is appeased; but the picked dish for the dogs, Ernest, and all the rest *alike*!"

This gentle reproach sunk, I perceived, into his heart; he placed the shell, filled with soup, upon the ground, and in the twinkling of an eye the dogs had licked up every drop. We on our parts were almost as sharp set as they, and every eye was fixed on the pot, watching when the steam would subside a little that we might begin dipping, when, on looking round, we saw Turk and Ponto standing over the agouti, gnawing and tearing him fiercely. The boys all screamed together. Fritz seized his gun and struck them with it, called them the unkindest names, threw stones at them, and was so furious that, if I had not interfered, it is probable he would have killed them. He had already bent his gun with the blows he had aimed at them, and his voice was raised so high as to be re-echoed from the rocks.

When he had grown a little cool I remonstrated with him on his violence of temper. I represented to him what distress he had occasioned his mother and myself; that his gun, which might have been so useful, was now entirely spoiled; and that the poor animals, upon whose assistance we should probably so much depend, he had, no doubt, greatly injured.

"Anger," continued I, "is always a bad counsellor, and may even lead the way to crimes. You are not ignorant of the history of Cain, who in a moment of violent anger killed his brother."

"Say no more, my dearest father," interrupted Fritz.

"Happy am I to recollect on this occasion," resumed I, "that they were animals and not human creatures you treated thus. But an angry person never reasons; he scarcely knows whom he attacks. Confess, too, that it was vanity which excited the furious temper you exhibited. If another than yourself had killed the agouti you would have been more patient under the accident."

Fritz agreed that I was right.

Soon after we had taken our meal the sun began to sink into the west. Our little flock of fowls assembled round us, pecking what morsels of our biscuit had fallen to the ground. Just at this moment my wife produced the bag she had so mysteriously huddled into the tub. Its mouth was now opened; it contained the various sorts of grain for feeding poultry— barley, peas, oats, &c., and also different kinds of seeds of vegetables for the table. In the fullness of her kind heart she scattered several handfuls at once upon the ground. I complimented her on the benefit her foresight had secured for us, but I recommended a more sparing use of so valuable an acquisition, observing that the grain, if kept for sowing, would produce a harvest, and that we could fetch from the ship spoiled biscuit enough to feed the fowls. Our pigeons sought a roosting-place among the rocks; the hens, with the two cocks at their head, ranged themselves in a line along the ridge of the tent; and the geese and ducks betook themselves in a body, cackling and quacking as they proceeded, to a marshy bit of ground near the sea, where some thick bushes afforded them shelter.

A little later we ourselves began to follow the example of our winged companions by beginning our preparations for repose. First we charged our guns and pistols, and laid them carefully in the tent; next we assembled all together, and joined in offering up our thanks to the Almighty for the succour afforded us. With the last ray of the sun we entered our tent, and laid ourselves close to each other on the grass and moss we had collected in the morning.

———

CHAPTER III

VOYAGE OF DISCOVERY

I was awaked at dawn by the crowing of the cocks. I awoke my wife, and we consulted as to our occupation for the day. We both agreed that the thing of the most importance was to seek for such traces as might be found of our late ship companions, and at the same time to examine the soil on the other side of the river before we came to a determination about a fixed place of abode. My wife perceived that such an excursion could not be undertaken by all the members of the family; and, full of confidence in the protection of Heaven, she consented to my proposal of my leaving her with the three youngest boys, and proceeding myself with Fritz on a journey of discovery. I entreated her not to lose a moment in giving us our breakfast. She gave us notice that the share of each would be but small, there being no more soup prepared.

" What then," I asked, " is become of Jack's lobster?"

" That he can best tell you himself," answered his mother. " But now, pray step and awake the boys, while I make a fire and put on some water."

The children were soon roused: even our slothful Ernest submitted to the hard fate of rising so early in the morning. When I asked Jack for his lobster, he ran and fetched it from a cleft in the rock in which he had carefully concealed it.

" I was determined," said he, " that the dogs should not treat my lobster as they did the agouti."

" I am glad to see, son Jack," said I, " that that giddy head upon your shoulders can be prevailed upon to reflect. But will you not kindly give Fritz the great claw which bit your leg (though I promised it to you), to carry with him for his dinner on our journey?"

" What journey?" asked all the boys at once. " Ah! we will go too. A journey! a journey!" repeated they.

" For this time," said I, " it is impossible for all of you to go. Your eldest brother and myself shall be better able to defend ourselves in any danger without you; besides, with so many persons we could proceed but slowly. You will, then, all three remain with your mother in this place, which appears to be one of perfect safety, and you shall keep Ponto to be your guard, while we will take Turk with us. With such a protector, and a gun well loaded, who shall dare treat us with disrespect? Fritz, make haste and tie up Ponto, that he may not follow us; and have your eye on Turk, that he may be at hand to accompany us, and get the guns ready."

At the word " guns " the colour rose in the cheeks

of my poor boy. His gun was so curved as to be of no
use; he took it up, and tried in vain to straighten it.
I let him alone for a short time, but at length I gave
him leave to take another. A moment after he attempted to lay hold of Ponto to tie him up; but the
dog, recollecting the blows he had so lately received,
began to snarl, and would not go near him. Turk
behaved the same, and I found it necessary to call
with my own voice to induce them to approach us.
Fritz then entreated for some biscuit of his mother,
declaring that he would willingly go without his breakfast to make his peace with the dogs. He accordingly
carried them some biscuit, stroked and caressed them,
and in every motion seemed to ask their pardon.

We now prepared for our departure. We took each
a game-bag and a hatchet; I put a pair of pistols in
the leather band round Fritz's waist in addition to the
gun, and provided myself with the same articles, not
forgetting a stock of biscuit and a flask of fresh river-
water. My wife now called us to breakfast, when all
attacked the lobster; but its flesh proved so hard that
there was a great deal left when our meal was finished,
and we packed it for our journey without further
regret from anyone.

In about an hour we were ready to set out. I had
loaded the guns we left behind, and I now enjoined my
wife to keep by day as near the boat as possible, which,
in case of danger, was the best and most speedy means
of escape.

The river we were about to pass was on each side
so steep as to be inaccessible, except by one narrow
slip near the mouth on one side, whence we had
already drawn our supply of fresh water; but there
was no means of effecting a passage across from this
place, the opposite shore being an unbroken line of

perpendicular rocks. We therefore walked on, following the river till we arrived at an assemblage of rocks at which the stream formed a cascade; a few paces beyond we observed some large fragments of rock which had fallen into the bed of the river. By stepping upon these, and making some hazardous leaps, we at length contrived to reach the other side. We had proceeded a short way along the rock we ascended in landing, forcing ourselves a passage through overgrown grass mixed with other plants, and rendered more capable of resistance by being half dried up by the sun. Perceiving, however, that walking on this kind of surface, joined to the heat, would soon exhaust our strength, we looked for a path by which we might descend and proceed along the river, in which direction we hoped to meet with fewer obstacles, and perhaps discover traces of our ship companions.

When we had walked about a hundred paces we heard a loud noise behind us, and perceived a rustling motion in the grass, which was almost as tall as ourselves. I was a good deal alarmed, thinking that it was probably occasioned by some serpent, a tiger, or other ferocious animal, which might devour us. But I was well satisfied with the courage of Fritz, who, instead of running away, stood firm to face the danger; the only motion he made being that of seeing that his piece was fit to be discharged, and turning himself to front the spot whence the noise proceeded. Our alarm, however, was of short duration; for what was our joy on seeing rush out, not an enemy, but our faithful Turk, whom in the moment of departure we had quite forgotten, and whom no doubt our anxious relatives had sent on to us! I received the poor fellow with lively joy, and did not fail to commend both the bravery and discretion of my son, in not yielding to even a rational alarm, and for waiting till he was sure of the object before he resolved to fire.

We again pursued our way. On our left was the sea, and on our right, at the distance of half a league, the continuation of the ridge of rocks, which extended from the place of our debarkation in a direction nearly parallel with the shore, the summit everywhere adorned with a fresh verdure and a great variety of trees; and the space between partly covered with tall grass and partly with small clumps of bushes, which on one side extended to the rocks, and on the other to the sea. We were careful to proceed on a course as near the shore as possible, fixing our eyes rather upon its smooth expanse than upon the land, in hopes to see something of the boats. We did not, however, wholly neglect the shore, where we looked about in all directions; but our endeavours were all in vain.

Fritz proposed to fire his gun from time to time, suggesting, that should they be anywhere concealed near us, they might thus be led to know of our pursuit.

"This would be very well," answered I, "if you could contrive for our friends to hear the report of the gun, and not the savages, who are most likely not far distant."

When we had gone about two leagues we entered a wood situated a little farther from the sea. Here we threw ourselves on the ground, and under the shade of a tree, by the side of a clear running stream, took out some provisions and refreshed ourselves. We heard on every side around us the chirping, singing, and the motion of birds, which in reality were more attractive by their splendid plumage than by any charm of note. Fritz assured me that between the branches of the bushes he saw some animals like apes. This indeed was further confirmed by the restless movements we had observed in Turk, who began to smell about, and to bark so loud that the wood resounded with the noise. Fritz stole softly about, and, raising his head to spy into the branches above his height, he stumbled on a small round body which lay on the ground. He took it up and brought it to me, observing that he thought it must be the nest of some bird.

" What makes you of that opinion?" said I.

" But I have read that there are some kinds of birds who build their nests quite round. And look, Father, how the outside is crossed and twined!"

" That is true, Fritz, but do you not perceive that what you take for straws crossed and twined by a bird is in fact a coat of fibres formed by nature? Do you not remember that the nut is enclosed within a round fibrous covering, which again is surrounded by a skin of a thin and fragile texture? I see that in the one you hold in your hand this skin has been destroyed by time, and this is the reason why the twisted fibres are so apparent. But now let us break the outside covering, and you will see the nut inside."

We soon accomplished this, but the nut, alas! from lying on the ground, had perished, and appeared but little different from a bit of dried skin, and not the least inviting to the palate.

Fritz was much amused at this discovery.

" How I wish Ernest could have been here!" cried he. " How he envied me the fine large coco-nuts I was to find, and the whole tea-cupful of sweet delicious milk, which was to spring out upon me from the inside! But, Father, I really believed that the coco-nut contained a sweet refreshing liquid, a little like the juice of almonds; travellers surely tell untruths!"

" Travellers do sometimes tell untruths, Fritz, but

on the subject of the coco-nut I believe them to be innocent. The coco-nut is known to contain the liquid you describe, just before a state of ripeness. It is the same with our European nuts, with only the difference of quantity: and the circumstance is common to both, that as the nut ripens the milk diminishes by becoming the same substance as the nut. If you put a ripe nut under the earth in a good soil, the kernel will shoot and burst the shell; but if it remain aboveground, or in a place that does not suit its nature, the nut rots and perishes as you have seen."

After looking for some time, we had at length the good luck to find another coco-nut. We opened it, and finding it sound we sat down and ate it for our dinner, by which means we were enabled to husband the provisions we had brought. The nut, it is true, was a little oily and rancid; yet, as this was not a time to be nice, we made a hearty meal, and then continued our route. We did not quit the wood, but pushed our way through it, being often obliged to cut a path through the bushes. At length we reached a plain, which afforded a more extensive prospect and a path less intricate.

We next entered a forest to the right, and soon observed in it some trees of a particular species. Fritz, whose sharp eye was continually on a journey of discovery, remarked that some of them were of so very extraordinary an appearance that he could not resist the curiosity he felt to examine them closely.

" Look here, Father!" he next exclaimed. " What a singular kind of tree, with wens growing all about the trunk!"

We walked up to some of them, and I perceived with surprise and satisfaction that they were of the gourd-tree kind, the trunks of which bear fruit. Fritz could not conceive the meaning of what he saw, and asked me if the fruit was a sponge or a wen.

"We will see," I replied, "if we cannot unravel the mystery. Try to get down one of them, and we will examine it minutely."

"I have got one," cried Fritz, "and it is exactly like a gourd, only the rind is thicker and harder."

"It then, like the rind of that fruit, can be used for making various utensils," observed I; "plates, dishes, basins, and flasks. We will give this tree the name of the gourd-tree."

"Hurrah!" cried he in ecstasy. "How happy Mother will be! She will no longer have the vexation when she makes soup of thinking that we shall scald our fingers."

"What, my boy, do you think is the reason that this tree bears its fruit only on the trunk and on its topmost branches?"

"I think it must be because the middle branches are too feeble to support such a weight."

"You have guessed exactly right."

"But are these gourds good to eat?"

"At worst they are, I believe, harmless; but they have not a very tempting flavour. The savages set as much value on the rind of this fruit as on gold, for its use to them is indispensable. These rinds serve them to keep their food and drink in, and sometimes they even cook their victuals in them."

"Oh, Father! it must be impossible to cook their victuals in them, for the heat of the fire would soon consume such a substance."

"I did not say the rind was put upon the fire, Fritz."

"Pray, how are the victuals to be cooked without fire?"

" Nor did I say that victuals could be cooked without a fire, and my meaning was, that there is no need to put the vessel that contains the food upon the fire."

" I have not the least idea of what you mean; there seems to be a miracle."

" So be it, my son. A little tincture of enchantment is the lot of man. Let me help you to understand this amazing phenomenon. When it is intended to dress food in one of these rinds, the process is to cut the fruit into two equal parts and scoop out the whole of the inside. Some water is put into one of the halves, and into the water some fish, a crab, or whatever else is to be dressed; then some stones red hot, beginning with one at a time, are thrown in, which impart sufficient heat to the water to dress the food, without the smallest injury to the pot."

" But is not the food spoiled by ashes falling in, or by pieces of the heated stones separating in the water?"

" Certainly it would not be very easy to make fine sauces or ragouts in such a vessel, but a dressing of the meat is actually accomplished, and the negroes and savages are not very delicate."

We next proceeded to the manufacture of our plates and dishes. I taught my son how to divide the gourd with a bit of string, which would cut more equally than a knife. I tied the string round the middle of the gourd as tight as possible, striking it pretty hard with the handle of my knife, and I drew tighter and tighter till the gourd fell apart, forming two regular-shaped bowls. Fritz, who had used a knife for the same operation, had entirely spoiled his gourd by the irregular strokes of his instrument. I recommended his making some spoons with the spoiled rind, as it was good for no other purpose. I on my part had soon completed two dishes, and some plates.

Fritz was in the utmost astonishment at my success. "I cannot imagine, Father," said he, "how this way of cutting the gourd could occur to you."

"I have read the description of such a process," replied I, "in books of travels, and also, that such of the savages as have no knives, and who make a sort of twine from the bark of trees, are accustomed to use it for this purpose."

"And the flasks, Father; in what manner are they made?"

"For this branch of their ingenuity the savages make preparation a long time beforehand. If a negro wishes to have a flask or bottle with a neck, he ties a very young gourd round in the proper place with a piece of string, of linen, bark of a tree, or anything he can get hold of; he draws this bandage so tight, that the part at liberty soon forms itself to a round shape, while the part which is confined contracts, and remains ever after narrow. By this method it is that they obtain flasks or bottles of a perfect form."

"Are then the bottle-shaped gourds I have seen in Europe trained by a similar preparation?"

"No, they are not; they are of another species, and what you have seen is their natural shape."

Our conversation and our labour thus went on together. Fritz had completed some plates, and was not a little proud of the achievement. "Ah, how delighted my mother will be to eat upon them!" cried he. "But how shall we convey them to her?"

"We must leave them here on the sand for the sun to dry them; this will be accomplished by the time of our return, and we can then carry them with us; but care must be taken to fill them with sand, that they may not shrink or warp in so ardent a heat."

My boy did not dislike this task, for he had no great fancy to the idea of carrying such a load. Our service was accordingly spread upon the shore.

We amused ourselves as we walked along in endeavouring to fashion some spoons from the fragments of the gourd-rinds. I had the fancy to try my skill upon a piece of coco-nut; but I must needs confess that what we produced had not the least resemblance to those I had seen in the Museum at London, and which were shown there as the work of some of the islanders of the Southern Seas. A European without instruments must always find himself excelled by the superior adroitness and patience of savages; in this instance, too, we had the assistance of knives, while the savages have only sharp flat stones to work with.

" My attempt has been scarcely more successful than your own," I cried; " and to eat soup with either your spoon or mine, we ought to have mouths extending from ear to ear."

" True enough, Father," answered Fritz; " but it is not my fault. In making mine, I took the curve of my bit of rind for a guide; if I had made it smaller, it should have been too flat, and it is still more difficult to eat with a shovel than with an oyster-shell. But I am thinking that they may serve till I have learned to improve, and I am quite sure of the pleasure they will afford Mother."

While these different conversations and our labours had been going on, we had not neglected the great object of our pursuit—the making every practicable search for our ship companions. But all, alas! was in vain.

After a walk of about four leagues, we arrived at a spot where a slip of land, on which we observed a hill of considerable height, reached far out into the sea.

We determined to ascend to its summit, which could not fail to give us a clear view; this would save us farther rambles.

We did not reach the top of the hill without much hard climbing, but when there it presented a magnificent scene over a vast extent of land and water. It was, however, in vain that we made use of our spyglass; no trace of man appeared. The shore, rounded by a bay of some extent, the bank of which ended in a promontory on the farther side; the blue tint of its surface; the sea, gently agitated with waves; the woods of variegated hues and verdure, formed altogether a picture of such new and exquisite delight, that if the recollection of our unfortunate companions had not intervened, we should have yielded to the ecstasy the scene was calculated to inspire. In reality, from this moment we began to lose the hope we had entertained, and a certain sadness stole into our hearts. We, however, became but the more sensible of the goodness of the Divine Being in the special protection afforded us, in permitting us to find a home where there seemed to be no cause for fear of danger from without, where we had not experienced even the want of food, and where there seemed to be a prospect of future safety for us all. I remarked to Fritz that we seemed destined to a solitary life, and that it was a rich country which appeared to be allotted us for a habitation; at least our habitation it must be, unless some vessel should happen to put on shore on the same coast.

" Having left our native country, fixed on the intention of inhabiting some more propitious soil, it was natural to expect that we must at first encounter difficult adventures. Let us therefore consider our present situation as no disappointment in any essential respect. We can pursue our scheme for agriculture. We shall learn to invent arts. Our only want is numbers."

" We, however, of ourselves," observed Fritz, " form a larger society than was the lot of Adam before he had children; and as we grow older, we will perform all the necessary labour, while you and Mother enjoy a serene repose."

" Your assurances are as kind as I can desire, and they encourage me to struggle with what hardships may present themselves. Who can foresee in what manner it may be the will of Heaven to dispose of us?"

We descended from the hill, and having regained the shore we made our way to the wood of palms, which I had just pointed out to Fritz; but not without considerable difficulty, for our path lay through a quantity of reeds, entwined with other plants, which greatly obstructed our march. We advanced slowly and cautiously, fearing at every step we might receive a bite from some serpent. We made Turk go before us, to give us timely notice of anything dangerous. I also cut myself a reed of uncommon length and thickness, the better to defend myself. It was not without astonishment that I perceived a glutinous kind of sap proceed from the divided end of the stalk. Prompted by curiosity, I tasted the sap, and found it sweet and of an agreeable flavour, so that not a doubt remained in my mind that we were passing through a fine plantation of sugar-canes. I determined not to tell Fritz immediately of the fortunate discovery I had made, preferring that he should find the pleasure out for himself. As he was at some distance on before, I called out to him to cut a reed for his defence. This he instantly did, and, without any remark, used it simply for a stick, striking lustily with it on all sides to clear a passage. This motion occasioned the sap to run out abundantly upon his hand, and he stopped to examine so strange a circumstance. He lifted it up, and still a larger quantity escaped. He now tasted what was on his fingers. Oh! then for the exclamations. " Father, Father! I have found some sugar! some syrup! I have a sugar-cane in my hand!"

In the meantime Fritz eagerly devoured the cane he had cut, till his relish for it was appeased.

" I will take home a good provision. I shall only just taste of them once or twice as I walk along. But it will be so delightful to regale my mother and my little brothers with them!"

" Certainly, Fritz; but do not take too heavy a load, for recollect you have other things to carry, and we have yet far to go."

Counsel was given in vain. He persisted in cutting at least a dozen of the largest canes, tore off their leaves, tied them together, and, putting them under his arm, dragged them as well as he was able through thick and thin to the end of the plantation. We arrived without accident at the wood of palms, which we entered in search of a place of shade, where we might stretch our limbs on the ground and finish our repast. We were scarcely settled, when a great number of large monkeys, terrified by the sight of us and the barking of Turk, stole so nimbly and quietly up the trees, that we scarcely perceived them till they had reached the topmost parts. From this height they fixed their eyes upon us, grinding their teeth, making most horrible grimaces, and saluting us with frightful screams. I observed that the trees were palms, bearing coco-nuts, and I instantly conceived the hope of obtaining some of this fruit by help of the monkeys. Fritz on his part prepared to shoot at them. He threw his burdens on the ground, and it was with difficulty I could prevent him from firing.

" What are you going to do," said I, " in this youthful ardour of yours? What use or what pleasure can it be to you to destroy one of these monkeys?"

" Ah, Father, why did you not let me kill him? Look how they raise their backs in derision of us !"

" And is it possible that this can excite your vengeance, my most reasonable Mr. Fritz? As long as an animal does no injury, or that his death can in no shape be useful in preserving our own lives, we have no right to destroy it, and still less to torment it for our amusement, or from an insensate desire of revenge."

" We could roast a monkey, could we not, Father?"

" Many thanks for the hint. A fine repast you would have provided us ! Thanks to our stars, too, we are each too heavily loaded to have carried the dead body to our kitchen. Does not your large bundle of sugar-canes convince you that I speak the truth? But the living monkeys we may perhaps find means to make contribute to our service. See what I am going to do; but step aside for fear of your head. If I succeed, the monkeys will furnish us with plenty of coco-nuts."

I now began to throw stones at the monkeys; and though I could not make them reach to half of the height at which they had taken refuge, they showed every mark of excessive anger. With their accustomed habit of imitation they furiously tore off, nut by nut, all that grew upon the branches near them, to hurl them down upon us, and in a short time a large quantity of coco-nuts lay round us. Fritz laughed heartily at the excellent success of our stratagem, and as the shower of coco-nuts began to subside we set about collecting them. We chose a place where we could repose at our ease to regale ourselves on this rich harvest. We opened the shells with a hatchet, but not without having first enjoyed the sucking of some of the milk through the three small holes, round which we found it easy to insert a knife and let the milk escape. The milk of the coco-nut has not a very pleasant flavour, but it is excellent for quenching thirst. What we liked best was a kind of solid cream which adheres to the shell, and which we scraped off with our spoons. We mixed with it a little of the sap of our sugar-canes, and it made a delicious repast. Turk obtained for his share what remained of the lobster, to which we added a small quantity of biscuit. All this, however, was insufficient to satisfy the hunger of so large an animal, and he sought about for bits of the sugar-canes and of the coco-nuts.

Our meal being finished, we prepared to leave the place. I tied together such of the coco-nuts as had retained the stalks, and threw them across my shoulder. Fritz resumed his bundle of sugar-canes. We divided the rest of the things between us, and continued our way towards home.

CHAPTER IV

RETURN FROM THE VOYAGE OF DISCOVERY— A NOCTURNAL ALARM

My poor boy now began to complain of fatigue. At last he stopped to take breath.

" I never could have thought," cried he, " that a few sugar-canes could be so heavy. I should, however, be so glad to get them home to Mother and my brothers."

" A little patience and a little courage, dear Fritz," replied I, " will enable you to accomplish this wish. Recollect Æsop's breadbasket, which at first was so overwhelming a burden, but which at last became so light. We can cause it to be the same with your sugar-canes if we diminish them by sucking a number on the road. As a beginning, you may give one to me. Take you one also; the rest we will bind together and put at your back, hanging them upon the barrel of your gun, by which means you will carry them more easily.

" But I am not without apprehensions, Fritz, that of our acquisition we shall carry them only a few sticks for firewood, for I must bring to recollection the circumstance that the juice of the sugar-cane is apt to turn sour soon after cutting. We may suck them, therefore, without compunction, and without regret at the diminution of our number of canes."

" Well, then, if we can do no better with the sugar-canes," said Fritz, " at least I will take them a good supply of the milk of coco-nuts, which I have here in a tin bottle."

" In this, too, my boy, I fear you will also be disappointed. You talk of milk, but the milk of the coco-nut, when exposed to the air and heat, turns soon to vinegar."

" Oh, dear, how provoking!" groaned poor Fritz. " I must taste it this very minute."

The tin bottle was lowered from his shoulder in the twinkling of an eye, and he began to pull the cork with all his strength. As soon as it was loose the liquid flew upwards in a brisk stream, and with a loud noise and frothing like champagne.

"Bravo, Mr. Fritz! You have manufactured a wine of some mettle. I must caution you not to let it make you tipsy."

"Oh, taste it, Father, pray taste it! It is really like wine; its taste is sweet, and it is so sparkling! Do take a little, Father! Is it not good? If all the milk remains in this state the treat will be better even than I thought."

"I wish it may prove so, but I have my fears. Its present state is what is called the first degree of fermentation. The same thing happens to honey dissolved in water, of which a beverage called hydromel is made. When this first fermentation is past and the liquid is clear, it is become a sort of wine, the quality of which depends on the materials used. By the application of heat there next results a second fermentation, which turns the fluid into vinegar. But this may be prevented by great care, and by keeping the vessel in a cool place. Lastly, a third fermentation takes place in the vinegar itself, which changes its character, and deprives it of its taste, its strength, and its transparency. In the intense temperature of this climate this triple fermentation comes on very rapidly, so that it is not improbable that, on entering our tent, you might find your liquids turned to vinegar, or even to a thick liquid of ill odour. We may therefore refresh ourselves with a portion of our booty, that it may not all be spoiled. Come then, I drink your health and that of our dear family. I find the liquor at present both refreshing and agreeable. But I am pretty sure that if we would arrive sober we must not venture on frequent libations."

The coco-nut wine gave our exhausted frames an increase of strength and cheerfulness, and we pursued our way with briskness to the place where we had left our gourd utensils. We found them perfectly dry, as hard as bone, and not the least misshapen. We now, therefore, could put them into our game-bags conveniently enough; and this done, we continued our way. Scarcely had we passed through the little wood in which we breakfasted, when Turk sprang furiously away to seize upon a troop of monkeys, who were skipping about and amusing themselves without observing our approach toward the place of their merriment. They were thus taken by surprise; and before we could get to the spot our ferocious Turk had already seized one of them. It was a female monkey, who held a young one in her arms, which she was caressing almost to suffocation, and which encumbrance deprived her of the power of escaping. The poor creature was killed, and afterwards devoured by Turk. The young one hid himself in the grass and looked on, grinding his teeth all the time.

Fritz flew like lightning to force the ferocious Turk from his prey. He lost his hat, threw down his tin bottle, canes, and other burdens, but all in vain.

The next scene was of a different nature, and comical enough. The young monkey, on perceiving Fritz, sprang nimbly on his shoulders, and fastened his feet securely in the stiff curls of his hair; nor could the squalls of Fritz, nor all the shaking he gave, make the little creature let go. I ran to Fritz, laughing heartily, for I saw that the animal was too young to be capable of doing him any injury, while the expression in the features of the boy made the most diverting contrast with the grimaces of the monkey, whom I in vain endeavoured to disengage.

" There is no remedy, Fritz," said I, " but to submit quietly and carry him. The conduct of the little animal displays a very surprising intelligence; he has lost his mother, and he adopts you for his father.

Perhaps he discovered in you something of the air of a father of a family."

"But I assure you, Father," cried Fritz, "he is giving me some terrible twitches. Do try once more to get him off!"

With a little gentleness and management I at last succeeded. I took the creature in my arms as one would an infant, and I confess I could not help pitying and caressing him.

"Father," cried Fritz, "do let me have this little animal in my own keeping. I will take the greatest care of him. I will give him all my share of the milk of the coco-nuts till we get our cows and goats. And, who knows? his monkey instinct may one day assist us in discovering some different kinds of wholesome fruits."

"I have not the least objection," answered I. "By and by we shall see whether he will be fittest to aid us with his intelligence, or to injure us by his malice."

We now again thought of resuming our journey, and accordingly left the ferocious Turk to finish his meal. The little orphan jumped again on the shoulder of his protector, while I on my part relieved my boy of the bundle of canes. Scarcely had we proceeded a quarter of a league when Turk overtook us full gallop. He showed no sign of giving himself any concern about his cannibal feast, but fell quietly behind Fritz with an air of cool and perfect satisfaction. The young monkey appeared uneasy from seeing him so near, and passed round and fixed himself on his protector's bosom, who did not long bear with so great an inconvenience without having recourse to his invention for a remedy. He tied some string round Turk's body, in such a way as to admit of the monkey's being fastened on his back with it, and then in a tone really pathetic addressed the dog as follows: " Now, Mr. Turk, since it was you who had the cruelty to destroy the mother, it is for you to take every care of her child." At first the dog was restive and resisted; but by degrees, partly by menaces and partly by caresses, we succeeded in gaining his goodwill, and he quietly consented to carry the little burden. The young monkey found himself perfectly happy. Fritz put another string round Turk's neck, by which he might lead him.

In happy expectation of our return we forgot the length of our journey, and found ourselves on the bank of the river before we were aware. Ponto on the other side announced our approach by a violent barking, and Turk replied so heartily, that his motions disturbed the tranquillity of his little burden, who, in his fright, jumped the length of his string from Turk's back to Fritz's shoulder, which he could not afterwards be prevailed upon to leave. Turk ran off to meet his companion and announce our arrival; and shortly after our much-loved family appeared in sight on the opposite shore. They advanced along by the course of the river, till they on one side and we on the other had reached the place where we had crossed it in the morning. We repassed it again in safety and greeted each other with joy. Scarcely had the young ones joined their brother than they began their exclamations of surprise.

" A monkey, a live monkey! Oh, how delightful! How did you catch him? What a droll face he has!"

" He is very ugly!" said little Francis, half afraid to touch him.

" He is much prettier than you!" retorted Jack. " Only see, he is laughing! I wish I could see him eat!"

" Ah ! If we had but some coco-nut !" said Ernest.
' Could you not find any? Are they nice?"

" Have you brought me any milk of almonds?" said
Francis.

" Have you met with any adventure?" asked my
wife.

At length, when all became a little tranquil, I
answered them thus: " Most happy am I to return
to you again, and God be praised, without having
encountered any new misfortune. We have even the
pleasure of presenting you with many valuable acquisitions. But in the object nearest my heart, the discovering what has become of our ship companions,
we have entirely failed."

" Since it pleases God that it should be so," said my
wife, " let us endeavour to be content, and let us be
grateful to Him for having saved us from their un-
happy fate, and for having once more brought us all
together. I have laboured this day under great uneasiness about your safety, and imagined a thousand
evils. The day appeared an age. But now I see you
once more safe and well, I am as happy as could be.
Put down your burdens, we will all help you; for
though we have not, I assure you, spent the day in
idleness, we are less fatigued than you. Now then,
sit down and tell us your adventures."

Jack received my gun, Ernest the coco-nuts, Francis
the gourd-rinds, and my wife my game-bag. Fritz
distributed the sugar-canes, and put his monkey on
the back of Turk, at the same time begging Ernest to
relieve him of his gun. But Ernest assured him that the
large heavy bowls with which he was loaded were the
most he had strength to carry. His mother, a little too
indulgent to his lazy humour, relieved him of them.
Thus we proceeded, all together, to our tent.

Fritz whispered me, that if Ernest had known what the large heavy bowls were he would not so readily have parted with them. " Why, Ernest," cried he, " do you know that these bowls are coco-nuts, your dear much-desired coco-nuts, and each containing the sweet nice milk you have so much wished to taste?"

" Are they indeed? Are they really and truly coco-nuts? Oh, Mother, return them to me quickly! I will carry them, if you please; and I can carry the gun too without finding it heavy!"

" No, no, Ernest," answered his mother. " I am certain you would begin to complain again before we had gone a hundred paces."

Ernest would willingly have asked his mother to give him the coco-nuts and take the gun herself, but this he dare not do. " I have only," said he, " to get rid of these sticks, and carry the gun."

" I would advise you not to give up the sticks either," said Fritz drily. " For the sticks are sugar-canes!"

" Sugar-canes!" cried Ernest.   " Sugar-canes!" exclaimed they all; and, surrounding Fritz, made him give them full instructions on the sublime art of sucking sugar-canes.

My wife was perfectly astonished, and earnestly entreated we would explain to her all about it. I instantly complied with her request, giving her every explanation and particular respecting our journey, and our new acquisitions, which I alternately exhibited for her inspection, no one of which afforded her more pleasure than the plates and dishes. We now adjourned to our little kitchen, and with great delight observed the preparations going forward in it for supper. On one side of the fire we saw a turn-spit, which my wife had contrived by driving two forked pieces of wood into the ground, and placing a long even stick sharpened at one end across them. By this invention she was enabled to roast different kinds of fish or other food, with the help of little Francis, who was entrusted with the care of turning it round from time to time. On the occasion of our return she had prepared us the treat of a goose, the fat of which ran down into some oyster-shells placed there to serve the purpose of a dripping-pan. There were also a dish of fish which the little ones had caught, and the iron pot was upon the fire, provided with a good soup. By the side of these most exhilarating preparations stood one of the casks which we had recovered from the waves, the head of which my wife had knocked out, so that it exposed to our view a cargo of the finest Dutch cheeses contained in round tins.

" You indeed but barely did yourselves justice, my dear ones, in saying that you had not been idle during our absence," cried I. " I see before me what must have cost you great labour. I am, however, a little sorry that you have killed one of our geese so soon; we must employ the utmost economy in the use of our poultry, which may be of service in a time of need."

" Do not make yourself uneasy on this subject," said my wife; " for what you see is not one of our geese, but a kind of wild bird, and is the booty of your son Ernest, who calls him by a singular name, and assures me that it is good to eat."

" Yes, Father. I believe that the bird is a kind of penguin, or we might distinguish him by the surname of *Stupid*. He showed himself to be a bird so wanting in intelligence, that I killed him with a single blow with my stick."

" What is the form of his feet, and of his beak?" asked I.

" His feet were webbed; the beak was long, small, and a little curved downwards. I have kept his head and neck. The bird reminds me exactly of the penguin, described as so stupid a bird in my book of natural history."

" I am glad you have read to such good purpose, my son. But now let us see what we can do with the coco-nuts. But first you will be obliged to learn from Fritz the best manner of opening them, so as to preserve the milk, and I recommend to you not to forget the young monkey."

We seated ourselves; my wife had placed each article of the repast in one of our newly-manufactured dishes. My sons had broken the coco-nuts, and already convinced themselves of their delicious flavour; and then they fell to making spoons with the shells. The little monkey had been served the first, and each amused himself with making him suck the corner of his pocket-handkerchief dipped in the milk of the coco-nut.

The boys were preparing to break some more of the nuts with the hatchet, after having drawn out the milk through the three little holes. I pronounced the word *halt*, and bade them bring me a saw. The thought struck me that by dividing the nuts carefully, the two halves when emptied would remain with the form of some well-looking tea-cups or basins already made to our hands. Jack, who was on every occasion the most active, brought me a saw. I performed my undertaking in the best manner I could, and in a short time each of us was provided with a convenient receptacle for food. Accordingly my wife put the share of soup which belonged to each into those basins. Fritz asked me if he might not invite our company to taste his fine champagne, which he said would not fail to make

us all the merrier. " I have not the least objection,"
answered I, " but remember to taste it yourself before
you serve it to your guests."

He ran to draw out the stopple, and to taste it. . . .
" How unfortunate!" said he. " It is already turned
to vinegar!"

" What is it?—vinegar did you say?" exclaimed my
wife. " How lucky! It will make the most delicious
sauce for our bird, mixed with the fat which has fallen
from it in roasting, and will be as good a relish as a
salad." No sooner said than done. This vinegar,
produced from coco-nut, proved a most agreeable
corrective of the wild and fishy flavour of the penguin,
and without it I am afraid we should have found it
not very palatable. The same sauce considerably
improved our dish of fish also. Each boasted most of
what he himself had been the means of procuring;
it was Jack and Francis who had caught the fish,
while Ernest was employed in securing his penguin.
My dear wife herself performed the most difficult task
of all, that of rolling the cask of Dutch cheeses into the
kitchen, and then knocking out its head.

By the time we had finished our meal the sun was
retiring from our view, and recollecting how quickly
the night would fall upon us, we were in the greatest
haste to regain our place of rest. Our whole flock of
fowls placed themselves as they had done the preceding evening; we said our prayers, and with an
improved serenity of mind lay down in the tent,
taking the young monkey with us, who was become
the little favourite of all. Fritz and Jack contended for
a short time which should enjoy the honour of his
company for the night, and it was at last decided that
he should be laid between them, after which each
would have a hand in covering him carefully that he

might not catch cold. We now all lay down upon the grass in the order of the night before, myself remaining last to fasten the sail-cloth in front of the tent, when I as well as the rest soon fell into a profound and refreshing sleep.

But I had not long enjoyed this pleasing state, when I was awakened by the motion of the fowls on the tent, and by a violent barking of the dogs. I rushed out instantly; my wife and Fritz, who had also been alarmed, followed my example, we each taking a gun.

" Shall you, my dearest, have the courage to fire if it should be necessary?" said I to my wife.

" Most certainly," said she, " if, as you say, it should be necessary. At the same time it would perhaps be better that I should leave to you the task of firing, while I can undertake to load your guns, and to hand them to you as fast as you may want them."

" That is best," said I, " so let us not lose a moment in examining what enemy it is we have to deal with."

Our dogs continued barking with the same violence, and at intervals even howled. We had not proceeded many steps from the tent, when, to our great astonishment, we perceived by the light of the moon a terrible combat. At least a dozen of jackals had surrounded our brave dogs, who defended themselves with an almost unexampled courage.

I had apprehended something much worse than jackals, and felt relieved. " We shall soon manage to set these gentlemen at rest," said I. " Let us fire both together, my boy; but let us take care how we aim for fear of killing the dogs." We fired, and two of the intruders fell instantly dead upon the sands. The others made their escape. My wife, seeing that all was now quiet, entreated us to lie down again and finish our night's sleep, but Fritz asked my permission to let him first drag the jackal he had killed towards the tent, that he might be able to exhibit him the next morning to his brothers. Having obtained my consent, he ran to fetch him, and with great difficulty succeeded in his plan, the animal being of the size of a large dog.

Having therefore nothing further to prevent us, we lay down till day began to break, and till the cocks awoke us both. The children being still asleep, afforded us an excellent opportunity to consult respecting the ensuing day.

CHAPTER V

RETURN TO THE WRECK

I broke a silence of some moments with observing to my wife that I could not conquer my alarm at the view of so many cares and such a variety of exertions to be made. In the first place, a journey to the vessel. " This is of absolute necessity; at least, if we would not be deprived of the cattle and various other useful things, all of which from moment to moment we run the risk of losing by the first approach of a heavy sea. On the other hand, there are so many things to think of, and so much to be done here, for the comfort of all in this desert spot! What ought we to resolve upon? For example, is it not, above all, necessary to contrive a better kind of habitation, and also the means of procuring a more secure retreat from wild beasts for ourselves, and some separate place of accommodation for our provisions? I own I am at a loss what to begin upon first."

" All will fall into the right order by degrees,"

observed my wife. " I cannot, I confess, help shudder-
ing at the thought of this voyage to the vessel; but if
you judge it to be of absolute necessity, it appears to
me that it cannot be undertaken too soon.   In the
meanwhile, nothing that is immediately under my
own care shall stand still, I promise you.   Let us not
be over-anxious about the morrow: sufficient unto
the day is the evil thereof."

" I will follow your advice," said I, " and without
further loss of time. You shall stay here with the three
youngest boys. Fritz, being so much older and stronger
than the others, shall accompany me in the undertaking."

I now woke the children. Fritz sprang nimbly out
of the tent, while his little brothers began to gape and
rub their eyes, to get rid of their sleepiness. Fritz ran
to visit his jackal, which during the night had become
cold and perfectly stiff. He fixed him upon his legs,
and placed him to look like a sentinel at the entrance
of the tent, joyously expecting the wonder and accla-
mations of his little brothers at so singular and unexpected an appearance. But no sooner had the dogs
caught a sight of him than they began a horrible
barking, and set themselves in motion to fall upon him
instantly, thinking he was alive. Fritz had enough to
do to restrain them, and succeeded only by dint of
coaxing and perseverance.   In the meantime their
barking had effectually awakened the younger boys,
and they all ran out of the tent, curious to know what
could be the occasion. Jack was the first who appeared, with the young monkey on his shoulders; but
when the little creature perceived the jackal, he sprang
away in terror, and hid himself at the farthest extremity
of the grass which composed our bed.

The children were much surprised at the sight of a

yellow-coloured animal standing without motion at the entrance of the tent.

" Oh, dear !" exclaimed Francis; " it is a wolf!"

" No, no," said Jack, going near the jackal and taking one of his paws; " it is a yellow dog, and he is dead."

" It is neither a dog nor a wolf," put in Ernest. " Do you not see that it is a golden fox?"

" Very near it, most learned professor !" exclaimed Fritz. " So you can tell an agouti when you see him, but you cannot tell a jackal. I killed him myself in the night."

" In the night, you say, Fritz? In your sleep, I suppose."

" No, Mr. Ernest, not in my sleep, as you suppose, but broad awake. But I cannot wonder at this mistake in one who does not know the difference between a jackal and a golden fox."

" Come, come, my lads, I will have no disputes," said I. " As to the animal, you all are right and all are wrong. He partakes at once of the nature of the dog, the wolf, and the fox; and for his skin, it is really of a *golden* tint."

The boys in an instant became friends; and then followed questions, answers, and wonder in abundance.

The next thing thought of was breakfast. To-day their mother had nothing to give them for their morning meal but some biscuit, which was so hard and dry that it was with difficulty we could swallow it. Fritz asked for a piece of cheese to eat with it, and Ernest spied about the second cask we had drawn out of the sea, and which was standing in our kitchen, to discover whether, as we had all imagined, it also contained some Dutch cheeses. In a minute or two he came up to us, joy sparkling in his eyes.

" Papa," said he, " if we had but a little butter spread upon our biscuit, do you not think it would improve it?"

" That indeed it would, Ernest."

" Perhaps, then, if we were to knock out the head of this cask, we might find some."

" What cask, my boy? And what are you talking of?"

" I am talking of this cask, which is filled with excellent salt butter. I made a little opening in it with a knife; and, see, I got out enough of it to spread nicely upon this piece of biscuit."

" That instinct of yours for once is of some general use," answered I, " and justice requires that I should also commend, with moderation, the excellence of your nose. But now let us profit by the event. Who will have some butter on their biscuits?"

The boys surrounded the cask in a moment, while I was in some perplexity as to the safest method of getting out its contents. Fritz proposed taking off the topmost hoop, by which means one of the ends could be got out. But this I objected to, observing that we should be careful not to loosen the staves, as the heat of the sun would not fail to melt the butter, which would run out. The idea occurred to me that I would make a hole in the bottom of the cask, sufficiently large to take out a small quantity of butter at a time; and I immediately set about manufacturing a little wooden shovel, to use it for the purpose. All this succeeded quite well, and we sat down to breakfast, some biscuits and a coco-nut shell full of salt butter being placed upon the ground, round which we all assembled. We toasted our biscuit, and while it was hot applied the butter, and contrived to make a hearty breakfast.

Meantime I did not fail to notice that their encounter with the jackals had not concluded without the dogs receiving several wounds. Fearing that the heat might bring on inflammation, I desired Jack, the valiant, to wash a small quantity of the butter thoroughly in fresh water, and then to anoint the wounds with it. This he effected with much skill and tenderness. The dogs did not attempt the least resistance, seeming to be sensible of the benefit he was conferring on them. They themselves assisted the cure by licking, so that in a few days they were as well as before.

"One of the things we must not forget to look for in the vessel," said Fritz, "is a spiked collar or two for our dogs, as a protection to them from wild beasts."

"Oh," says Jack, "I can make some spiked collars if Mamma will give me a little help."

"That I will most readily, my boy, for I should like to see what new fancy has come into your head," cried Mamma.

"Yes, yes," pursued I, "as many inventions as you please! But now we must think of setting ourselves to some occupation. You, Mr. Fritz, who, from your superior age and discretion, enjoy the high honour of being my privy counsellor, must make haste and get yourself ready, and we will undertake to-day our voyage to the vessel, to save and bring away whatever may be possible. You younger boys will remain under the wing of your mother. I hope I need not mention that I rely on your perfect obedience to her, and general good behaviour."

While Fritz was getting the boat ready I looked about for a pole, and put a piece of white linen to the end of it. This I drove into the ground, in a place where it would be visible from the vessel. I agreed with my wife that in case of any accident that should require my immediate presence, they should take down the pole and fire a gun three times as a signal of distress. But I gave her notice, that there being so many things to do on board the vessel, it was very probable that we should not be able to return the same day; in which case I, on my part, also promised to make them signals. My wife had the courage and the good sense to consent to my plan. She, however, extorted from me a promise that we should pass the night in our tubs, and not on board the ship. We took nothing with us but our guns and a supply of powder and shot, relying on it that we should find provisions on board. Yet I did not refuse to indulge Fritz in the wish he expressed to let him take the young monkey.

We embarked in silence, often looking back at the dear ones we were quitting. When we had reached to a considerable distance, I remarked that besides the opening by which we had the first time made land, there was another that formed the mouth of the river, running not far from that spot, the current of which was visible a good way into the sea.

To take advantage of this current was my first thought and my first care. Little as I knew of the management of sea affairs, I succeeded in keeping our boat in the direction in which the current ran, by which means we were drawn gently on, till the current had conducted us to within a short distance of the wreck. There we were again obliged to have recourse to our oars. But our arms having now rested for some time, we were ready for new exertions. A little afterwards we found ourselves safely arrived at the breach of the vessel, and fastened our boat securely to one of the timbers.

Scarcely had we got out of the boat than Fritz proceeded with his young monkey on his arm to the main deck, where he found all the animals we had left on board. I followed him, pleased to observe the impatience he betrayed to relieve the wants of the poor creatures, who all now saluted us by the cry or the sounds natural each to its species. It was not so much the want of food as the desire of seeing once more their accustomed human companions which occasioned them to manifest their joy, for they had a portion of the food and water we had left them still remaining. We next examined the food and water of the other animals, taking away what was half-spoiled and adding a fresh supply. Nor did we neglect the care of renewing our own strength by a plentiful repast.

While we were seated and appeasing the calls of hunger, Fritz and I consulted what should be our first occupation, when, to my great surprise, the advice he gave was that we should immediately contrive a sail for our boat. " What," cried I, " makes you think of such a thing at so critical a moment?"

" Father," said Fritz, " let me confess the truth, which is, that I found it very difficult to perform the task of rowing for so long a time, though I assure you I did my best, and did not spare my strength. I observed that, though the wind blew strong in my face the current nevertheless carried us on. Now, as we cannot be benefited on our return by the current, I was thinking that we might make the wind supply its place."

" Ah ha, Mr. Fritz! So you wish to spare yourself a little trouble, do you? But I perceive a great deal of good sense in your argument. The best thing we can do is to take care and not overload the boat, and thus avoid the danger of sinking, or of being obliged to throw some of our stores overboard. Come then, let us set to work upon your sail, and let us look about for what we want."

I assisted Fritz to carry a pole strong enough to serve for a mast, and another for a sail-yard. I directed him to make a hole in a plank with an auger, large enough for the mast. I then went to the sail-chamber, and cut off from an ample piece of sail-cloth enough to make a triangular sail: in the edges I made holes, and passed cords through them. I then sought for a pulley, that I might fasten it to the top of the mast, and thus be enabled to raise and lower my sail at pleasure. Thus prepared I hastened to join Fritz, who was earnestly working at the mast. As soon as he had done we placed the plank that he had perforated across the centre of our craft, and made it fast. The pulley was suspended from a ring at the top of the mast, and the cord, attached to the sharpest angle of the sail, was passed through it. The sail formed a right-angled triangle, one side of which touched the mast and was fastened to it. The shortest side was also fastened with cords to a pole, stretching from the mast beyond the circumference of our bark, and of which one end was fastened to the mast, while the other had a cord running to the stern to be held in my hand.

While I was thus occupied, Fritz had been taking observations through a telescope of what was passing on land. He imparted the agreeable tidings that all was still well. He soon after brought me a small streamer which he had cut from a piece of linen, and which he entreated me to tie to the extremity of the mast, and appeared as much delighted with the streamer as with the sail itself.

"But now, Father," said Fritz, looking kindly on me as he spoke, " as you have eased me of the labour of rowing, it is my turn to take care of you. I am thinking about making a better rudder."

"Your thought would be a very good one," said I,

" but that I am unwilling to lose the advantage of being able to proceed this way and that, without being obliged to veer. I shall therefore fix our oars so as to enable me to steer from either end."

During these exertions the day became far advanced, and I perceived that we should be obliged to pass the night in our tubs. We had promised to hoist a flag if our intention was to pass the night from home, and we decided that our streamer was precisely the thing for this purpose.

We employed the rest of the day in emptying the tubs of the useless ballast of stone, and putting in their place what would be of service, such as nails, pieces of cloth, and different kinds of utensils, &c. The prospect of entire solitude, made us devote our principal attention to the securing as much powder and shot as might fall in our way, that we might thus secure the means of killing animals for food, and of defending ourselves against wild beasts. Utensils also for every kind of workmanship were also objects of incalculable value to us. The vessel, which was now a wreck, had been sent out as a preparation for the establishment of a colony in the South Seas, and for that reason had been provided with a variety of stores not commonly included in the loading of a ship. The quantity of useful things which presented themselves in the store-chambers made it difficult for me to select among them, and I much regretted that circumstances compelled me to leave some of them behind. Fritz, however, already meditated a second visit. We took good care not to lose the present occasion for securing knives and forks and spoons, and a complete assortment of kitchen utensils. In the captain's cabin we found some services of silver, dishes and plates of high-wrought metal, and a little chest filled with bottles of all sorts of excellent wine.

Each of these articles we put into our boat. We next descended to the kitchen, which we stripped of gridirons, kettles, pots of all kinds, a small roasting-jack, &c. Our last prize was a chest of choice eatables, intended for the table of the officers, containing West-phalia hams, Bologna sausages, and other savoury food. I took good care not to forget some little sacks of maize, of wheat, and other grain, and some potatoes. We next added such implements as shovels, hoes, spades, rakes, harrows, &c., &c. Fritz reminded me that we had found sleeping on the ground both cold and hard, and prevailed upon me to increase our cargo by some hammocks and a certain number of blankets; and as guns had hitherto been the source of his pleasures, he added such as he could find of a particular costliness or structure, together with some sabres and clasp-knives. The last articles we took were a barrel of sulphur, a quantity of ropes, some small string, and a large roll of sail-cloth. The ship appeared to us to be in so wretched a condition, that with the least storm she would go to pieces.

Our cargo was so considerable that the tubs were filled to the very brim, and no inch of the boat's room was lost. The first and last of the tubs were reserved for Fritz and me to seat ourselves in and row the boat, which sunk so low that, if the sea had been otherwise than calm, we should have been obliged to ease her of some of the loading: we, however, used the pre-caution of putting on our swimming-jackets.

It will easily be imagined that every moment of the day had been employed. Night suddenly surprised us, and it was no longer possible to think of returning the same evening. A large fire on shore soon greeted our sight—the signal we had agreed upon for assuring us that all was well. We returned the compliment by tying four lanterns to the mast-head. This was answered on their part, according to agreement, by the firing of two guns; so that both parties had reason to be satisfied and easy.

After offering up our earnest prayers for the safety and happiness of all, yet not without some apprehension for the night, we resigned ourselves to sleep in our tubs. The night passed tranquilly enough: my boy Fritz slept as soundly as if he had been in a bed, while I, notwithstanding my fatigue, could neither close my eyes nor keep them from the direction of the shore, perpetually haunted by the recollection of the nocturnal visit of the jackals. I had, however, great reliance that our valiant dogs would do their duty, and was thankful to Heaven for having enabled us to preserve so good a protection.

CHAPTER VI

A TROOP OF ANIMALS IN CORK-JACKETS

Early the next morning, though it was scarcely light, I was already on deck, endeavouring to have a sight of the tent through a spying-glass. Fritz prepared a good breakfast of biscuit and ham; but before we sat down to this refreshment, we recollected that in the captain's cabin we had seen a telescope of a much superior size and power, and we hastily conveyed it upon the deck. While this was doing, the brightness of the day had succeeded to the imperfect light of an earlier hour. I eagerly fixed my eye to the glass, and discovered my wife coming out of the tent and looking attentively

towards the vessel, and we at the same moment perceived the motion of the flag upon the shore. A load
of care was thus taken from my heart. A great object
of my anxiety now was to endeavour to save the live-
stock and get them to shore.

" Would it be impossible to construct a raft," said
Fritz, " and sail them ashore upon it?"

" But think what a difficulty we should find in completing such a raft, and that a greater still would be
to induce a cow, an ass, and a sow, either to get upon
a raft, or, when there, to remain quiet. The sheep and
goats one might perhaps find means to remove, but
for the larger animals, I am quite at a loss how to
proceed. Do consider the point, and tell me what
occurs to your imagination."

" I think, Father, we should tie a long rope round
the sow's neck and throw her into the sea. She is sure
to be able to swim, and we can easily get hold of
the other end of the rope and draw her after the
boat. Then here is another idea, Father: let us tie a
swimming-jacket round each animal, and throw them
into the water; you will see that they will swim like
fish."

We accordingly hastened to carry out our design.
We fixed on a jacket to one of the lambs and threw it
into the sea, and full of anxious curiosity, I followed
the poor animal with my eyes. He sunk at first, and
I thought he was drowned; but he soon reappeared,
shaking the water from his head, and in a few seconds
we perceived that he could swim quite well. After
another interval he appeared fatigued, gave up his
efforts, and suffered himself without resistance to be
borne along by the current, which conducted and
sustained him to our complete satisfaction. " Victory!"
exclaimed I; " these useful animals are all our own!

Let us not lose a moment in adopting the same measures with those that remain, but take care not to lose our little lamb." Fritz now would have jumped eagerly into the water to follow the poor creature, but I stopped him till I had seen him tie on one of the swimming-jackets, and then I suffered him to go. He took with him a rope, first making a slip knot in it, and, soon overtaking the lamb, threw the noose round his neck, and thus drew him to our boat, and lifted him out of the water.

We then went and looked out four small casks, such as had been used for keeping fresh water. I emptied their contents, and then closed them again. Then I bound them together with a piece of sail-cloth. I strengthened this with a second piece, and this con-trivance I destined to support the cow and the ass, two casks to each, the animal being placed in the middle. The weight of the animal pressed down the sail-cloth, and would have brought the casks into close contact on each side, but that I took care to insert a wisp of hay or straw, to prevent friction or pressure. I added a thong of leather, stretching from the casks across the breast and haunches of the animal, to make the whole secure; and thus both my cow and my ass were equipped for swimming.

It was next the turn of the smaller animals. Of these, it was the sow who gave us the most trouble; we were first obliged to put a muzzle on her to prevent her biting, and this being done, we tied a large piece of cork under her body. The sheep and goats were more docile, and we had soon accoutred them. And now we had succeeded in assembling our whole company on the deck, in readiness for the voyage. We tied a cord to either the horns or the neck of each, and to the other end of the cord a piece of wood. We struck

away some more of the shattered pieces of wood from
the side of the vessel, which only served to encumber
the breach by which we had entered, and were again
to pass to put out to sea. We began our experiment
with the ass, by conducting him as near as possible to
the edge of the vessel, and then suddenly shoving him
off. He fell into the water, and for a moment disappeared; but he soon rose again.

Next came the cow's turn. As she was infinitely more
valuable than the ass, my fears increased in proportion.
The ass had swam so courageously, that he was already
at a considerable distance from the vessel, so that there
was room for our experiment on the cow. We had
more difficulty in pushing her overboard, but she
reached the water in as much safety as the ass; she
did not sink so low in it, and was perfectly sustained
by the empty barrels; and she made her way on the
surface with, if I may so express it, a dignified composure. According to this method we proceeded with
our whole troop, throwing them one by one into the
water, where by and by they appeared in a group
floating at their ease, at a short distance from the
vessel. The sow was the only exception; she became
quite furious, set up a loud squalling, and struggled
with so much violence in the water that she was carried
to a considerable distance, but fortunately in a direction towards the landing-place. We had now not a
moment to lose; our last act was to put on our cork-
jackets, and then we descended through the breach,
took our station in the boat, and were soon out to sea,
surrounded by our troop. We carefully took up from
the water each of the floating bits of wood which we
had fastened to the ends of the ropes round the animals,
and thus drew them all after us. When everything was
adjusted and our company in order, we hoisted our

sail, which, soon filling, conducted us and our escort safe to the land.

We now perceived how impossible it would have been for us to have executed our enterprise without the assistance of the sail; for the weight of so many animals sunk the boat so low that all our exertions to row to such a distance would have been ineffectual, while by means of the sail she proceeded to our satisfaction, bearing in her train our suite of animals, which produced the most singular effect. Proud of the success of so extraordinary an enterprise, we were in high spirits, and seated ourselves in the tubs, where we made an excellent dinner. Fritz amused himself with the monkey, while I was wholly occupied in thinking of those I had left on land, and of whom I now tried to take a view through my telescope. My last act on board the vessel had been to take one look more at them, and I perceived my wife and the three boys setting out on some excursion; but it was in vain that I endeavoured to conjecture what their plan might be. I therefore seized the first moment of quiet to make another trial with my glass, when a sudden exclamation from Fritz filled me with alarm. " Oh, Father," cried he, " look! A fish of an enormous size is coming up to the boat!"

" Be ready with your gun, Fritz, and the moment he is close upon us, let us both fire upon him at the same instant."

Our guns were each loaded with two balls, and we got up from our tubs to give the intruder a hearty reception. He had nearly reached the boat, and with the rapidity of lightning had seized the foremost sheep: at this instant Fritz aimed his fire so skilfully that the ball lodged in the head of the monster, an enormous shark. The fish half turned himself round in the water and hurried off to sea, leaving us to observe the lustrous smoothness of his belly, and that as he proceeded he stained the water red. I determined to have the best of our guns at hand the rest of the way, lest we should be again attacked.

Fritz had reason to be proud of his achievement, while I on my part felt surprise. I had always understood that this kind of sea-monster was not easily frightened, and also that the heaviest load of shot was rarely known to do him any injury, his skin being so hard as to present an extraordinary degree of resistance. I resumed the rudder, and as the wind drove us straight towards the bay, I took down the sail and continued rowing till we reached a convenient spot for our cattle to land. I then untied the end of the cords, and they stepped contentedly on shore. Our voyage thus happily concluded, we followed their example.

I had already been surprised at finding none of my family looking out for us, and was at a loss to conjecture in what they could be occupied to prevent them. We could not, however, set out in search of them till we had disencumbered our animals of their swimming apparatus. Scarcely had we entered upon this employment, when I was agreeably relieved by the exclamation and joyful sounds which reached our ears. It was my wife and the youngest boys who uttered them, the latter of whom were soon close up to us, and their mother followed not many steps behind, each and all in excellent spirits. When the first burst of happiness had subsided, we all sat down on the grass, and I began to give them an account of our different plans and their success, in the order in which they occurred. My wife could find no words to express her surprise and satisfaction at seeing so many useful animals round us.

" I had been ransacking my poor brains," said she, " every moment of your absence, to conceive some means by which you might succeed in protecting the poor animals, but I could fix on none."

" Ha! ha!" cried little Francis suddenly, " what is that I see in your boat? Look, Mother, there is a sail and a new flag floating about in the air. How pretty they are!"

Ernest and Jack now ran to the boat, and bestowed no less admiration than Francis had done upon the mast, the sail, and the flag. In the meantime we began to unpack our cargo, while Jack stole aside and amused himself with the animals; took off the jackets from the sheep and goats, bursting from time to time into shouts of laughter at the ridiculous figure of the ass, who stood before them adorned with his two casks and his swimming apparatus, and braying loud enough to make us deaf. Jack tried a long time to disengage the ass, but found difficulties he knew not how to overcome; till at last, tired out and longing to be in some way a more effectual actor in the scene, he got upon the ass's back between the casks, and kicked so violently against his sides that he at last succeeded in causing the animal to advance to the place where we were all assembled.

We laughed heartily at the sight of so singular an equipage, when, as I was assisting him to get down from the ass's back, I perceived with surprise that he had round his waist a belt of metal covered with yellow skin, in which were fixed a pair of pistols.

" Hullo, Jack!" exclaimed I, " where did you procure this curious costume, which gives you the look of a smuggler?"

" From my own manufactory," replied he. " And if you cast your eyes upon the dogs you will see more of my specimens."

I looked at them, and perceived that each had on

a collar similar to the belt round Jack's waist, with, however, the exception of the collars being armed with a number of nails, the points of which were outwards, and exhibited a most formidable appearance.

" But where did you get the metal, and the thread, and the needle?"

" Fritz's jackal furnished the first," answered my wife; " and as to the last, a good mother is always provided with them. Then have I not an enchanted bag, from which I draw out such articles as I stand in need of? So, if you have a fancy for anything, you have only to acquaint me with it."

Fritz was somewhat angry and discontented on finding that Jack had taken upon him to dispose of his jackal, and to cut his beautiful skin into slices. He, however, concealed his ill-humour as well as he could. But, as he stood quite near to his brother, he called out suddenly, holding his nose as he spoke:

" What a horrid smell! It is enough to give one the plague! Does it come from you, Mr. Currier?"

" It is rather yours than mine," replied Jack in a resentful tone, " for it was your jackal which you hung up in the sun to dry."

" And which would have been dried in a whole skin if it had not pleased your fancy to cut it to pieces."

" Fritz," said I, in a somewhat angry tone, " this is not generous on your part. Of what importance is it who cut up the skin of the jackal, if it has contributed to our use? My dear children, we are here in this desert island in just such a situation as that of our first parents when they were driven out of the garden of Eden. Let us then share one with the other in every benefit bestowed upon us, and from this moment may the words *yours* and *mine* be banished from our happy circle! It is quite certain, Jack, that the belt round

your waist, not being dry, has an offensive smell.
The pleasure of wearing what you had contrived
makes you willing to bear with the inconvenience,
but we should never make our own pleasures the pain
of another. I therefore desire that you will take it off
and place it in the sun to dry; and then you can join
your brothers, and assist them to throw the jackal
into the sea."

Fritz's ill-humour was already over; but Jack, whose
temper was less docile, persisted in keeping on the belt,
assuming an air which was meant to express that he
was not disposed to yield. His brothers, however,
continued their warfare by pretending to avoid him,
and crying out " What a smell! What a smell!" till
at length Jack, tired with the part he had been acting, stripped off the belt, and ran to assist his brothers
in dragging the dead jackal to the sea.

Perceiving that no preparations were making for
supper, I ordered Fritz to bring us the Westphalia
ham. The eyes of all were now fixed upon me with
astonishment, everyone believing I could only be in
jest. Fritz returned, displaying with exultation a large
and excellent ham, which we had begun to cut in the
morning.

" A ham!" cried one and all, clapping their hands.
" A ham! and ready dressed! What a nice supper
we shall have!"

" It comes quite in the nick of time too," said I,
" for, to judge by appearances, a certain careful steward
I could name seems to have intended to send us supper-
less to bed."

" I will tell you presently," replied my wife, " what
prevented me from providing a supper for you all.
Your ham, however, makes you ample amends, and
I have something which will make a pretty side-dish."

She now showed us about a dozen of turtles' eggs, and then hurried away to make an omelette.

"Oh, look, Father!" said Ernest, "if they are not the very same sort which Robinson Crusoe found in his island! See, they are like white balls, covered with a skin like wetted parchment! We found them upon the sands along the shore."

"Your account is perfectly just, my dear boy," said I. "By what means did you make so useful a discovery?"

"Oh, that is a part of our history," called out my wife; "for I also have a history to relate, when you will be so good as to listen."

"Hasten then, my dear, and get your pretty side-dish ready, and we will have the history for the dessert. In the meanwhile I will relieve the cow and the ass from the encumbrance of their sea accoutrements. Come along, boys, and give me your help."

I got up, and they all followed me gaily to the shore, where the animals had remained. We were not long in effecting our purpose with the cow and the ass, who were both animals of a quiet and kind temper. But when it was the turn of the sow, our success was neither so easy nor so certain. We had no sooner untied the rope than she escaped from us. The idea occurred to Ernest of sending the two dogs after her, who caught her by the ears and brought her back, while we were half deafened with the hideous noise she made. At length, however, she suffered us to take off her cork-jacket quietly enough. We now laid the swimming apparatus across the ass's back and returned to the kitchen, Ernest particularly delighted at finding that we were to have our loads carried for us.

In the meanwhile my wife had prepared the omelette, and spread a table-cloth on the end of the cask of butter, upon which she had placed some of the plates and silver spoons we had brought from the ship. The ham was in the middle, and the omelette and the cheese opposite to each other. The whole made a figure not to be despised by the inhabitants of a desert island. By and by the two dogs, the fowls, the pigeons, the sheep, and the goats had all assembled round us, which gave us something like the air of sovereigns of the country. It did not please the geese and ducks to add themselves to the number of our subjects; they seemed to prefer their natural element, and confined themselves to a swamp, where they found a kind of little crab in great abundance.

When we had finished our repast, I bade Fritz present our company with a bottle of Canary wine, which we had brought from the captain's cabin, and I then desired that my wife should tell us the promised history.

CHAPTER VII

SECOND JOURNEY OF DISCOVERY PERFORMED BY THE MOTHER OF THE FAMILY

" You pretend," said my wife, with a smile, " to be curious about our history. Well, then, on the first day of your absence nothing took place, except that we were anxious on your account. But this morning, after catching sight of the signal you had promised, and having set up mine in return, I looked about before the boys were up, in hopes to find a shady place in which I might sit down and rest myself; but the only bit of shade which presented itself was behind our tent. This occasioned me to reflect on our situation. 'It will be impossible,' said I to myself, ' to remain in this place, without any other shelter than a miserable tent, inside which the heat is even worse than outside. Courage then,' said I, ' my husband and my eldest son are at this moment actively employed for the general good, why then should not I be active also? Why not undertake, with my younger sons, to do something that shall add some comfort to our existence? I will pass over with them to the other side of the river, and examine the country respecting which my husband and Fritz related such wonders. I will try to find out some well-shaded, agreeable spot, in which we may all be settled.'

" In the course of the morning Jack had slipped away to the side of the tent where Fritz had hung his jackal, and cut some long slips of skin, lengthways, from the back of the animal, and afterwards set about cleaning them.

" Jack completed the cleaning of his skins very cleverly. When he had finished, he looked out from the chest of nails those that were longest, and which had the largest and flattest heads; these he stuck through the bit of skin intended for the collar. He next cut a strip of sail-cloth the same breadth as the skin, and laying it along on the heads of the nails, politely proposed to me the agreeable occupation of sewing them together to prevent the heads of the nails from injuring the dogs. I begged leave to be excused; but observing afterwards the good humour with which he set about trying to sew them for himself, I conquered my repugnance, and rewarded him by completing the job myself.

" The next thing was a belt for himself, it being intended to contain his two pistols. ' But, my dear

Jack,' said I, ' you do not foresee what will happen—
a piece of skin not entirely dry is always liable to
skrink.   So you will not be able to make use of it.'
My little workman, as I said this, struck his forehead
and betrayed other marks of impatience.   ' What you
say is true,' said he.   ' But I know what to do.' He then
took a hammer and some nails, and stretched his strips
of leather on a plank, which he then laid in the sun to
dry quickly, thus preventing their shrinking.

" I next assembled them all three round me, and
informed them of my plans, and you may believe I
heard nothing like a dissenting voice.   They lost not a
moment in preparing for our departure; they examined their arms, their game-bags, looked out the best
clasp-knives, and cheerfully undertook to carry the
provision-bags.   I, for my share, was loaded with a
large flask of water and a hatchet, for which I thought
it likely we might find a use.   I also took the light
gun which belongs to Ernest, and gave him in return a
carbine.   Turk seemed well aware that he knew the way,
and proceeded at the head of the party.   We arrived
at the place at which you had crossed the river, and
succeeded in passing over as securely as you had done.

" Ernest was first in reaching the other side, and
met with no accident.   Little Francis entreated me to
carry him on my back, which appeared difficult
enough, but Jack relieved me of my gun and hatchet.
I had great difficulty to keep myself steady with the
little burden at my back, who leaned with all his
weight upon my shoulders.   After having filled my
flask with river-water, we proceeded on our way;
and when we had reached to the top of the ascent on
the other side, which you described to us as so enchanting, I myself experienced the same delight from
the scenery around.

" In casting my eyes over the vast extent before me, I had observed a small wood of the most inviting aspect. I had so long sighed for shade, that I resolved to take our course towards it. For this, however, it was necessary to go a long way through a strong kind of grass, which reached above the heads of the little boys; an obstacle which we found too difficult to overcome. We therefore resolved to pursue a direction along the river, till it was necessary to turn upon the wood. We found traces of your footsteps, and took care to follow them till we had come to a turn on the right, which seemed to lead directly to it. Here again we were interrupted by the grass, which we had great difficulty in getting through. Jack was now loitering a little behind, and I frequently turned round to observe what he could be doing. At last I saw him tearing off some handfuls of grass and wiping his clothes with it; and then I perceived him shake his pocket-handkerchief and lay it on his shoulders to dry. I hastened back to him to inquire what had happened.

" ' Oh, Mother!' said he, ' I believe all the water of the river has got into my pockets. Only see, everything I had in them is wet—pistols, everything!'

" ' Mercy on us!' interrupted I in great alarm, ' have you put your pistols in your pocket? They are not loaded, I hope?'

" ' I do not know, Mother. I only put them there while my belt was drying, that I might always have them about me.'

" ' Thoughtless, yet fortunate boy!' exclaimed I. ' If with the suddenness of your motions the pistols had gone off, they would infallibly have killed you. Take care, I entreat you, not to commit such an imprudence in future.'

" In reality I perceived that there was little danger

of their going off. While we were conversing about what had happened, our attention was interrupted by a sudden noise, and we perceived a large bird issuing from the thickest part of the grass and mounting in the air. Each of the boys prepared to fire, but before they could be ready the bird was out of the reach of shot. Ernest was bitterly disappointed, and instantly changed the gun for the carbine I had given him, crying, ' What a pity! If I had but had the lightest gun! if the bird had not got away so fast, I am sure I should have killed him. Ah, if one would but come at this very moment!'

" ' A good sportsman, Ernest,' said I, ' always holds himself in readiness, this being the great art of a sportsman; for you must know that birds never send messages to give notice of their coming.'

" ' I wish I could but know,' said Jack, ' what bird it was.'

" ' I am sure it was an eagle,' said Francis; ' for I have read that an eagle can carry off a sheep, and this bird was terribly large.'

" ' Oh yes,' said Ernest mockingly; ' as if all large birds must be eagles! Why, do you not know that there are some birds much larger even than eagles? The ostrich, for example; and there are others.'

" The boys now scampered away to the place where the bird had risen, when a second like the first, rushed out with a great noise, and mounted above their heads.

" The boys remained stupid with astonishment, following him with their eyes and open mouths, while I could not help laughing heartily.

" ' Oh, such fine sportsmen as we have here!' cried I. ' They will never let us be in want of game, I plainly perceive. *Ah, if one would but come at this very moment!* These were your own words, Ernest!'

" Jack, with a comic look on his face, darted his eager eyes upon the flying bird, and taking off his hat made a profound bow, roaring out:

" ' Have the goodness, Mr. Traveller, to pay just one more little visit, only for a single minute. I beg that we may have the pleasure of seeing you once again——'

" We now examined the place from which the birds had mounted, and found a large nest formed of dried plants, the workmanship of which was clumsy enough. The nest was empty, with the exception of some broken shells of eggs. I inferred from this that their young had lately been hatched, and observing at this moment a rustling motion at some distance, I concluded that the young covey were scampering away in that direction.

" Continuing our journey, we reached the little wood. A prodigious number of unknown birds were skipping and warbling on the branches of the trees without betraying the least alarm at our presence. My dear husband, you cannot possibly form an idea of the trees we now beheld! In my whole life I have never seen a tree so immense. What appeared to us at a distance to be a wood, was only a group of about fourteen, the trunks of which looked as if they were supported in their upright position by so many arches on each side, the arches being formed by portions of the roots of the trees, of great thickness and extent. Meanwhile the tree itself is further supported by a perpendicular root, placed in the midst of the others, and of a smaller compass.

" Jack climbed with considerable trouble upon one of these arch-formed roots, and with a packthread in his hand measured its circumference, which he found was some twenty-two inches and a half. I made thirty-two steps in going round one of those giant trees at the roots. The twigs are strong and thick; its leaves moderately large in size, and bearing some resemblance to the hazel-tree; but I was unable to discover that it bore any fruit. The soil immediately round the tree and under its branches produced in great abundance a short, thick kind of plant, and of a perfectly smooth surface. Thus every circumstance seemed inviting us to use this spot as a place of repose, and I resolved to go no farther, but to enjoy its delicious coolness till it should be time to return. I sat down in this verdant elysium with my three sons. We took out our provision-bags; a charming stream flowed at our feet. Our dogs were not long in reaching us. They had remained behind, about the skirts of the wood. To my great surprise they did not ask for anything to eat, but lay down quietly, and were soon asleep at our feet. I felt that I could never tire of this enchanting spot. It occurred to me that if we could but contrive a kind of tent that could be fixed in one of the trees, we might safely come and make our abode here. I had found nothing in any other direction that suited us so well. When we had shared our dinner, and rested, we set out on our return, again keeping close to the river, half expecting to see along the shore some other vestiges of the vessel.

" But before we left our enchanting retreat, Jack entreated me to stay a little longer and finish sewing the linen strips to his leather belt. The little coxcomb had so great an ambition to strut about in his belt, that he had taken the trouble to carry the piece of wood, on which he had nailed his skin to dry, along with him. Finding that the skin was really dry, I granted his request. When I had finished my task, he eagerly fastened the belt round him, and placed his pistols in it. He set himself before us in a marching step, with the knuckles of his hand turned back upon his hip, leaving to Ernest the care of putting on the dogs' collars, which he insisted should be done, for it would give them, he said, a martial air. The little hero was all impatience for you and Fritz to see him in his new accoutrement, so that I had enough to do to walk quick enough to keep sight of him. In a country where no track of the foot of man is to be found, we might easily lose each other. I became more tranquil respecting him when we had got once more all together on the sea-shore, for, as I expected, we found there pieces of timber, poles, large and small chests, and other articles from the vessel. None of us, however, was strong enough to bring them away. We therefore contented ourselves with dragging all we could beyond the reach of the highest tide. Our dogs were fully employed in fishing for crabs, which they drew with their paws to the shore as the waves washed them up, and on which they made an excellent repast. I now understood that it was this sort of prey which had appeased their hunger before they joined us at dinner.

" We now suddenly cast our eyes on Ponto, whom we perceived employed in turning over a round substance he had found in the sands, some pieces of which he swallowed from time to time. Ernest also perceived what he was about, and did us the favour, with his usual composure, to pronounce: ' They are turtles' eggs.'

" ' Run, my children," cried I, ' and get as many of them as you can. They are excellent, and I shall have the greatest pleasure in being able to regale our dear travellers with so delicious a dish.'

" We found it difficult to make Ponto come away from the eggs, to which he had taken a great fancy. At length, however, we succeeded in collecting nearly two dozen. When we had concluded this affair, we

by accident cast our eyes upon the ocean, and to our
great astonishment we perceived a sail, which seemed
to be approaching the land. I knew not what to think.
But Ernest, who always thinks he knows everything,
exclaimed that it was you and Fritz. Little Francis
was terribly afraid that it must be the savages come to
eat us up, like those described in Robinson Crusoe's
island. We soon, however, had the happiness of being
convinced that Ernest was right. We ran eagerly
towards the river, which Jack and Ernest recrossed as
before, while I also resumed my burden of little Francis
at my back, and in this manner soon arrived at the
place of your landing, when we had nothing to do but
to throw ourselves into your arms! This, my dear
husband, is a faithful narration of our journey; and
now, if you wish me happiness, you will conduct me
and your sons, with our whole train of animals, to the
spot I have described."

My dear wife's story finished, I assured her how
much I admired her courage.

" Tell me," said I, " if I shall make you a balloon
of sail-cloth, to enable you to arrive at your country-
seat?"

" Yes, yes," said she, " laugh as much as you like,
but I assure you my plan is not so silly as you imagine.
One advantage, at least, it is certain we should derive
—the being out of reach of wild beasts. Do you recollect the large lime-tree in the public walk of the
town we lived in, and the pretty little room which had
been built among its branches, and the flight of stairs
which led to it? What should hinder us from effecting
such a contrivance in one of my giant trees?"

" I think it is a very good idea," said I.

Having finished our conversation, we performed our
devotions and retired to rest.

CHAPTER VIII

CONSTRUCTION OF A BRIDGE

When my wife and I were awake next morning we resumed the question of our change of abode. I observed to her that it was a matter of great difficulty. "First," I said, "we must contrive a place among the rocks where we can leave our provisions and other things, which may serve both for a fortress and a storehouse, and to which, in case of any danger, we can retreat. The next thing is to throw a bridge across the river, if we are to pass it with all our family and baggage."

"A bridge!" exclaimed my wife; "can you possibly think of such a thing? What reason can there be that we should not cross the river as we did before? The ass and the cow will carry all our goods upon their backs."

"But do you recollect, that to preserve dry what they carry they must not perform their journey as they did from the vessel? For this reason, then, if for no other, we must contrive a bridge. We shall want also some sacks and baskets; you may therefore set about making these, and I will undertake the bridge, which the more I consider the more I think to be of indispensable necessity, for the stream will, no doubt, at times increase, and the passage become impracticable in any other way."

"Well, then, a bridge let there be," said my wife. "But let us not allow ourselves a moment of leisure till we have completed all that is necessary for our departure. You will leave our stock of gunpowder here, I hope, for I am not easy with a large quantity of it so near us. A thunderstorm, or some thoughtless action of one of the boys, might expose us to serious danger."

" You are right, my dear; and I will carefully attend to your suggestion."

Thus, then, we decided the important question of removing to a new abode; after which we fixed upon a plan of labour for the day, and then awaked the boys. Their joy on hearing of our project may easily be conceived; but they expressed their fear that it would be a long while before a bridge could be built, a single hour appearing an age to them, with such a novelty in view as the prospect of removing to the wood. In the fullness of their joy they entreated that the place might be called *The Promised Land.*

We now began to look about for breakfast, Fritz taking care not to neglect his monkey, who sucked one of the goats as quietly and as contentedly as if she had been his mother. My wife undertook to milk another, and then the cow, and afterwards gave some of the milk to each of the children: with a part of what remained she made a sort of soup with biscuits, and the rest she put into one of the flasks, to accompany us in our expedition. During this time I was preparing the boat for another journey to the vessel, to bring away planks and timbers for the bridge. After breakfast we set out; and this time I took with me Ernest as well as Fritz, that we might accomplish our object in a shorter time. We rowed stoutly till we reached the current, which soon drew us on beyond the bay; but scarcely had we passed a little islet lying to one side of us, than we perceived a prodigious quantity of sea-gulls, whose various and discordant sounds so disagreeably assailed us that we were obliged to stop our ears. I had a great curiosity to discover what could possibly be the reason of so numerous an assembly of these creatures. I therefore steered to the spot, but finding that the boat made but little way, I hoisted my sail that we might have the assistance of the wind.

To Ernest our expedition afforded the highest delight. Fritz on his part did not for a moment take his eyes from the islet where the birds had assembled. Presently he suddenly exclaimed: " I see what it is! The birds are all pecking at a monstrous fish, which lies dead upon the soil!"

I approached sufficiently near to step upon the land, and after bringing the boat to an anchor with a heavy stone, we walked cautiously up to the birds. We soon perceived that the object which attracted them was in reality an enormous fish, which had been thrown by the sea upon the islet, and whose body lay there for the birds. Indeed, so eagerly were they occupied with the feast, that though we were within the distance of half gun-shot, not one of them attempted to fly off. We observed the extreme voracity of this plumed group; each bird was so intent upon its prey, that nothing could have been more easy than to have killed numbers of them with our sticks alone. We did not, however, envy them their prize. Fritz did not cease to express his wonder at the monstrous size of the animal, and asked me by what means he could have got there.

" I believe," answered I, " you were yourself the means; there is every appearance that it is the shark you wounded yesterday. See, here are the two balls which you discharged."

" I do believe it is the very same!" cried Fritz, skipping about for joy. " I well remember I had two balls in my gun, and here they are. lodged in his hideous head!"

" I grant it is hideous enough," continued I. " Its aspect even when dead makes one shudder. See what a horrible mouth he has, and what a rough and prickly skin! Nor is he small of his kind, for I fancy that he measures more than twenty feet. We ought to be thankful to Providence, and a little to our Fritz also, for having delivered us from such a monster! But let us each take away with us a bit of his skin, for I have an idea that it may be useful to us. But how to drive away these eager intruders so as to get at him is the difficulty."

Ernest instantly drew out the iron ramrod from his gun, and in a few moments killed several of the birds, while all the others took their flight. Fritz and I then cut several long strips of the skin from the head of the shark, with which we were proceeding to our boat, when I observed, lying on the ground, some planks and timbers which had recently been cast by the sea on this little island. I therefore made choice of such as seemed proper for my purpose; and, with the assistance of the crowbar and a lever which we had brought with us, I found means to get them into the boat, and thus spared ourselves the trouble of proceeding farther to the vessel. I bound the timbers together, with the planks upon them, in the manner of a raft, and tied them to the end of the boat; so that we were ready to return in about four hours after our departure, and might with justice boast of having done a good day's work. I accordingly pushed again for the current, which soon drove us out to sea. Then I tacked about, and resumed the direct route for the bay and for our place of embarkation, by this means avoiding the danger of touching upon shallows. All this succeeded to my utmost wishes; I unfurled my sail, and a brisk wind soon conveyed us to our landing-place.

While we were sailing, Fritz at my request had nailed the strips of skin we cut from the shark to the mast to dry. Before very long he took a look at the drying strips. " Look, Father," he said, " you were wrong in telling me to nail my skins to the mast, for they have curled round in drying."

" That was precisely my intention," replied I; " they will be much more useful to us round than flat. Besides, you have still some left which you may dry flat; and then we shall have a fine provision of shagreen, if we can find out a good method to rub off the sharp points, and afterwards to polish it."

Ernest asked his brother if he knew why the mouth of the shark is not, as in other animals, placed in the middle of the snout, but directly under. Fritz confessed his inability to answer this question. " All I know is how to kill them," he growled.

" I suppose," rejoined Ernest, " that the mouth of the shark is thus placed with the intention of preventing him from depopulating the sea. With so voracious an appetite, nothing would escape him if he had the power to seize his prey without turning his body. But, as it is, there is time enough for a smaller animal to make his escape."

Presently we were once more landed safely on our shore, but no one of our family appeared. We called out to them and were answered by the same sounds in return, but in a few minutes my wife appeared between her two little boys returning from the river, a rising piece of ground having concealed her from our sight.

After we had all partaken of refreshment, we proceeded with our plans. I imitated the example of the Laplanders in harnessing their reindeer for drawing their sledges. Instead of traces, halters, &c., I put a piece of rope with a running knot at the end round the neck of the ass, and to the other end, which I passed between its legs, I tied the piece of wood which I wished to be removed. The cow was harnessed in the same manner, and we were thus enabled to carry our planks from the boat, piece by piece, to the spot which our architect, Jack, had chosen at the river as the most eligible for our bridge; and, to say the truth, I thought his judgment excellent. It was a place where the shore on each side was steep and of equal height. There was even on our side an old trunk of a tree, on which I rested my principal timber.

"Now then, boys," said I, "the first thing is to see if our timbers are long enough. By my eye I should think they are."

"Mother has some balls of packthread with which she measured the height of the giant tree," interrupted Ernest, "and nothing would be more easy than to tie a stone to the end of one of them and throw it to the other side of the river; then we could draw it to the very brink, and thus obtain the exact length."

"Your idea is excellent," cried I. "Run quickly and fetch the packthread."

He returned without loss of time. The stone was tied to its end and thrown across as we had planned. We drew it gently back to the river edge, marking the place where the bridge was to rest. We next measured the string, and found that the distance from one side to the other was eighteen feet. It appeared to me necessary, that to give a sufficient solidity to the timbers I must allow three feet at each end of extra length, amounting therefore in all to twenty-four feet; and I was fortunate enough to find that several of those we had brought did not fall short of this length. There now remained the difficulty of getting them across the stream; but we determined to discuss this part of the subject while we ate our dinner.

We all now proceeded homewards, and entering the kitchen we found our good steward had prepared a large dish of lobsters for us. But before she would let us taste them she insisted we should see another useful labour she had been employed about. She accordingly displayed two sacks intended for the ass, which she had seamed with packthread. The work, she assured us, had with difficulty been accomplished, since for want of a needle large enough to carry pack-thread, she had been obliged to make a hole with a nail for every stitch. We might therefore judge by her perseverance in such a task of the ardour with which she longed to see her plan of a removal executed. She received on this occasion, as was well her due, abundance of compliments and thanks, and also a little good-humoured raillery. For this time we hurried through our meal, all being deeply interested in the work we were about to undertake. The impatience we all felt to begin scarcely left us time to strip the lobsters of their shells, each thinking only of the part which might be assigned him towards the execution of the bridge.

Having consulted together as to the means of laying our timbers across the river, the first thing I did was to attach one of them to the trunk of the tree of which I have already spoken, by a strong cord, long enough to turn freely round the trunk. I then fastened another cord to the other end of the beam. This cord I fastened round a stone, and then threw the stone across the river. I next passed the river as I had done before, furnished with a pulley, which I secured to a tree. I passed my second cord through the pulley, and recrossing the river with this cord in my hand, I

contrived to harness the ass and the cow to the end of
the cord. I next drove the animals from the bank of
the river. They resisted at first, but I made them go
by force of drawing. I first fixed one end of the beam
to the trunk of the tree, and then they drew along the
other end, so as gradually to advance over the river.
Presently, to my great joy, I saw it touch the other
side, and at length become fixed by its own weight.
In a moment Fritz and Jack leaped upon the timber,
and, in spite of my paternal fears, crossed the stream
with a joyful step upon this narrow bridge.

The first timber being thus laid, the difficulty of our
undertaking was considerably diminished; a second
and a third were fixed with the greatest ease. Fritz
and I placed them at such distances from each other
as was necessary to form a broad and handsome bridge.
What now remained to be done was to lay some short
planks across them quite close to each other, which
we executed so expeditiously that our whole undertaking was completed in a much shorter time than I
should have imagined possible. I had not fastened
the cross planks to each other, for they appeared to be
close and firm without it; and, besides, I recollected
that in case of danger from any kind of invasion, we
could with the greatest ease remove them, and thus
render the passage of the river more difficult. Our
labour, however, had occasioned us so much fatigue,
that we found ourselves unable for that day to enter
upon new exertions, and, the evening beginning to set
in, we returned to our home, where we partook heartily
of supper and went to bed.

CHAPTER IX

CHANGE OF ABODE

As soon as we had breakfasted the next morning, I assembled all the family together, to take with them a solemn farewell of this our first place of reception from the horrible disaster of the shipwreck. I thought it right to represent strongly to my sons, particularly to the youngest, the danger of exposing themselves as they had done the evening before, along the river.

" We are now going," said I, " to inhabit an unknown country. We are unacquainted both with the soil and its inhabitants, whether human creatures or beasts. It is therefore necessary to use the utmost caution; to make it a rule never to remain separate from each other. Particularly you young ones must take care not to run on before or stray too far behind."

I directed my sons to assemble our animals, and to leave the ass and the cow to me, that I might load them with the sacks as we had planned. I had filled these at the two ends, and made a slit longways in the middle of each of them, and to each side of the slit I tied several long pieces of cord, which, crossing each other and being again brought round and fastened, served to hold the sacks firmly on the back of the animal. We next began to put together all the things we should stand most in need of, for the two or three first days, in our new abode. I put these articles into the two ends of each sack, taking care that the sides should be equally heavy, and then fastened them on. I next added our hammocks and other coverings to complete the load, and we were about to begin our march when my wife stopped me.

"I cannot prevail upon myself," said she, "to leave our fowls behind us to pass the night by themselves, for I fear they would become the prey of the jackals. We must contrive a place for them among the luggage, and also one for our little Francis, who cannot walk so far. There is also my enchanted bag, which I recommend to your particular care," said she smiling, "for who can tell what may yet pop out of it for your good pleasure!"

Fortunately I had already thought of making the ass's load as light as possible, foreseeing that it would be necessary he should carry our little one a part of the way. I now placed the child upon his back, fixing the enchanted bag in such a way as to support him; and I tied them together upon the ass with so many cords, that the animal might have galloped without his falling off.

In the meanwhile the other boys had been running after the cocks and hens and the pigeons, but had not succeeded in catching one of them. "Well," said their mother, "see how you have heated yourselves in running after the fowls. I could have put you in a way to catch them in a moment."

"Yes, yes, you may think so, Mother," said Jack, a little sulky, "but I will give you leave to roast me in the place of the first fowl that you shall be able to catch."

"Poor Jack!" said his mother laughing, "you will then soon be on the spit, which would be a pity, considering what better things we might do with you."

She now stepped into the tent, and brought out two handfuls of peas and oats, and calling to the birds in her accustomed tones, they flocked round her in a moment. She then walked slowly before them, dropping the grain all the way, till they had followed her into the tent. When they were all in, and busily employed in picking up the grain, she shut the entrance, and caught one after the other without difficulty.

" Grant me a reprieve from the spit, Mother," cried Jack, " and I will do all I can to help you in securing your prisoners."

Accordingly he soon caught the whole of the fowls. They were then tied by the feet and wings, and in a basket covered with a net, placed on the top of our luggage. Ernest suggested placing two bent sticks archways across the basket, and throwing a blanket over it, that the want of light might incline them to sleep, for with the clatter they made it was impossible to hear each other speak.

We packed up everything we were obliged to leave and placed it in the tent, which we carefully closed, and for greater security fastened down the ends of the sail-cloth at the entrance by driving stakes through them into the ground. We ranged a number of vessels, both full and empty, round the tent to serve as a rampart, and thus we confided to the protection of Heaven our remaining treasures. At length we set ourselves in motion. Every one of us carried a gun upon his shoulder and a game-bag at his back. Children are always fond of a change of place; ours were full of joy and good-humour. Nor was their mother less affected with the same cause. She walked before with her eldest son, the cow and the ass being immediately behind them. The goat, conducted by Jack, came next. The little monkey was seated on the back of his nurse, and made a thousand grimaces. After the goats came Ernest, conducting the sheep; while I, in my capacity of general superintendent, followed behind and brought up the rear. Our march was slow, and there was something patriarchal in the spectacle we exhibited. I fancied we must resemble our forefathers journeying in the deserts.

"Now then, Fritz," cried I, "you have the specimen you wished for of the patriarchal mode of life; what do you think of it?"

"I like it much, Father," replied he. "I never read the Bible without wishing I had lived in those good times."

We had now reached our bridge and advanced half-way across it, when the sow for the first time took the fancy of joining us, and contributed to the pictorial effect of our procession. At the moment of our departure she had shown herself so restive and indocile, that we had been compelled to leave her behind us. But when she saw that we had all left the place, she set out to overtake us.

On the other side of the river we experienced an inconvenience wholly unexpected. The nutritious aspect of the grass was too strong a temptation for our animals, who strayed in every direction to feed upon it, so that, without the assistance of our dogs, we should not have been able to bring them back to the line of our procession. The dogs, indeed, were of great use to us, and when everything was restored to proper order we were able to continue our journey. For fear, however, of a similar occurrence, I directed our march along the seaside, where there was not sufficient grass to attract the animals.

Scarcely had we advanced a few steps on the sands, when our two dogs, which had stayed behind, set up a loud barking, mixed at intervals with howling, as if they had been wounded, or were engaged in an encounter with some formidable animal. Fritz in an instant lifted his gun to his cheek, and was ready to fire; Ernest, always somewhat timid, drew back a step; Jack ran bravely after Fritz with his gun upon his shoulder; while I prepared myself to run to their assistance. Youth is always full of ardour, and in spite of all my exhortations that they would advance with caution, my boys, eager for the event, made but three jumps to the place from which the noise proceeded. In an instant Jack had turned to meet me, clapping his hands and calling out, " Come quickly, Father, come quickly! Here is a monstrous porcupine!"

I soon reached the spot, and perceived that it was really as they said, bating a little exaggeration. The dogs were running to and fro with bloody noses; and when they approached too near him, he made a frightful noise, and darted his quills so suddenly at them, that a great number of them had penetrated the skins of our valiant dogs, and remained sticking in them.

While we were looking on, Jack determined on an attack, which succeeded marvellously well. He took one of the pistols which he carried in his belt, and fired it so exactly at the head of the porcupine that he fell dead at once.

The boys were absolutely at a loss what means to use for carrying away the carcass. They thought of dragging it, but as often as they attempted to take hold there was nothing but squalling, and running to show the marks made by the quills on their hands. " We must leave him behind," said they.

" Not for an empire," cried Jack, " shall he be left there, for Mother must have a sight of him."

In saying this, he tied one corner of his handkerchief round the neck of the animal, and drew him by the other to the place where we had left the dear mother in care of our possessions.

" Here is the monster, Mother," said he, " armed

with his hundred thousand spears. But I was a match for him, and at one shot too! His flesh is excellent food, at least Father says so."

Meanwhile my wife and I had hastened to relieve the dogs, by drawing out the quills and examining their wounds. Having done this, we joined the boys round the porcupine. Jack took upon him to do the honours, as if he was showing the animal at a fair.

" Observe," cried he, " what a terrible creature it is! How long and hard his quills are, and see what strange feet he has! I am sure he must have run like a hare, but I killed him for all that! And what a singular sort of crest he has on his head!"

" That," said I, " is the reason why naturalists call him the crested porcupine. But now tell me, were you not afraid in going so near him that he would dart some of his quills at you?"

" Oh no, Father; I knew that the stories about his shooting his quills at you were merely fabulous."

" But you saw that many of them had stuck in the dogs."

" That was because the dogs attacked the animal and ran against his quills."

" Well, Jack, what do you mean to do with your prize?"

" Oh, take it with us, take it with us, certainly, Father, for you say its flesh is good to eat."

I could not resist his importunity, and I resolved to lay the porcupine on the back of the ass, behind little Francis, first having wrapped his bloody head in a quantity of grass, and then rolled him up in a blanket to protect my boy from his quills. We now resumed our journey, but had not proceeded far when the ass began to kick furiously with his hind legs, tore himself away from my wife, who was guiding him, and set off full gallop, braying so loud as almost to deafen us, and scampering from side to side in so extraordinary a way that the boys were thrown into fits of laughter, in which my wife and I should probably have joined, if we had not conceived the idea that the situation of Francis was not quite safe. A sign we made to the dogs made them set off like lightning after the deserter, whom they in a moment overtook, and stopped his way with a tremendous barking. We took our boy from the ass's back, delighted to find that he had scarcely even experienced any alarm.

"But tell me, Francis," said I jocosely, "have you been clapping spurs to your horse?"

I no sooner pronounced these words than suddenly I recollected the porcupine. I immediately examined if the quills had not penetrated through the covering in which I wrapped it. This I found was actually the case; though I had folded it three times double, the quills had pierced through all, and produced the effect of the sharpest spur. I soon found a remedy for this, by placing my wife's enchanted bag, which was filled with articles of a nature to be absolutely impenetrable, between the ass's back and the dead animal. I now restored Francis to his place, and we then resumed our journey.

Fritz had run on before with his gun, hoping he should meet with prey. What he most desired, was to find one or two of those large bustards which his mother had described. We followed him at our leisure, till at last, without further accident or adventure, we arrived at the place of the giant trees. Such, indeed, we found them, and our astonishment exceeded all description. "What trees! what a height! what trunks! I never heard of any so prodigious!" exclaimed one and all. "I must confess I had not myself formed

an idea of the reality. To you be all honour, my dear
wife, for the discovery of this agreeable abode. The
great point we have to gain, is to fix a tent large enough
to receive us all in one of these trees."

We began now to release our animals from their
burdens, having first thrown our own on the grass.
We next used the precaution of tying their two fore-
legs together with a cord, that they might not go far
away. We restored the fowls to liberty, and then,
seating ourselves upon the grass, held a family council.
I was myself somewhat uneasy on the question of our
safety during the ensuing night. I accordingly observed
to my wife, that I would make an endeavour for us
all to sleep in the trees that very night. While I was
deliberating with her on the subject, Fritz, who thought
of nothing but his sporting, had stolen away to a short
distance, and we heard the report of a gun. This
would have alarmed me, if at the same moment we
had not recognized Fritz's voice crying out " Hit!
hit!" and in a moment we saw him running towards
us, dragging a dead animal of uncommon beauty by
the paws. " Father, Father, look! Here is a superb
tiger-cat!" said he, proudly raising it off the ground.

" Bravo! bravo!" cried I; " bravo, Nimrod the
undaunted! Your achievements will call forth the
unbounded gratitude of our cocks and hens and
pigeons, for you have rendered them important service. If you had not killed this animal, he would no
doubt have destroyed our whole stock of poultry. I
charge you look about in every direction, and try to
destroy as many of the species as fall in your way, for
we cannot have more dangerous intruders."

" How did you kill him, Fritz?"

" With my pistol, Father, as Jack killed the porcupine. What is the exact name of the animal, Father?"

" You may for the present give it the name of the tiger-cat. I do not, however, think that it is the animal which is so denominated at the Cape of Good Hope. I rather think it is the margay, a native of America, an animal of extremely vicious dispositions and singular voraciousness; he destroys the birds of the forest, and neither a man, a sheep, nor goat that should fall in his way would escape his rapacity. We ought to be thankful to you for having destroyed so formidable an enemy."

" All I ask, Father, is, that you will let me keep the skin, and I wish you would tell me what use I can make of it."

" One idea occurs to me, and it is this: you must skin the animal yourself, taking the greatest care not to injure it in the operation, particularly those parts which cover the fore-legs and the tail. If you will do this, you may make yourself a belt with it, like your brother Jack's, except that it will be much more beautiful. The odd pieces will serve admirably to make bags to contain our knives, forks, spoons."

" And I too, Father, will make some cases with the skin of my porcupine," said Jack.

" And why should you not, my boy? The skin of the tiger-cat can only furnish us with four, and we ought to have six at least. So set to work, and show us quickly what you can do. I should like you to preserve some of the quills for me, for I think I can contrive to convert them into packing-needles, or into arrows. Those bits of skin that are left may serve to repair the dogs' collars when they begin to wear, or might be joined together and made into a sort of coat of mail, as a protection to them when they have to encounter wild beasts."

The boys left me no moment of repose till I had

shown them how to take off the skins of the animals. In the meanwhile Ernest looked about for a flat stone as a sort of foundation for a fireplace, and Francis collected some pieces of wood for a fire. Ernest was not long in finding what he wanted, and then he ran to join us and advise on the subject of skinning animals, and then on that of trees, making various comments and inquiries respecting the name of those we intended to inhabit. " It is my belief," said he, " that they are large hazel-trees. See if the leaf is not of the same form."

" But that is no proof," interrupted I, " for many trees bear leaves of the same shape, but nevertheless are of different kinds. Besides, it appears to me that there is not so great a resemblance as you think between the leaves of the trees which grow here and those of the hazel, the former being of a paler colour, and white underneath. I recollect, too, that there is the wild mango and also the fig-tree, whose roots grow in the same manner as our giant trees, forming a beautiful arch."

" I thought, Father, that the mango-tree only grew on the sea-shore, and in marshy soils?"

" You are not mistaken, Ernest; the black mango-tree loves the water. But there is, besides, the red mango, which bears its fruit in bunches, something like our currant-bushes. This kind of the mango-tree is found at a considerable distance from the sea, and its wood is used for a red dye. There is a third sort, which is called the mountain mango, or yellow wood, and this is the kind whose roots produce the beautiful arches you now see around us."

Little Francis presently came running loaded with dry branches for his mother, his mouth crammed full of something, and calling out, " Mamma, Mamma,

I have found a nice fruit to eat, and I have brought you home some of it!"

His mother, quite alarmed, made him open his mouth, and took out with her finger what he was eating with so keen a relish. With some difficulty she drew out the remains of a fig.

"A fig!" exclaimed I. "Where did you find it? Thank God, this is no poison! But nevertheless remember, Francis, that you are never to put anything in your mouth without first showing it to your mother or to me. And tell us where you got this fig."

"I got it among the grass, Father, and there are a great many more. I thought it must be good to eat, for the fowls and the pigeons, and even the pig, came to the place and ate them."

"You see, then, my dear," said I to my wife, "that our beautiful trees are fig-trees, at least the kind which are thus named at the Antilles, though they do not in the least resemble the tree called by that name in Europe, except that they both bear a fruit having some resemblance to the European fig. I now recollect that the leaves of the mango-tree are round, and not oval like these."

I took this occasion to give the boys a lesson on the necessity of being cautious, and never to venture on tasting anything they met with till they had seen it eaten by birds and monkeys. At the word monkeys they all ran to visit the little orphan, whom they found seated on a root of a tree, and examining with the oddest grimaces the half-skinned porcupine and the tiger-cat. Francis offered him a fig, which he first turned round and round, then smelled at it, and concluded by eating it voraciously

In the meanwhile my wife had been employed in making a fire, in putting on the pot, and preparing for our dinner. She had put a large piece of the porcupine into it, and the rest she had laid in salt for another time. The tiger-cat was bestowed upon the dogs. While our dinner was dressing, I employed my time in making some packing-needles with the quills of the porcupine. I put the point of a large nail into the fire till it was red-hot. Then taking hold of it, with some wet linen in my hand by way of guard, I perforated the thick end of the quills with it. I had soon the pleasure of presenting my wife with a large packet of long, stout needles, which were the more valuable in her estimation, as she had formed the intention of contriving some better harnessing for our animals. I recommended her to be frugal in her use of the packthread, for which I should soon have so urgent a need in constructing a ladder for ascending the tree we intended to inhabit. I had singled out the highest and thickest fig-tree, and while we were waiting for dinner, I made the boys try how high they could throw their sticks and stones in it. I also tried, but the very lowest branches were so far from the ground that none of us could touch them. I perceived, therefore, that we should be under the necessity of inventing some method to reach so far, as otherwise it would be impossible to fasten the ends of my ladder to them. I allowed a short pause to my imagination on the subject, during which I assisted Jack and Fritz in carrying the skins of the two animals to the adjacent stream, where we confined them under water with some large stones. By this time we were called to dinner, and we all partook with pleasure of our porcupine, which had produced an excellent soup, and had no fault but that of being a little hard. My wife, however, could not prevail upon herself to eat of it; which occasioned Jack a little mortification.

CHAPTER X

CONSTRUCTION OF A LADDER

Our repast being ended, I observed to my wife that I did not think it would be possible for us to sleep that night in the tree. I however desired her immediately to begin preparing the harness for the animals, that they might go to the seashore and fetch the pieces of wood and such articles as I might find necessary for enabling us to ascend the tree, if, contrary to my expectation, it should be found practicable. She lost not a moment in beginning her work. In the meantime I set about suspending our hammocks to some of the arched roots of the trees. I next spread over the same arched roots a piece of sail-cloth large enough to cover all the hammocks, to preserve us from the dew and from the insects. Having thus made the best provision I could for the night, I hastened with the two eldest boys to the sea-shore to examine what pieces of wood might have been thrown up by the waves, and to choose out such as were most proper for the steps of my ladder. The dry branches of the fig-tree I would not use, for they appeared to me too fragile; and I had not observed any other kind of wood growing near that was sufficiently solid. There were, no doubt, on the sands, numberless pieces, the quality of which was fit for my object. Unfortunately, however, there was none that would not require considerable labour to be adapted to my purpose, and thus my undertaking would have experienced a considerable delay, if Ernest had not been lucky enough to discover a number of bamboo-canes in a sort of bog. I took them out, and with the boys' assistance completely cleared them from the dirt, and stripping off their leaves, I found that they were precisely what I wanted. I then began to cut them with my hatchet in pieces of four or five feet long; the boys bound them together in faggots proportioned to their strength for carrying, and we prepared to return with them to our place of abode. I next secured some of the straight and most slender of the stalks to make arrows. At some distance I perceived a thicket, in which I hoped I might find some young twigs, which I thought might also be useful. We proceeded to the spot, but apprehending it might be the retreat of some dangerous reptile or animal, we held our guns in readiness. Ponto, who had accompanied us, went before. We had hardly reached the thicket when we observed him make several jumps, and throw himself furiously into the middle of the bushes. Instantly a troop of large-sized flamingoes sprang out, and mounted into the air. Fritz, always too ready with his gun, instantly fired, when two of the birds fell down among the bushes. One of them was quite dead, but the other, slightly wounded in the wing, soon got up, and giving himself a shake, and finding that he could not fly, began to make use of his long legs, and to run so fast towards the water that we were afraid he would escape us. Fritz, in the joy of his heart, ran to pick up the flamingo he had killed. He plunged up to his knees in the water, and with great difficulty was able to get out again. Warned by his example, I proceeded more cautiously in my pursuit of the wounded bird. Ponto came to my assistance, and without him I should have lost all trace of the creature; but Ponto ran on before, caught hold of the flamingo, and held him till I reached the spot. All this was effected with considerable trouble, for the bird made a stout resistance, flapping his wings with violence for some time. However, at last I succeeded in securing him.

Fritz was not long in extricating himself from the swamp. He now appeared holding the dead flamingo by the feet, but I had more trouble in the care of mine, as I had a great desire to preserve him alive. I had tied his feet and his wings with my handkerchief, notwithstanding which he still continued to flutter about, and tried to make his escape. I held the flamingo under my left arm, and my gun in my right hand. I made the best jumps I was able to get to the boys, at the risk of sinking every moment into the mud, which was extremely deep.

The joy of the boys was excessive when they saw that my flamingo was alive. " If we can but cure his wound and contrive to feed him, what a happiness it will be!" said they. " Do you think that he will like to be with the other fowls?"

" I know," answered I, " that he is a bird that may be easily tamed. But he will not thank you for such food as we give our fowls; he will make his humble petition to you for some small fish, a few worms, or insects."

" Our river will furnish him with all these," said Ernest.

" I hope you will take great care of him, boys."

" How delightful it will be," said Fritz, " if we can catch some other sorts of wild birds, and have a yard to keep them in! But look, Father, he is web-footed like aquatic birds, while his legs are long like the stork. Is not this rare and extraordinary?"

" Not at all, Fritz; many birds are able to both run and swim."

" But, Father," said Ernest, " are all flamingoes like this, of such a beautiful red colour, and the wings with purple? I think I have seen the flamingo in my *Natural History*, and the colours were not like these, so perhaps this is not a flamingo at all."

" I believe it is a flamingo, Ernest, and that this difference in the plumage denotes the age; when very young they are grey, at a more advanced age, white, and it is only when they are full grown that they are adorned with this beautiful tinted plumage."

" This dead one, then, is an old fellow, Father, and I am afraid he will make a tough dish. Shall we take him home to Mother?"

" Yes, certainly. I leave to you the care of carrying him in the best manner you can; in the meantime I shall repeat my visit to the canes, for I have not done with them yet."

I accordingly selected now some of the oldest of the stalks, and cut from them their hard-pointed ends, which I thought would serve for the tips of my arrows.

When I had done all I wanted, I began to think of returning. Ernest took the charge of all the canes; Fritz carried the dead flamingo, and I took care of the living one. We had not gone far when Fritz, addressing himself to Ponto, said, " Oho, lazy bones! so you think you are to be excused from any part of the burden; have the goodness to carry my flamingo on your back."

As he said this, he tied the dead bird upon his back without the least resistance from the patient animal.

" So then," said I, " Mr. Fritz intends to return quite at his ease, and without any part of our load, while his old father and his young brother carry each a heavy portion!"

" Your reproach is very just, Father," said Fritz. " Give me your live bird, and I will take care of him. See, he already gives me a kind look!"

We were now returned to the spot where we had left the three bundles of bamboo-canes, and as my sons were sufficiently loaded, I took charge of them myself.

We were at length arrived once more at our giant trees, and were received with a thousand expressions of interest and kindness. All were delighted at the sight of our new conquests. My wife immediately asked where we should get food enough for all the animals we brought home. "You should consider," said I, "that some of them feed us instead of being fed, and the one we have now brought need not give you much uneasiness, if, as I hope, he proves able to find food for himself." I now began to examine his wound, and found that only one wing was injured by the ball, but that the other had also been slightly wounded by the dog's laying hold of him. I anointed them both with an ointment composed of a mixture of butter and wine, which seemed immediately to ease the pain. I next tied him by one of his legs with a long string to a stake driven into the ground, quite near to the stream.

I now set Fritz and Ernest to work to measure our stock of thick ropes, of which I wanted no less than some eighty feet for the two sides of the ladder; the two youngest I employed in collecting all the small string we had used for measuring, and carrying it to their mother. For my own part, I began to make arrows with a piece of the bamboo and the short, sharp points of the canes. As the arrows were hollow, I filled them with moist sand to give them weight, and lastly I tipped them with a bit of feather from the flamingo to make them fly straight. Scarcely had I finished my work than the boys came jumping round me.

"A bow! a bow! and some real arrows!" cried

they. " Tell us, Father," continued they, " what you
are going to do with them? Do let me shoot one!
And me; and me too !"

" Have patience, boys; I say, have patience. This
once I must claim the preference for myself, in order
to make trial of my work, which I undertook rather
for use than for amusement."

" Have you, my dear, any strong thread?" said I
to my wife.

" Come," said she, " my pretty bag, give me what
I ask you for! My husband wants some thread, and
it must be very strong—See now, did I not promise
you should have your wish?"

Just at this moment Fritz joined us, having finished
measuring the rope. He brought me the welcome
tidings that our stock in all was about five hundred
fathoms. I now tied the end of the ball of strong
thread to an arrow, and fixing it to the bow, I shot it
off in such a direction as to make the arrow pass over
one of the largest branches and fall on the other side.
By this method I lodged my thread across the main
branch, while I had the command of the end and the
ball below. It was now easy to tie a piece of rope to
the end of the thread, and draw it upwards till the
knot should reach the same branch. We were thus
enabled to measure the height it was from the ground,
and it proved to be forty feet. Having now made
quite sure of being able to raise my ladder by means
of the string already suspended, we all set to work with
increased confidence. The first thing I did was to cut
a length of about a hundred feet from my ropes an
inch thick; this I divided into equal parts, which I
stretched along on the ground in two parallel lines, at
the distance of a foot from each other. I then directed
Fritz to cut pieces of bamboo-cane, each two feet in

length. Ernest handed them to me, one after another; and as I received them I inserted them into my cords at the distance of twelve inches respectively, fixing them with knots in the cord, while Jack, by my order, drove into each a long nail at the two extremities, to hinder them from slipping out again. Thus in a very short time I had formed a ladder of forty rounds in length, and in point of execution firm and compact. I now proceeded to fasten it firmly to one end of the rope which hung from the tree, and pulled it by the other till one end of our ladder reached the branch, and seemed to rest so well upon it that the joyous exclamations of the boys and my wife resounded from all sides. All the boys wished to be the first to ascend upon it, but I decided that it should be Jack, he being the nimblest and of the lightest among them. Accordingly the rest of us held the end of the rope with all our strength, while our young adventurer tripped up the ladder with as much ease as if he were a cat, and presently took his post upon the branch; but he had not strength enough to tie the rope firmly to the tree. Fritz now assured me that he could ascend the ladder as safely as his brother; but, as he was much heavier, I was not altogether without apprehension. I gave him instructions how to step in such a way as to divide his weight, by occupying four rounds of the ladder at the same time with his feet and hands. I made him take with him some large nails and a hammer, to nail the ladder firmly to the branch. He set out courageously upon the undertaking, and was almost instantly side by side with Jack, forty feet above our heads, and both saluting us with cries of exultation. Fritz immediately set to work to fasten the ladder by passing the rope round and round the branch, and this he performed with so much skill and intelligence, that I felt sufficient reliance to determine me to ascend myself, and conclude the business he had begun. But before I ascended I tied a large pulley to the end of the rope, and carried it with me. When I was at the top I fastened the pulley to a branch which was within my reach, that by this means I might be able to draw up the planks and timbers for building my aerial castle. I executed all this by the light of the moon, and felt the satisfaction of having done a good day's work. I now gently descended my rope-ladder, and joined my wife.

I had directed the boys to descend first. My astonishment, therefore, on reaching the ground and finding that neither Fritz nor Jack had made their appearance, it is easier to conceive than to describe, their mother having seen nothing of them since they ascended the ladder. While I was endeavouring to conjecture where they could be, we suddenly heard the sound of voices which seemed to come from the clouds, chanting the evening hymn. I soon recognized the trick our young rogues had played me. Seeing me busily employed in the tree, instead of descending, they had climbed upwards till they reached a great height. My heart was now lightened of my apprehensions for their safety, and I called out to them as loudly as I could to take great care in coming down. It was almost night, and the light of the moon scarcely penetrated the foliage. They presently descended without any accident. I now directed them to assemble all our animals, and to get together what dry wood we should want for making fires, which I looked to as our defence against the attacks of wild beasts.

When these preparations were finished, my wife presented me with the result of the day's work she had performed. It was a set of traces and a breast-leather each for the cow and the ass. I promised her, as a reward for her zeal, that we should all be settled in the tree the following day. And now we began to think of our supper, in which she and Ernest and little Francis had been busily engaged. Ernest had made two wooden forks, and driven them into the ground to support a spit, upon which was a piece of the porcupine, which he kept turning at the fire. Another piece of the animal was boiling for soup, and both exhaled an odour which gave us an excellent appetite.

All our animals had now come round us, one after the other. My wife threw some grain to the fowls, to accustom them to assemble in a particular spot, and when they had eaten it we had the pleasure of seeing our pigeons take their flight to the top of the giant tree, and the cocks and hens perching and settling themselves, and cackling all the time, upon the rounds of the ladder. The quadrupeds we tied to the arched roots of the tree, quite near to our hammocks, where they lay down on the grass to ruminate in tranquillity. Our flamingo was not forgotten, Fritz having fed him with crumbs of biscuit soaked in milk, which he ate heartily. Afterwards, putting its head under its right wing and raising its left foot, the beautiful bird gave itself with confidence to sleep.

At last we had notice that our supper was served. My wife, still keeping her resolution of not tasting the porcupine, contented herself with bread and cheese. The children brought us some figs for dessert, which they had picked up under the trees, and of which we all partook with pleasure. And now the gaping of one of the boys, and the outstretched arms of another, gave us notice that it was time for our young labourers to retire to rest. We performed our evening devotions. I set fire to several of the heaps of branches, and then threw myself contentedly upon my hammock. My young ones were already cased in theirs, and we were soon greeted with their murmurs at being obliged to lie so close to each other that they could not move their limbs.

" Ah, boys," cried I, " you must try to be contented. No sailor is ever better accommodated than you are now."

I then directed them how to put themselves in a more convenient posture, and to swing their hammocks gently to and fro.

They profited by my advice, and all except myself were soon asleep.

CHAPTER XI

THE SETTLING IN THE GIANT TREE

I had thought it necessary to keep watch during this first night. Every leaf that stirred gave me the apprehension that it was the approach of a jackal or a tiger, who might attack some member of my family. As soon as one of the heaps was consumed I lighted another. At length, finding that no animal appeared, I by degrees became assured, and at last fell into so sound a sleep that I did not awake early enough for the execution of my project of that day. The boys were all up and about me. We took our breakfast and fell to our work. My wife, having finished her daily occupation of milking the cow and preparing the breakfast, set off with Ernest, Jack, and Francis, attended by the ass, to the sea-shore. They had no doubt of finding some more wood, and thought it would be prudent to replenish our store. I ascended the tree with Fritz, and made preparations for my undertaking, for which I found the tree in every respect convenient. The branches grew extremely close to each other, and in an exactly horizontal direction. Such as grew in a manner to obstruct my design, I cut off either with the saw or hatchet, leaving none but what presented me with foundation for my work. I left those which spread themselves evenly away from the trunk, and had the largest circuit, as a support for my floor. Above these, at the height of forty-six feet, I found others upon which to suspend our hammocks; and higher still there was a further series, destined to receive the roof of our tent, which for the present was to be formed of a large surface of sail-cloth.

The progress of these preparations was slow. It was necessary to hoist up to this height of forty feet beams that were too heavy for my wife and her little assistants to raise from the ground without great effort. I had, however, the resource of my pulley, which served to excellent purpose. My wife and her little boys fastened the beams to pieces of cord, while Fritz and I contrived to draw them up to the elevation of the tent. When I had placed two beams upon the branches, I hastened to fix my planks upon them. I made the floor double, that it might have solidity if the beams should be in any way warped from their places. I then formed a wall something like a park-paling all round, to prevent accidents to ourselves or children. This operation, and a third journey to the sea-shore to collect timber, filled our morning so completely that not one of us thought about dinner. For this once it was requisite to be content with ham and milk. Dinner ended, we returned to finish our aerial palace, which now began to make an imposing appearance. We unhooked our hammocks, and by means of the pulley hoisted them up to our new habitation. The sail-cloth roof was supported by the thick branches above. As it was of great compass, and hung down on every side, the idea occurred to me of nailing it to the paling on two sides, and thus getting not only a roof, but two walls also; the immense trunk of the tree forming a third side, while the fourth side contained the entrance of our apartment. This I left open, both as a means of seeing what passed without, and as a means of admitting air. We enjoyed an extensive view of the ocean and shore. The hammocks were soon suspended, and now everything was ready for our reception. Well satisfied with the execution of my plan I descended with Fritz, who had assisted me through the whole. As the day was not far advanced, and I observed we had still some planks remaining, we set about contriving a table to be placed between the roots of the trees, and surrounded with benches; and this place, we said, should be our dining-parlour.

Entirely exhausted by the fatigues of the day, I threw myself at full length on a bank, saying to my wife that as I had worked like a galley-slave to-day, I should allow myself some rest to-morrow.

My wife answered, that not only was I entitled to a day of rest, but that it was a duty to take it on the following day. " For," said she, " I have calculated that to-morrow is Sunday."

Unfortunately we had already passed one Sabbath day without recollecting that it was so.

" I thank you, my dear," said I, " for making this discovery, and I promise you that the day shall be celebrated by us as it ought to be. Now that we seem to have surmounted many difficulties, and to have secured ourselves an habitation, we should indeed be culpable not to celebrate the day He has consecrated."

The little company was soon assembled round the supper-table. Their mother followed, holding in her hand an earthen pot, which we had before observed upon the fire, and the contents of which we were all curious to be informed of. She took off the cover, and with a fork drew out of it the flamingo which Fritz had killed. She informed us that she had preferred dressing it this way to roasting, because it was an old bird, which would prove tough. The bird was excellent, and was eaten up to the very bones.

While we were thus enjoying our repast, the live flamingo stalked up to the place where we were sitting, in the midst of our flock of fowls, to receive his part of the repast, little thinking that it was his late companion that had furnished it. The live flamingo had now become so tame that we had released him from the stake. He took his walks gravely from place to place, and looked perfectly contented with his company. His fine plumage was most pleasing to look upon; while, on the other hand, the sportive tricks and the grimaces of our little monkey afforded the most agreeable spectacle imaginable. The little animal had become quite familiar with us: jumped from the shoulder of one to that of another; always caught adroitly the meat we threw him, and ate it in so pleasant a way as to make us laugh heartily. To increase our merriment, the old sow, which hitherto had shown an unconquerable aversion to our society, and which we had missed for two whole days, was now seen advancing towards us, grunting at every step. For this time, however, her grunting indicated her joy at having found us once more: and the joy was mutual, of which my wife gave her a substantial proof, by serving her instantly with what remained of our daily allowance of milk.

I thought her too generous, till she explained that it was necessary to contrive some utensils for making butter and cheese, and that till this was done, it was better to turn the milk to profit, than to let it be spoiled. And it was the more necessary as our grain began to run short, and that, as pigs are very fond of milk, it might be a means of preventing her wandering from us again.

" I always find you right, my dear," said I. " It shall not be long ere we again undertake another visit to the vessel to fetch a new provision of grain for your poultry."

" Again the subject of the vessel !" said she. " I shall never enjoy a moment's happiness till it is gone to the bottom, and you have banished it from your thoughts ! You never make a voyage that does not leave me filled with agonizing alarm."

" I cannot deny," replied I, " that there may be reason for this. But I must remind you that we always choose a day of calm weather for our excursion; and we should be unpardonable, if we allowed ourselves to neglect the means of obtaining a variety of useful things which Providence seems to have reserved for our use."

During this conversation the boys had lighted one of the heaps of wood. Everyone was now eager to retire to rest, and the signal for ascending the ladder was given. The three eldest boys were up in an instant; then came their mother's turn, who proceeded cautiously, and arrived in safety. My own ascension was the last. I carried little Francis on my back, and the end of the ladder had been loosened at the bottom, that I might be able to draw it up during the night. Every step, therefore, was made with the greatest difficulty, in consequence of the swinging motion. At last, however, I got to the top, and drew the ladder

after me. It appeared to the boys that we were in one
of the castles of the ancient chevaliers, in which, when
the drawbridge is raised, the inhabitants are secured.
Notwithstanding this apparent safety, I kept our guns
in readiness. We now abandoned ourselves to repose;
our hearts experienced a full tranquillity; and the
fatigue we had all undergone induced so sound a sleep,
that daylight shone full in the front of our habitation
before our eyes were opened.

CHAPTER XII

THE SABBATH

On awaking in the morning, we were all sensible of
an unusual refreshment, and a new activity of mind.

" Well, young ones," cried I jocosely, " you have
learned, I see, how to sleep in a hammock."

" Ah," answered they, stretching and yawning,
" we were so fatigued yesterday that it is no wonder
we slept so soundly."

" Here, then, my children, is another advantage
derived from labour; that of procuring a sweet and
peaceful sleep."

" Yes, yes, Father, that is very true," said they,
" so let us go to work again to-day. What is there to
do?"

" Nothing at all, my children."

" Oh, Father, you are joking."

" No, my boys, I am not joking. This day is Sunday,
and God said *six days shalt thou labour, but the seventh
is the Sabbath of the Lord thy God*; and we will therefore

refrain from all serious labour. Now let us descend to breakfast, and see to our animals."

Accordingly, after saying our prayers, we descended the ladder, and breakfasted on warm milk.

All now standing up, I repeated aloud the church service, which I knew by heart, and we sung some verses from the hundred-and-nineteenth psalm, which the boys had before learned.

My wife then brought from her enchanted bag a copy of the Holy Bible, which, most thoughtful of women, she had brought with her from the wreck. I read some passages from it to my family. In this solitude, in which for so long a time we had heard only our own thoughts expressed in simple enough language, we were singularly affected with the words of Scripture. I explained as well as I could what I read, and I gave the book in turn to each of the boys that they might read for themselves. I chose in preference such passages as were applicable to our circumstances. We then raised our hearts to God to thank Him for so signal a benefit as the preservation of our Bible.

My young folks remained for a time thoughtful and serious, but by and by each slipped away to seek the recreation he liked best.

Jack desired me to lend him my bow and arrows. Little Francis laid my activity under contribution, by requesting me to make him a bow and arrows, he being yet too young to be entrusted with a gun. I began with giving Jack the bow and arrows, as he desired, and told him how to put on the sharp points, and tie them securely round with packthread, and then to dip them into glue.

" Yes, yes, I understand," said Jack. " I know how to do it very well, Father. But will you tell me where there is a glue-shop."

" I will show you," said little Francis, laughing as he spoke. " Ask Mamma to give you one of her soup-cakes, which are exactly like good strong glue."

" Oh indeed !" replied Jack. " I want glue, not soup."

" Jack," cried I, " you will do well to follow Francis's advice. I believe that one of the cakes, with a little water added, and afterwards melted upon the fire, would produce a good substitute for glue. Give yourself therefore the trouble of making the experiment."

While Jack was preparing his glue, and Francis, proud of being the inventor, was busied in assisting his brother, Fritz came to me for advice about the making of his case. " Run," said I, " and fetch your skin, and we will work at it together." I sat down on the grass, took up my knife, and with the remains of a bamboo-cane began to make a bow for Francis. I was well satisfied to observe the boys, one and all, take a fancy to shooting with the bow, having been desirous to accustom them to this exercise, which might possibly become our only means of protection and subsistence.

While these reflections were passing through my mind, we heard the firing of a gun from the tent in the tree, and two birds fell at our feet. We were at once surprised and alarmed, and all eyes were turned upwards to the place. There we saw Ernest standing outside the tent, a gun in his hand, and heard him triumphantly exclaim, " I have hit them ! You see, I did not run away for nothing."

One of the dead birds proved to be a sort of thrush, and the other was a very small kind of pigeon, which in the Antilles is called an *ortolan*. They are very fat, and of a delicious taste. We now observed that the wild figs began to ripen, and that they attracted a great number of these birds. I foresaw, in consequence, that we were about to have our table furnished with a dish which even a nobleman might envy us. My wife set about stripping off the feathers of the birds to dress them for our supper. I proceeded in my work of arrow-making for Francis, and observed to my wife that she would find in the figs an excellent substitute for grain to feed our fowls.

Thus finished our day of rest. The birds proved excellent; but in point of quantity, we ran no risk of indigestion.

CHAPTER XIII

CONVERSATION, A WALK, AND IMPORTANT DISCOVERIES

Jack had finished the trial of his arrows: they flew to admiration. Little Francis waited with impatience for the moment when he should do the same, and followed with his eyes everything I did. When I had finished my bow, and prepared some little arrows for him, I must next undertake to make him a quiver; " for," said he, " an archer can no more be without a quiver than a sportsman without a game-bag."

I found I must submit. I took some bark from the branch of a tree, and, folding the edges over each other, I stuck them together with glue produced from the soup-cakes. I next stuck on a round piece to serve for the bottom, and then tied on a loop of string, which I hung round his neck. He put his arrows into it, and took his bow to try his skill by the side of his brother. Fritz had also cleaned and prepared his materials for the cases, when his mother summoned us to dinner. We cheerfully placed ourselves round the table I had manufactured. At the end of the repast, I made the following proposition to the boys.

" What think you," said I, " of giving a name to our abode, and to the parts of the country which are known to us?"

They all exclaimed joyfully that the idea was excellent.

Jack. " Oh pray, Father, let us invent some very long names, and that are very difficult to be pronounced. I should be glad that those who shall read about us should be a little puzzled to remember the names of the places and things that belonged to us. What pains has it not cost me to remember their *Monomotapa*, their *Zanguebar*, their *Coromandel*, and many other still more difficult names!"

Father. " This would all be very well, but you forget that our own tongues will be fatigued by pronouncing such names as you propose."

Jack. " What pretty names can we find?"

Father. " We will name the places by different words from our own language, that shall express some particular circumstance with which we have been concerned."

Jack. " Where shall we begin?"

Father. " We shall begin with the bay by which we entered this country. What shall we call it? What say you, Fritz? You must speak first, for you are the oldest."

Fritz. " Let us call it *Oyster Bay*: you remember what quantities of oysters we found in it?"

Jack. " Oh, no! let it be called *Lobster Bay*; you cannot have forgot what a large one caught hold of my leg."

Ernest. " Why, then, we may as well call it the *Bay of Tears*, for you must remember that you roared loud enough."

My Wife. " My advice would be that we ought to call it *Providence Bay*, or the *Bay of Safety*."

Father. " This name is both appropriate and pleasing. Let it be *Providence Bay*. But what name shall we give to the spot where we first set up our tent?"

Fritz. " Let us call it simply *Tent House*."

Father. " That name will do very well. And the little islet at the entrance of Providence Bay?"

Ernest. " It may be called *Sea-Gull Island* or *Shark Island*."

Father. " I am for the last of those names, *Shark Island*, and it will also be a means of commemorating the courage and the triumph of Fritz, who had killed the monster."

Jack. " For the same reason we will call the marsh, in which you cut the canes for our arrows, *Flamingo Marsh*."

Father. " Quite right, I think; and the plain through which we passed *Porcupine Field*. But now comes the great question—what name shall we give to our present abode?"

Ernest. It ought to be called simply *Tree Castle*."

Fritz. " No, no; that will not do at all. That is the same as if, when we wanted to name a town, we called it *The Town*. Let us invent a more noble name."

Jack. " Yes, so we will. I say *Fig Town*."

Fritz. " Ha, ha, ha! a noble name! Let us call it *The Eagle's Nest*, which has a much better sound. Besides, our habitation in the tree is really much more like a nest than a town, and the eagle cannot but ennoble it."

Father. " Will you let me decide the question? I

think our abode should be called *The Falcon's Nest*; for, my boys, you are not arrived at the dignity of eagles. Like the falcon you are, I trust, obedient, docile, active, and courageous. Ernest can have no objection, for, as he knows, falcons nest in large trees."

All exclaimed, clapping their hands, " Yes, yes, we will have it *The Falcon's Nest*! So, health to *Falcon's Nest Castle*!" cried they all, looking up to the tree and making low bows.

" And how," said I, " shall we name the promontory where Fritz and I in vain wearied our eyes in search of our companions of the vessel? I think it may properly be called *Cape Disappointment*."

All. " Yes, this is excellent. And the river with the bridge?"

Father. " If you wish to commemorate one of the greatest events of our history, it ought to be called *The Jackal's River*. The bridge I should name *Family Bridge*, because we were all employed in its construction, and all crossed it together on our way to this place. It will be quite a pleasure to converse about the country we inhabit now that we have instituted names."

Ernest. " It will be just as if we had farms and country houses all dependent upon our castle."

Francis. " It is the same as if we were kings."

My Wife. " And the queen-mother is not without hope that her little slips of majesty will conduct themselves mercifully towards their subjects—the birds, the agoutis, the geese, and the flamingoes; the—— What more shall I say, for I do not know the family names of all your vassals? Let me therefore end by hoping that you will not depopulate your kingdom."

Fritz. " No, Mother, we will take care of that. We will extirpate only those among our subjects who are wicked."

After dinner Jack ran off, and returned presently, dragging after him the skin of his porcupine. He spread it at my feet, entreating me to assist him in making some coats of mail or cuirasses of it for the dogs, as I had before recommended to him. After making him clean the skin completely on the inside with some cinders and sand mixed together, I assisted him in cutting it, and his mother helped him in the sewing. When this was done we put the first that was dried on the back of the patient Turk, which gave him a warlike appearance, and no one could doubt that he was sufficiently well armed to encounter even a hyena.

His companion Ponto had less reason to be pleased with this spiked accoutrement. Turk, unconscious of one particular quality in his new dress, approached near to Ponto, who sprang off in a fright, searching for some place where he might be sheltered from the perforating familiarities of his companion. Jack's concluding business was stripping the skin from the head of the porcupine, and stretching it on one of the roots of our trees to dry, intending to make a cap of it, like those worn by the savages.

During our employment Ernest and Francis had been exercising themselves in shooting their arrows. The evening was advancing, and the intense heat of the day began to diminish. "Leave your work for this time, my boys," said I, "and let us make a short excursion. Where shall we go?"

Fritz. "Let us go to Tent House, Father. We are in want of powder and shot."

My Wife. "I too vote for Tent House. My butter is nearly gone, for Fritz took an unreasonable share for his tanning."

Ernest. "If we go to Tent House, let us try to bring away some of the geese and ducks."

Father. " To Tent House, then, we will go. But we will not take our accustomed road along the seashore, but rather explore some other way. We will keep along our own little stream as far as the wall of rocks, whose shade will accompany us almost as far as the cascade formed by Jackal's River. We will return with our provisions by the road of Family Bridge, and along the seashore; the sun, if not gone down, will then be at our backs."

All was soon arranged for our setting out. Fritz was adorned with a fine belt, made from the skin of his tiger-cat. Jack walked gravely on, his porcupine cap upon his head, and his jackal belt, armed with his two pistols, round his waist. Each carried a gun and a game-bag. Even little Francis had his bow in his hand and his quiver on his shoulder. My wife was the only person not burdened with a gun, but she carried her large butter-pot. Turk marched before us with his coat of mail studded with spikes, but it was apparent that he felt ill at ease. The monkey also, having a great desire to accompany us, leaped without ceremony on his accustomed seat, the back of Turk. But when he perceived the projecting spikes, he sprang forward four times, making the most comical grimaces. He was not long, however, in deciding what to do. Ponto, he saw, was without such a frightful saddle. So he jumped upon him in a trice, and clung so closely to his back that the dog could not shake him off. Even our new friend, the flamingo, prepared to make one of the party. The pretty kind-tempered creature had become every day more tame, and attached himself to us with a confidence which increased our goodwill towards him. The boys all contended for being his companion; but the flamingo adopted the prudent measure of coming up to me, and showing his reliance on my protection by walking gravely by my side.

Our route at first lay along the stream, sheltered by the shade of large trees. To prolong the pleasure of our walk we proceeded slowly, amusing ourselves with looking about us. The eldest boys made frequent escapes, running on before so that we sometimes lost sight of them. In this manner we reached the end of the wood. The country now appearing to be less open, we thought it would be prudent to bring our whole company together. On looking forward we saw the boys approaching us full gallop, and this time, for a wonder, the grave Ernest was first. He reached me panting for breath, and so full of joy and eagerness that he could not pronounce a word distinctly. He held out his hand, which contained three little balls of a light green colour.

" We have found a prize, Father!" cried he at last when he had recovered his voice. " We have found some potato-seed!"

" What say you—potato-seed?" inquired I joyfully. " Come near, every one of you, and let me see what you have."

I scarcely dared believe in so happy an event.

Ernest explained where he had found the plants, and we all hastened to the place. With extreme joy we found there a large plantation of potato plants. A part of them were covered with their lilac and yellow blossoms, the sight of which conveyed more pleasure to our hearts than if they had been the most fragrant roses. Another portion of the plantation was in seed. And in several places some younger plants were pushing through the earth. Our petulant Jack bawled out, jumping for joy:

" They are really potatoes! and though it was not

I who discovered them, at least it shall be I who will dig them up!"

Saying this, he knelt down and began to scratch up the earth with all his ten fingers. He would not, however, have made much progress, if the monkey, excited by his example, had not also set himself to work. He dug up several potatoes with great dexterity. After smelling at them he was going to throw them to a distance, but Jack snatched them out of his paws and gave them to his mother. Afterwards the monkey and he continued digging up the potatoes together, and soon obtained enough to serve up for a dinner. The rest of us, unwilling to be idle, set to work also. With our knives and sticks we soon procured a sufficient number to fill our bags and our pockets. When we were well loaded we again began to think of our walk to Tent House. Some of our company raised their voices in favour of returning immediately to Falcon's Stream to prepare our booty for a delicious meal. But so many motives presented themselves for proceeding to our store-house, that it was decided we should continue our route.

CHAPTER XIV

CONTINUATION OF THE PRECEDING CHAPTER, AND MORE DISCOVERIES

Presently we reached the long chain of rocks, over which our pretty Falcon's Stream made its escape in the form of a cascade. We kept along the chain of rocks which led to Jackal's River, and from thence to Tent House, having first with difficulty pushed through the high grass. We saw many specimens of the Indian fig, with its large broad leaf; aloes of different forms and colours; the superb prickly candle or cactus, bearing straight stalks, taller than a man, and crowned with long straight branches, forming a sort of star. The broad plantain spread along the rocks, its innumerable boughs twisted with each other, hanging down perpendicularly, and ornamented with flowers, which grew in large tufts, and were of the brightest rose-colour; while that which pleased us best, and which was found there in great abundance, was the king of fruits, both for figure and relish, the crowned pine-apple. We immediately fell on this fruit with avidity, because we knew its value. The monkey was not the last to seize one for himself; and as he could make higher jumps than the boys, they formed the scheme of making him angry by little tricks, so as to induce him to fling pine-apples at them. This game they continued so long that I thought it prudent to interrupt them, fearing that the unripe state of the fruit might affect their health.

Soon after, I was fortunate enough to discover, among the multitude of plants which grew either at the foot or in the clefts of the rock, the karata, many of which were now in blossom, and of others the flowers had lately fallen off. Travellers have given so perfect a description of them in their books of natural history that it was impossible I should mistake them. But what further confirmed their identity was their straight slender stalk, crowned with blossoms, and proceeding from a tuft of leaves like the pine-apple, with its large foliage terminating in a sharp point, and forming altogether a plant remarkably pleasing to the eye. I pointed out to the boys the immense size of these leaves, which were hollowed in the middle

like a saucer, in which the rain is for a long time preserved; and also its beautiful red flowers. As I was
acquainted with the properties of this useful plant, the
pith of which is used as tinder by the negroes, who also
make a strong kind of thread from the fibres of its
leaves, I was not less satisfied with my discovery than
I had been with that of the potatoes. I did not hesitate to assure the boys that I preferred it to the pine-
apples. All answered me, their mouths at the same
time full of the fruit, that they would resign these trees
with all their flowers to me if I would leave them the
pine-apples.

" The pine-apples are better than all the rest," said
they, " even than the potatoes."

For answer I called to Ernest.

" Here," said I, " take out my flint and steel and
strike me a light."

Ernest. " But, Father, what am I to do for tinder?"

Father. " This is precisely to the purpose. When the
tinder which we brought from the vessel is all consumed, how shall we be able to make a fire?"

Ernest. " Oh, do like the savages—rub two pieces
of wood against each other till at length they catch
fire."

Father. " I think I can show you a better way."

I then took a dried stalk of the tree, stripped off the
bark, and disclosed a dry spongy pith, which I laid
upon the flint. Striking a spark with a steel, the pith
instantly caught fire. The boys began to caper about,
exclaiming, " Long live the tinder-tree!"

" Here, then," said I, " we have an article of greater
usefulness than if it served merely to gratify the appetite. Your mother will next inform us what she will
use for sewing your clothes when her thread from the
enchanted bag is exhausted."

My Wife. " I have long been uneasy upon this subject, and would give all the pine-apples in the world for hemp or flax."

" And your wish shall be accomplished," said I. " If you examine, you will find some excellent thread under the leaves of this extraordinary plant, where all-provident nature has placed a store-house of this valuable article." I accordingly examined one of the leaves, and drew out of it a strong piece of thread of a red colour, which I gave to my wife. " We shall put the leaves to dry," said I, " either in the sun, or by a gentle fire. The useless part of the leaf will then separate by being beaten, and the mass of thread will remain."

I next drew attention to a specimen of the Indian fig or prickly-pear, a tree of no common interest. It grows in the poorest soils, even upon the rocks; the poorer the soil the more its leaves are thick and succulent. " I should be tempted," said I, " to believe that it was nourished by the air, rather than by the earth. This plant bears a kind of fig, which is said to be sweet and palatable when ripened in its native sun, and it is a wholesome and refreshing food." Scarcely had I pronounced these words, than our light-footed Jack was on the rock trying to gather some of the fruit; but this time he had reason to repent his precipitation, for the fruit of this tree is covered with fine prickles. Poor Jack soon came down again, shaking his hand with the pain the prickles occasioned. I showed how to gather the fruit without incurring such inconvenience. I threw up a stone and brought down a fig, which I caught upon my hat. I cut off its two ends, and was thus enabled to hold it, while I peeled off the skin. I then resigned it to the curiosity of my young companions.

The novelty rather than the taste of the fruit made them think it excellent. They all found means to gather the figs, each inventing the best method of taking off the skins.

In the meantime, I perceived Ernest holding a fig upon the end of his knife, turning it about in all directions, and bringing it close to his eye with a look of inquiry. " I wish I could know," said at length our young observant, " what little animals these are in the fig, which feed so eagerly upon it, and are as red as scarlet."

Father. " Ha, ha! This, too, will perhaps turn out an additional source of usefulness which this plant possesses. Let me look at your fig. I believe it is the insect called the cochineal."

Jack. " What is the cochineal, Father?"

Father. " It is an insect that feeds upon the Indian fig, which, no doubt, is the cause of his beautiful colour, which forms an object of considerable importance in the trade of the dyer, for nothing else produces so fine a scarlet.

There is another respect in which the prickly-pear is of great value. It is used for making hedges, its prickly surface preventing the approach of animals. You see that, besides those prickles which took such a fancy to Jack's hand, there is a large thorn at each of the knots which appear in the plant."

" The largest serve very well for pins," said my wife, " and even for nails. See how they keep my gown fastened."

" This, then," I continued, " is still another useful-ness the Indian fig-tree can boast. You must perceive of what importance these enclosures are, and the rather as they are made with so little trouble. If you plant only one of the leaves in the ground it immediately takes root, and grows with astonishing rapidity."

" Oh, Father," said Ernest, " do let us make such a hedge round our tree ! We shall then have no further occasion to light fires to preserve us from wild beasts, or even from the savages, who from one day to another may arrive in their canoes."

" And we could then easily gather the cochineal," said Fritz.

Conversing thus we reached Jackal's River, which we crossed, and very shortly arrived at our old habitation. We immediately dispersed, each in quest of what he intended to take away. Fritz loaded himself with powder and shot. My wife and I and Francis employed ourselves in filling our pot with butter, the carrying of which on our return it was agreed was to fall on me. Ernest and Jack looked about for the geese and ducks, but the boys did not succeed in catching one of them. The idea then occurred to Ernest of taking a small bit of cheese and tying it to the end of a piece of string, and holding it to float in the water. The voracious animals hastened eagerly to seize it. In this way Ernest drew them towards him, one by one, with the cheese in its mouth, till he had caught the whole. We tied their legs together and fastened them to our game-bags, so that each had his share in carrying them.

We had thought of taking a stock of salt, but could not carry so much as we wished, the sacks being occupied with potatoes. I, however, thought of throwing a quantity into one of the sacks to fill up the space between the potatoes. In this way we secured a supply, but it made the sack so heavy that no one was willing to be encumbered with it. Fritz proposed that Turk should carry it; and accordingly we took off his coat of mail and left it at Tent House, and the sack was tied on the back of the kind-tempered animal.

We set out on our return, loaded with treasures, and the appearance of our caravan was even more amusing than it had been before. The ducks and geese, with their heads and necks stretching out at our shoulders, cackling with all their might, gave us a truly singular and ludicrous appearance. We could not help laughing immoderately as we passed the bridge, one after the other, loaded in so strange a fashion. Our jokes, and the general good-humour which prevailed, served to shorten the length of the walk, and we none of us were sensible of fatigue till we were seated under our tree at Falcon's Stream.

CHAPTER XV

THE SLEDGE

I had remarked on our return to the seashore, a quantity of wood, of which I thought I could make a conveyance for our cask of butter and other provisions from Tent House to Falcon's Stream. I had determined to go early the next morning, before my family should be awake, to the spot. I had fixed upon Ernest for my assistant, thinking that his indolent temper required to be stimulated. He felt as a great favour the preference I gave him, and he promised to be ready at a very early hour.

As soon as I perceived the first dawn I quietly awoke Ernest. He raised himself, stretching and gaping in his hammock. We descended the ladder without being perceived by the rest of the family. The first thing we had to do was to loose the ass, who was to be of our party. That he might not go without a load, I made him draw a very large branch of a tree, which I wanted for my undertaking.

When we reached the seashore we found the wood in great abundance. I determined to cut pieces of the proper length, and to lay them cross-ways on the branches which the ass had drawn to the place, and make them serve as a kind of sledge. We lost no time in setting to work, and we added to the load a little chest which we found quite close to the waves. We also provided ourselves with some poles which lay there, that we might use them as rollers, should we stand in need of them for passing difficult places, and then we set out on our return. When we were within a certain distance of our abode we heard a loud firing, which informed us that the attack upon the ortolans was in good train. On seeing us approach, all ran to meet us. The chest was soon opened by a hatchet, for all were eager to see what was within. It contained only some sailor's suits of clothes and linen, which was quite wet with the sea.

I next inspected the booty of the three sportsmen, who had shot in all no less than fifty ortolans and thrushes. They had had various luck, now missing and now hitting, and had used so large a quantity of powder and shot, that when they were about to get up the tree and fire from thence, my wife and I stopped them, recommending a more frugal use of those materials. I taught them how to make snares to be suspended from the fig-tree, and advised them to use the thread of the karata for the purpose. What is new always amuses young persons, and the boys took a great fancy to this mode of sporting. Jack succeeded in his first attempt. I left Francis to assist him, and

took Fritz and Ernest to help me in making the sledge.
As we were all hard at work, for my wife had joined
the youngest boys, we suddenly heard a prodigious
clatter among the fowls; the cock crowed louder than
all the rest together, and the hens ran to and fro as
if they were pursued by a fox.

" I wonder what is the matter," said my wife, rising.
" Every day I hear the hens clucking as if they had
been laying eggs."

At this moment Ernest happened to look at the
monkey, and remarked that he fixed his piercing eyes
on the hens. When he saw my wife approaching,
driving the hens before her, the young rascal jumped
quickly into a hollow place under one of the roots of
the tree, and hid himself. Ernest ran to the place as
soon as he, and was fortunate enough to seize him,
seeing that he held a new-laid egg in his paw. The
monkey sprang immediately to another hole, and
Ernest followed. Here also he found some eggs, and
brought them in his hat to his mother. The monkey
was so greedy of this food, that he was sure to seize the
eggs as soon as the hens had laid them. We inflicted
no other punishment upon him for this knavery than
that of tying him up when the hens were about to lay.
By this means my wife soon collected a considerable
number of eggs.

Meantime I was busily employed upon my sledge,
which was soon completed; and I found that necessity
had converted a preacher of moderate talents into a
tolerably good carpenter. Two bent pieces of wood,
the segments of a circle, formed the outline of my
machine, which I fixed in their places by a straight
piece of wood, placed across and firmly fixed to the
bent pieces in the middle and at the rear. I then
fastened two ropes to the front of my work, and my

sledge was finished. As I had not raised my eyes from my work, I did not know what my wife and the two youngest boys had been about. On looking up, I perceived that they had been stripping off the feathers from a quantity of birds which the boys had killed, and that they afterwards spitted them on an officer's sword, which my wife had turned into this useful kitchen utensil. I approved of the idea, but I remarked on her profusion in dressing more birds at once than we could eat. She reminded me that I had myself advised her to half-roast the birds before putting them into the butter, to be preserved for future use. She was in hopes, she said, that as I had now a sledge, I should not fail of going to Tent House after dinner to fetch the cask of butter, and in the meanwhile she was endeavouring to be ready with the birds. I had no objection to this, and immediately determined on going to Tent House the same day, and requested my wife to hasten the dinner for that purpose. She replied that this was already her intention, as she also had a little project in her head, which I should be informed of at my return. I, for my part, had one too, which was to take a bathe in the sea. I wished that Ernest should bathe also; while Fritz was to remain at home for the protection of the family.

CHAPTER XVI

A BATHING, A FISHING, THE JUMPING-HARE, AND A MASQUERADE

As soon as Ernest and I had dined, we prepared for our departure. Fritz presented each with one of the

neat skin-bags of his own workmanship, which we
hung to our belts, and which held nicely spoons and
knives and forks.

We now set about harnessing the ass and cow to
our sledge. Each of us took a piece of bamboo-cane
in hand, to serve as a whip; and, resting our guns
upon our shoulders, we began our journey. Ponto was
to accompany us, and Turk to remain behind. We
took the road by the seashore, where the sands afforded
better travelling for our vehicle than did the thick
wild grass. We reached Family Bridge on Jackal's
River, and arrived at Tent House without adventure.
We immediately unharnessed the animals to let them
graze, while we set to work to load the sledge with the
cask of butter, the cask of cheese, a small barrel of
gunpowder, different instruments, some ball, some
shot, and Turk's coat of mail. These exertions had so
occupied our thoughts, that it was late when we first
observed that our animals, attracted by the quality
of the grass on the other side of the river, had repassed
the bridge, and wandered out of sight. I was in hopes
they would be easily found, and I directed Ernest to
go with Ponto and bring them back, intending in the
meantime to look for a convenient place to have our
bathe. In a short time I found myself at the extremity
of Providence Bay, which ended, as I now perceived,
in a marsh producing the finest bulrushes. Farther
on a chain of steep rocks advanced into the sea, forming a kind of creek, as if expressly contrived for bathing.
Enchanted with this discovery, I called out to Ernest
to come and join me, and in the meantime I amused
myself with cutting rushes. Ernest neither replied
nor came, so I resolved to go in pursuit of him. I at
length discovered him at a distance, extended at his
length on the ground, in the shade of Tent House. I

approached him with a beating heart, and was agreeably surprised at finding him in a sound sleep, while the ass and the cow were eating the grass close by.

" Come, come, you must awake," cried I, shaking him. " While you are sleeping, your animals may once more escape."

He instantly awoke starting, and was soon on his feet.

" Oh, but I defy them to cross the bridge," said he, rubbing his eyes; " for I have taken away some of the planks, and left a space which they will have no inclination to jump."

Father. " Since your idle fit has rendered you inventive, I forgive it. But did you not promise your mother to carry her some salt?"

Ernest. " But, Father, I was planning something."

Father. " Pray tell me what study made you go to sleep?"

Ernest. " I was thinking how difficult it would be to bring away from the vessel everything which it contains."

Father. " And did you hit upon some method?"

Ernest. " No, Father; I fell asleep in the middle of my reflections."

Father. " So this is the hard work your head was engaged in. Discovering a difficulty, and finding no means for conquering it!"

Ernest. " At this very moment an idea strikes me. We ought to have a raft; but the beams of the ship are too heavy for the purpose. I think it would be better to take a number of empty casks, and nail planks upon them to keep them together."

Father. " This is a sound idea, but for the present, my boy, we must make up for lost time. Run and fill this little bag with salt, which you will then empty into the large one that the ass is to carry. During this time I will take the refreshment of bathing, and then it will be your turn to bathe and mine to take care of the animals."

I returned to the rocks, and was not disappointed in my enjoyment; but I did not stay long, fearing my boy might be impatient. When I had dressed I returned to see if his work had advanced; but he was not there, and I supposed that he had again fallen asleep. Presently, however, I heard his voice calling out:

" Father, Father, a fish! A fish of monstrous size! Run quickly, Father, I can hardly hold him!"

I ran to the place from which the voice proceeded, and found Ernest lying along the ground on his face, upon the extremity of a point of land, and pulling in his line, to which a large fish was hanging, and beating about. I hastily snatched the rod out of his hand, for I had some apprehension that the fish would pull him into the water. I gave a certain liberty to the line, to calm the fish, and then contrived to draw him gently along till I had got him into a shallow, from which he could no longer escape. We examined him thoroughly, and it appeared to me that he could not weigh less than fifteen pounds; our capture would afford the greatest pleasure to our steward of provisions at Falcon's Stream.

" You have now really laboured," said I to Ernest, " not only with your head, but with your whole body, so I would advise you to wipe the perspiration from your face, and keep a little quiet before you venture into the water. You have procured us a dish of great excellence."

" It was at least fortunate," observed he in a modest tone, " that I thought of bringing my fishing-rod."

Father. " Certainly it was. But tell me how you

came to see this large fish, and what made you think
you could catch it?"

Ernest. " I used to remark that there were many
fish just hereabouts. This made me determine to
bring my fishing-tackle. On my way to the place
where we keep the salt, I saw a great number of little
crabs, upon which fishes feed, near the water's brink.
I thought I would try to bait my hook with one of
them. So I hurried my task of fetching the salt, and
came to this spot, where at first I caught only some very
little fish, which are there in my handkerchief. Then I
remarked that these were chased in the water by fishes
of larger size. This gave me the idea of baiting my
hook with one of the small ones. I put a larger hook
to my line, and in a short time the fish seized the bait."

We now examined the smaller fishes he had
caught, which for the most part appeared to me little
herrings, while I felt certain that the large one was a
cod. I immediately cut them all open, and rubbed
them in the inside with salt. While I was thus employed
Ernest went to the rocks and bathed, and I had time
to fill some more bags with salt before his return. We
then resumed the road to Falcon's Stream.

When we had proceeded about half-way, Ponto
suddenly escaped, and by his barking gave notice that
he scented some game. We soon after saw him pursuing an animal which seemed endeavouring to escape,
and made the most extraordinary jumps. The dog
continuing to follow, the creature in trying to avoid
him passed within gunshot of the place where I stood.
I fired, but its flight was so rapid that I missed. Ernest,
who was at a small distance behind, hearing the
report of my gun, prepared his own, and fired at the
instant the animal was passing near him. He aimed so
well that the animal fell dead. I ran hastily to ascer-

tain what kind of quadruped it might be. We found
it most remarkable. It was of the size of a sheep, with
a tail resembling that of a tiger. Both its snout and
hair were like those of a mouse, and its teeth were like
a hare's, but much larger. The fore-legs resembled
those of the squirrel, and were extremely short. But
to make up for this, its hind-legs were very long.
Ernest, after a long and close examination, interrupted
our silence by an exclamation of joy. " And have I
really killed this extraordinary animal?" said he,
clapping his hands together. " What do you think is
its name, Father? I would give all the world to know."

" And so would I, my boy; but I am as ignorant as
you. So let us both examine this interesting stranger
with attention, that we may be certain to what family
of quadrupeds it belongs."

Ernest. " I think it can hardly be a quadruped, for
the little fore-legs look more like hands, as is the case
with monkeys."

Father. " They are legs, nevertheless, I can assure
you. Let us look for its name among the mammalia.
On this point we cannot be mistaken. Now let us
examine its teeth."

Ernest. " Here are the four incisor teeth, like the
squirrel."

Father. " Thus we see that it belongs to the order of
Nibblers. Now let us look for some names of animals
of this kind."

Ernest. " Besides the squirrels, I recollect only the
mice, the marmots, the hares, the beavers, the por-
cupines, and the jumpers."

Father. " The jumpers ! That word furnishes the
clue; the animal is completely formed like the gerboa
or jumping-hare, except that it is twice the size of
those. . . . Wait a moment, an idea strikes me. I

will lay a wager that our animal is one of the large
jumpers, called kangaroo; it belongs properly to the
genus *Didelphis* or *Philander*, because the female, who
never bears more than one young one, carries it in a
kind of purse placed between her hind-legs. To the
best of my knowledge this animal has never been seen
but on the coast of New Holland, where it was first
observed by the celebrated navigator Captain Cook."

I now tied the fore-legs of the kangaroo together,
and by means of two canes, we contrived to carry it
to the sledge.

Ponto was still scampering about in the tall grass.
We called him to us, and having continued our road,
Ernest entreated me to tell him all I knew about the
kangaroo. " It is," said I, " a most singular creature.
Its fore-legs, as you see, have scarcely the third part of
the length of the hind ones, and the most it can do is
to make them serve to help in walking. But the hind-
legs enable it to make prodigious jumps. The food of
the kangaroo consists of herbs and roots, which they
dig up very skilfully with their fore-legs. They place
themselves upon their hind-legs, which are doubled
under them, as if on a chair, and by this means are
able to look above even the tall kinds of grass. They
rest too upon their tail, which is exceedingly strong,
and is also of great use to them in jumping, by assisting
the spring from the ground.

We at length arrived happily, though somewhat
late, at Falcon's Stream, having heard from a great
distance the kind welcome of the salutations of our
family. Our companions all ran to meet us. But it
was now, on seeing the ludicrous style of the dress of
the three boys, our turn for laughter. One had on a
sailor's shirt, which trained round him like the robe of
a spectre. Another was buried in a pair of pantaloons,

which were fastened round his neck and reached to the ground. The third had a long waistcoat which came down to the instep. They all tried to jump about, but finding this impossible from the length of their garments, they next resolved to carry off the whole with an air, by strutting slowly to and fro in the manner of a great personage in a theatre. After some hearty laughing, I inquired of my wife the cause of this masquerade, and whether she had assisted them in attempting to act a comedy. She disclosed the mystery by informing me that her three boys had also been into the water to bathe, and that while they were thus engaged she had washed all their clothes; but as they had not dried so soon as she expected, her little rioters had become impatient, and had fallen on the chest of sailor's clothes, and each had taken from it what article he pleased. " I preferred," said she, " that you should see them in this odd sort of a disguise rather than quite naked, like little savages." In which opinion I assured her that I heartily joined.

It was now our turn to give an account of our journey. In proportion as we advanced in our narrative, we presented, one after another, casks, bulrushes, salt, fish, and lastly, our beautiful kangaroo. In a trice it was surrounded, examined, and admired by all, and such a variety of questions asked, that Ernest and I scarcely knew which to answer first. Fritz was the only one who was a little silent. I saw plainly by his countenance what was passing in his mind. He was jealous of his brother Ernest. But I also saw that he was struggling manfully against so mean a passion. In a short time he had succeeded so completely that he joined frankly in our conversation, and I am persuaded no one but myself perceived what was passing in his mind. He came near the kangaroo and examined it with great attention. Then, turning to his brother, he observed to him in a kind tone that he had had good luck, and that he must be a good shot. " But, Father," said he, " when you go again to Tent House, or on any other excursion, will it not be my turn to go with you? For here at Falcon's Stream there is nothing new to amuse us; a few thrushes and some pigeons."

" I promise you what you desire, my dear boy," said I, " for you have valiantly combated the ill-humour which assailed you on witnessing your brother's success. I promise that you shall accompany me in my next excursion, which will probably take place to-morrow. It will be another journey to the vessel."

We concluded the day with our ordinary occupations. I gave some salt to each of our animals, to whom it was an acceptable treat. We next skinned our kangaroo, and put it carefully aside till the next day, when we intended to cut it to pieces, and lay such parts in salt as we could not immediately consume. We made an excellent supper on our little fish, to which we added some potatoes. The labours of the day had more than usually disposed us all to seek repose; we therefore said our prayers at an early hour, mounted our ladder, and were soon asleep.

CHAPTER XVII

MORE STORES FROM THE WRECK

I rose with the first crowing of the cock, before the rest of the family were awake, descended the ladder, and employed myself in carefully skinning the kangaroo. This gave me so much trouble that all my little family were assembled about me and their mother, and calling out "Famine!" before I had finished my work. Having completed it, I went to the stream to wash, and then to the sailor's chest to change my coat, that I might make a decent appearance at breakfast, and give my sons an example of cleanliness. Breakfast over, I ordered Fritz to prepare everything to go to Tent House, and prepare our boat, that we might proceed to the vessel. At the moment of departure I found that Ernest and Jack were wanting. Their mother knew no more than myself what was become of them, but she thought they were gone to get some potatoes. I charged her to reprove them a little for this, to prevent their accustoming themselves to stray from home alone and without leave in an unknown country. But they had taken Turk along with them this time, and I was therefore the less uneasy.

We began our journey after having taken an affectionate leave of my wife and of my little Francis. I left Ponto with her, and I entreated her not to be uneasy, and to commit herself to the care of Providence.

We soon reached and crossed the bridge. At this moment, to our astonishment, we heard the shrill sounds of human voices, and almost at the same time we saw Ernest and Master Jack come forth from a bush, delighted to have half-alarmed us. "Ah! did not you think we were savages?" said Jack.

"Rather," said I, "two little rogues I am much inclined to chide for having left their home without permission."

"Oh, Father," said Ernest, "we do wish so much to go with you to the vessel, and we were afraid you would refuse us; but we thought that when you saw us so near, you would consent."

" Very badly argued, my young gentleman," replied I. " At Falcon's Stream I might perhaps have consented, although I have so many things to take that it would be wrong to let you occupy a place in the boat, but as it is, I would on no account leave your mother in anxiety the whole day as to what is become of you. I have a commission to give you for her that I have much at heart."

I then requested them to tell her that it was probable we should be forced to pass the night on board the vessel.

It was essential that we should get out of the vessel, if it yet remained afloat, all that could be saved, as every moment might complete its destruction. With this view I told my sons what they should say to their mother. I exhorted them to obey and assist her; and made them collect some salt, and I enjoined them to be at Falcon's Stream before noon. To be sure of the fulfilment of this order, I requested Fritz to lend Ernest his silver watch, and told him he would find a gold one in the vessel, in which case he would allow his brother to keep the one he lent him, and that we might perhaps get another for Jack. This hope consoled them for not going on with us.

After having bid adieu to our dear boys, we got into the boat, and we left the shore to gain the current. We quickly cleared Safety Bay, and reached the vessel. As soon as we had got on board and our boat was securely fastened, our first care was to look out for fit materials to construct a raft. I wished to begin by executing the idea suggested by Ernest. Our boat of staves had neither room nor solidity enough to carry a considerable burden. We soon found a sufficient number of water-casks, which appeared to me very proper for my new enterprise. We emptied them, then replaced the bungs, and threw the casks overboard, after securing them by means of ropes and cramps, so as to keep them together at the vessel's side. This completed, we placed planks upon them to form a firm and commodious platform, to which we added a gunwale of a foot in depth all round to secure the lading. Thus we contrived to possess a raft in which we could stow thrice as much as in our boat. This laborious task had taken up the whole day. We scarcely allowed ourselves a minute to eat a mouthful of cold meat we had provided for the expedition. In the evening Fritz and I were so weary that it would have been impossible for us to row back to land, even if our business had not detained us. We therefore came to the resolution of passing the night on board; and having taken all precautions in case of a storm, we reposed in the captain's cabin, on a good elastic mattress. In fact, it induced such sound repose, that our design to watch in turn quite escaped us, and we slept heavily side by side, till broad daylight opened our eyes, when we awoke with gratitude to that Providence to whom we were indebted for the quiet night. We rose and actively set to work to load our raft.

In the first place, we completely stripped the cabin which had been occupied by my family on board the vessel, removing everything it contained which belonged to us. Then we proceeded to the cabin in which we had slept and carried off the very doors and windows. Some valuable chests of the officers were there; but this discovery, and the rich lace clothes which seemed to court our grasp, were less acceptable to us than the carpenter's and gunner's chests, containing tools and implements. Those which we could remove with levers and rollers were put entire upon the raft, and we took out of the others the things that made them too heavy. One of the captain's chests was filled with costly articles, which no doubt he meant to dispose of to the opulent planters of Port Jackson, or among the savages. In the collection were several gold, and silver watches, snuff-boxes of all descriptions, buckles, shirt-buttons, necklaces, and rings—in short, an abundance of all the trifles of European luxury. There was also a strong-box full of louis d'or and dollars, which attracted our notice less than another containing a very pretty table-service of fine steel, which we had substituted for the captain's, that were silver, and for which my wife had shown no small regard. But the discovery that delighted me most, and for which I would readily have given the box of louis d'or, &c., was a chest containing some dozens of young plants of every species of European fruits. I perceived pear, plum, almond, peach, apple, apricot, chestnut-trees, and vine-shoots. I beheld with a feeling I cannot describe those productions of my dear country, which, if God vouchsafed to bless them, would thrive in a foreign soil. We discovered a number of bars of iron and large pigs of lead, grinding-stones, cart-wheels ready for mounting, a complete set of farrier's instruments, tongs, shovels, ploughshares, rolls of iron and copper wire, sacks of maize, pease, oats, vetches, and even a little hand-mill. The vessel had been freighted with everything likely to be useful in an infant colony so distant. We found a saw-mill in a separated state, but each piece numbered and so accurately fitted that nothing was easier than to put it together.

I had now to consider what of all these treasures I

should take. It was impossible to carry with us in one trip such a quantity, and to leave them in the vessel, threatened every moment with destruction, was exposing ourselves to be wholly deprived of them.

" Ah," said Fritz, " let us leave, in the first place, this useless money and the chest of trinkets."

" It gives me pleasure, my boy, to hear you speak thus. We will do, then, as you wish, and determine upon taking with us what is useful, such as the powder, lead, iron, the corn and the fruit-trees, implements for gardening and agriculture. Let us take as many as possible of these last. If we should have any room left, we can then select a few of the objects of luxury. However, begin by taking from the chest the two watches I have promised, and one for yourself."

We then loaded our raft, we, moreover, stowed away a large and handsome fishing-net, quite new, and the vessel's great compass. With the net, Fritz found luckily two harpoons and a rope windlass, such as they use in the whale fishery. Fritz asked me to let him place the windlass, with the harpoons attached to the end of the rope, over the bow of our tub-boat, and thus hold all in readiness in case of seeing any large fish. I indulged him in his innocent fancy.

It was afternoon before we had finished our lading, for not only our raft was as full as it could hold, but our boat likewise.

Having completely executed our undertaking, both as to construction and lading, we stepped into the tub-boat, and with some small difficulty pushed out for the current, drawing our raft triumphantly after us with a stout rope.

CHAPTER XVIII

THE TORTOISE HARNESSED

The wind was in a humour favourable to our undertaking, and briskly swelled our sail. The sea was calm, and we advanced at a considerable rate. Fritz had been looking steadfastly for some time at something of a large size which was floating on the water, and now desired me to take the glass and see what it could be. I soon perceived distinctly that it was a tortoise, which, agreeably to the habits of its singular species, had fallen asleep in the sun on the surface of the water. No sooner had Fritz learned this, than he earnestly entreated me to steer softly within view of so extraordinary a creature, that he might examine it. I readily consented. But as his back was towards me, and the sail was between us, I did not observe what he was about till I felt a violent jerk, a sudden turning of the windlass, accompanied by a rapid motion of the boat.

" Whatever are you about, Fritz?" exclaimed I.

" I have caught him!—I touched him!" cried Fritz, without hearing one word I had been saying. " The tortoise is ours! Is not this a valuable prize, for it will furnish dinners for weeks?"

I soon admitted that the harpoon had secured the animal, which thus agitated the vessel in its endeavours to be disengaged, for the rope of the harpoon was fastened to the windlass. I quickly pulled down the sail, and seizing a hatchet sprang to the boat's head to cut the rope and let the harpoon and the tortoise go; but Fritz caught hold of my arm, begging me to wait a moment, and not bring upon him the mortification of losing, at one stroke, the harpoon, the rope, and the tortoise.   He proposed watching himself with the hatchet in his hand to cut the rope should any danger appear. I yielded to his entreaties, after a due exhortation to him to take care.

Thus then, we proceeded with a hazardous rapidity, and having no small difficulty to keep the head of the boat in a straight direction, and keep her steady.   In a little time I observed that the creature was making for the sea. I therefore again hoisted the sail. As the wind was to the land, and very brisk, the tortoise found resistance of no avail.   He accordingly fell into the track we desired to take, and we soon gained the current which had always received us. He drew us straight towards our usual place of landing, and by good fortune without striking upon any of the rocks. We, however, did not disembark without encountering one adventure.   I perceived that the state of the tide was such that we should be thrown upon one of the sand-banks, which indeed took place.   We were at this time within a gunshot of the shore.   The boat, though driven with violence, remained upright in the sand.   I stepped into the water for the purpose of conferring upon our conductor his reward for the alarm he had caused us, when he suddenly gave a plunge, and I saw him no more. Following the rope I however soon found the tortoise at the bottom, where it was so shallow that I was not long in finding means to put an end to his pain by cutting off his head with the hatchet. Being now near Tent House, Fritz gave a halloo and fired a gun, to apprise our relatives that we were arrived in triumph. The good mother and her three young ones soon appeared, running towards us.   Upon which Fritz jumped out of the boat, placed the head of our prize on the muzzle of his gun, and walked to shore, which I reached at the same moment.

After some gentle reproaches from my wife for leaving her and the boys for so long a time, the history of the tortoise was related in due form. The tender-hearted mother began to shudder at the thought of the danger we had been exposed to. We all now fell to a new examination of the adventure, and were struck with surprise that Fritz should so exactly have hit the vulnerable part of the animal; next, that the tortoise should have gone to sleep and left this part exposed, contrary to his habit of drawing the neck within his shell; and lastly, that with the harpoon stuck in his flesh, and sunk still deeper by the act of drawing in his head to save himself, he should yet have been able to pull along a heavy-laden boat and a raft tied to it.

Our conversation being ended, I requested my wife to go with two of the younger boys to Falcon's Stream and fetch the sledge and the beasts of burden, that we might not fail of seeing at least a part of our booty put safely under shelter. A tempest, or even the tide, might sweep away the whole during the night. We took every precaution in our power against the latter danger by fixing the boat and the raft as securely as we could. I rolled two heavy masses of lead, with the assistance of levers, from the raft upon the shore, and then tied a rope to each, the other ends of which were fastened, one to the raft and the other to the boat.

While we were employed on this scheme the sledge arrived, and we immediately placed the tortoise upon it, and also some articles of light weight, such as mattresses, pieces of linen, &c. The strength of our whole party was found necessary to move it, we therefore all set out together to unload it at Falcon's Stream. We pursued our way thither with the utmost gaiety of heart, and Fritz and I found the time pass quickly in answering the questions with which the three youngest boys assailed us as to the nature and amount of the treasures we had brought. The chest containing the articles in silver, and another filled with trinkets and utensils, most powerfully excited their interest, for Fritz had dropped a hint of what was in them.

" Are they left on the raft or in the boat?" asked Ernest. " We will open them to-morrow and I shall have my watch."

Jack. " I assure you I shall not be content with only a watch. I must have, since I hear there are so many, a snuff-box also."

Francis. " And I shall ask for a pretty purse filled with louis."

Father. " Well imagined, my young ones. Jack intends, I presume, to take now and then a pinch of the snuff he has not got, and Francis means to sow his louis that they may produce a crop."

In this trifling kind of talk we beguiled the time till we reached the foot of our castle. Our first concern now was the tortoise, which we turned on his back that we might strip off the shell, and make use of some of the flesh.

My wife asked leave to take away the *green*-coloured part of the flesh, which she said she could not even look at without distaste. I answered that she was wrong in this. I informed her that the green was the fat, and would add to the fine flavour of the dish.

" But," added I, " if you think it is too abundant, you can take a part and preserve it by melting. We will then," said I, " put what we mean to keep in salt, and distribute the head, the entrails, and the feet to the dogs; for all, you know, must live."

" Oh," cried Francis, " do give me the shell, Father !"

" No, no !" bawled out another, all contending for preference.

I imposed silence, declaring that the right was entirely in Fritz, since it was he who had harpooned the animal. " But," continued I, " it may be well to ask what Fritz would think of doing with the shell."

" I thought, Father, of cleaning it and fixing it by the side of our river, and keeping it always full of pure water for my mother's use when she had to wash the linen or cook."

" Excellent, excellent, my boy ! This is what I call *thinking for the general good.* And we will execute the idea as soon as we can prepare some clay as a foundation."

" Hah, hah !" cried Jack. " Now then, it is my turn, for I have got some clay."

" And where did you get it, my boy?" said I.

Mother. " Oh, to my cost I know where the clay was got. This morning early my young hero falls to digging on the hill you see to the right, and home he comes with the news that he has found a bed of clay, but so dirty himself that we were obliged to think next of the washing-tub."

Jack. " And if I had minded a little dirt, Mother, I should not have discovered this clay, which will be of great use to us. As I was returning from looking for potatoes I thought I would take the high path along the river. By and by I came to a large slope watered by the river. It was so slippery that I could not keep upon my legs, so I fell and dirtied myself all over. The ground was all of clay, and almost liquid, so I made some into balls and brought them home."

Ernest. " When the water-tub is complete I will put the roots I have found to soak a little in it, for they are now quite dry. I do not exactly know what they are—they look something like the radish or horse-radish, but the plant from which I took them was almost the size of a bush. As I don't know its nature, I have not tasted the roots, though I saw our sow eat heartily of them."

Father. " It was quite right to be cautious, my son. But let me look at these roots. How did you first discover them?"

Ernest. " I was rambling about, Father, and met the sow, who was turning up the earth under the plant I have been speaking of, and stopped only to chew and swallow greedily something she seemed to find there. I drove her away, and on looking into the place I found a knot of roots, which I tore out and brought home."

Father. " If my suspicion is right you have made a discovery, which, with our potatoes, may furnish us the means of existence as long as we remain in this land. I am tolerably certain that these roots are *manioc*, of which the natives of the West Indies make a sort of bread which they call *cassave*. But if we would make this use of it we must first carry it through a certain preparation, without which these roots possess pernicious properties."

By the time of ending this discourse we had also finished unloading the sledge, and I bade the three eldest boys accompany me to fetch another load before dark. We left Francis and his mother busy in preparing a refreshing supper, the tortoise having presented itself most opportunely for this purpose.

When we reached the raft, we took from it as many effects as the sledge could hold, or the animals draw along. The first object of my attention was to secure two chests which contained the clothes of my family;

which I knew would afford the highest gratification
to my wife. I reckoned also on finding in one of the
chests some books, and principally a large handsomely-
printed Bible. I added to these four cart-wheels and
a hand-mill tor grinding, which, now that we had
discovered the manioc, I considered of signal importance.

On our return to Falcon's Nest we found my wife
looking anxiously for our arrival, and ready with the
welcome of an ample and agreeable repast. Nor was
her kind humour diminished by the acquisitions we
now added to her store.

Before she had well examined them, she drew me,
with one of her sweetest smiles, by the arm. " Step
this way," said she, " and I too will produce something that will both refresh and please you." And
leading to the shade of a tree, " This," continued she,
" is the work I performed in your absence," pointing
to a cask of tolerable size half-sunk into the ground,
and the rest covered over with branches of trees. She
then applied a small corkscrew to the side, and filling
the shell of a coco-nut with the contents, presented it
to me. I found the liquor equal to the best Canary.

" How then," said I, " have you performed this
new miracle? I cannot believe the enchanted bag
produced it."

" Not exactly," replied she, " for this time it was an
obliging wave which threw on shore the agreeable
liquid. I took a little ramble in your absence yesterday, and behold how well my trouble was rewarded!
The boys ran for the sledge, and had but little difficulty in getting it to Falcon's Stream, where our next
care was to dig a place in the earth to keep it cool.
We guessed it must contain wine, but to be quite sure
Ernest and Jack bored a small hole in the side, and

inserting a hollow reed they contrived to taste it, and assured me the cask was filled with a most delicious beverage."

After supper I completed my day's work by drawing up the mattresses from the ship to our chamber in the tree. When I had laid them along to advantage, they looked so inviting that I was glad the time had come to commit ourselves to the kind relief they offered to our exhausted strength.

CHAPTER XIX

ANOTHER TRIP TO THE WRECK

I rose before day to go to the sea-side and inspect our two vessels. My family did not hear me depart, and I was unwilling to disturb their sleep. I therefore gently descended the ladder. Above, the scene was all repose; below, I found everything in life and motion. The dogs jumped about me for joy, perceiving that I was going out; the cock and the hens flapped their wings and chuckled; and our goats shook their long beards as they browsed; but the ass, the only creature amongst them I was likely to want at that time, still lay stretched at full length on the grass, and discovered no inclination for the morning jaunt I designed for him. I quickly roused and harnessed him singly to the sledge. It was unnecessary to call the dogs after me. As I walked towards the shore I saw with pleasure that the boat and raft had resisted the tide. I got quickly on the raft, took a small loading, and returned to Falcon's Stream in time for breakfast.

Judge of my surprise when arrived, that I neither saw nor heard a single creature of its inhabitants, though the sun had climbed high above the horizon. Thinking it time for our fellow-labourers to be stirring, I gave a shout as loud as a war-whoop. My wife awoke first, and wondered to see the day so far advanced.

" Really, my dear," said she, " I think it must be the magic charm of the good mattress you brought home yesterday that has lulled me into such a long, sound sleep, and that appears to be still exerting its influence upon our boys."

In fact, they yawned, stretched, turned round, and turned back again.

" Come, come, up, my lads !" exclaimed I once again. " Brave youths like you ought to awake at the first call and leap gaily out of bed."

After this short admonition all came down. Prayers and breakfast over, we returned to the sea-side to complete the unloading of the raft, that it might be ready for sea on the ebbing of the tide. I was not long, with the additional assistance I had, in taking two cargoes to Falcon's Stream. At our last trip the tide was nearly up to our craft. I immediately sent back my wife and three children, and remained with Fritz waiting till we were quite afloat, when, observing Jack hovering round us, I perceived his wish, and assented to his embarking with us. Shortly after the tide was high enough for us to row off. Instead of steering for Safety Bay to moor our vessels there, I was tempted by the fineness of the weather to go out again to the wreck, which it was with considerable difficulty we reached, though aided by a fresh sea-breeze. On our getting alongside it was too late to undertake much, and I was unwilling to cause my wife uneasiness by passing another night on board. I therefore determined to bring only what could be obtained with speed. In this intention we searched hastily through the ship for any trifling articles that might be readily removed. Jack was up and down everywhere, at a loss what to select. When I saw him again he drew a wheel-barrow after him, rejoicing at having found such a vehicle for our potatoes. Fritz next disclosed that he had discovered behind the bulkhead amidships a pinnace taken to pieces, with all its appurtenances, and even two small guns. This intelligence so delighted me that I ran to the bulkhead, when I was convinced of the truth of the lad's assertion. But I perceived that to put it together and launch it into the sea would be a Herculean task, which I relinquished for the present. I then collected some house utensils and whatever else I thought most useful, such as a large copper boiler, some plates of iron, tobacco-graters, two grinding stones, a small barrel of gunpowder, and another of flints. Jack's barrow was not forgotten. Two more were afterwards added. All these articles were hurried into the boat, and we re-embarked with speed to avoid meeting the land wind that invariably rose in the evening. As we were drawing near to shore, we were struck with the appearance of an assemblage of small figures ranged in a long line on the strand. They were dressed in black, and all uniform, with white waistcoats and full gravats. The arms of these beings hung down carelessly. Now and then, however, they seemed to extend them tenderly, as if they wished to embrace or offer us a token of friendship.

"I really think," said I to the boys, who were steadfastly gazing at so novel a spectacle, "that we are in the country of the pygmies."

"But I begin to see," said Fritz, "that the pygmies have beaks and short wings. What strange birds!"

" You are right, son; they are penguins or ruffs. They are of the *stupid* species. Ernest killed one soon after our arrival. They are excellent swimmers, but cannot fly; and so confused are they when on land, that they run in the silliest way into danger."

While we were talking I steered gently towards the shore to enjoy the uncommon sight the longer. But the very moment we got into shallow water, my giddy boy Jack leaped out of his tub up to his waist, and was quickly on land battering with his stick among the penguins, so that half a dozen of them were immediately laid flat. They were not dead, but only stunned. The remainder plunged into the sea, dived, and disappeared.

Fritz murmured at his brother for having frightened them away before he could fire. I could not help laughing at this perpetual shooter of guns, who was so disposed to waste his powder on animals who were to be taken with the hand. I also taunted Jack a little for having jumped into the water at the risk of being drowned. While I was making these observations, the birds gradually recovered, rose upon their legs and began a tottering sort of march with a gravity which irresistibly excited our laughter. I did not allow Jack's game to escape. I took hold of them, tied their legs together with reeds without hurting them, and laid them on the beach while we were landing our treasures. But as the sun declined, and we despaired of finishing before night set in, each of us filled a barrow in order to take home something. I requested that the tobacco-graters and iron plates might be in the first load. To these we added the penguins, living and dead, and then set out. As we drew near Falcon's Stream I heard the watchful dogs proclaim our approach with loud barking. My wife was highly pleased with the

wheel-barrows, and for the most part with their contents, but she had no partiality for the tobacco-graters.

"What is the use of these graters?" she exclaimed.
"Are our four sons to become snuff-takers?"

"No, dear wife," I replied; "and pray do not be
uneasy about them. These graters are not for the
gratification of our noses. Come, children," said I,
pointing to the penguins, "look after the newcomers
to the poultry-yard."

I then directed them to fasten the birds one by one
to a goose or a duck, as a means of taming them and
inuring them to the society of their companions. This
essay, however, was inconvenient to our feathered
animals, who were but slowly reconciled to their
singular companions. My wife now showed me a good
store of potatoes which she had got in, and a quantity
of the roots I had taken for manioc, and in which I
was not mistaken.

"Father, we have worked very hard," said little
Francis. "What will you say when we have a fine
crop of maize, melons, dates, and gourds? Mother has
planted all these in the potato holes."

Mother. "I took the grain and seeds from my
enchanted bag, and your thirst after booty and your
trips to the wreck are the sources of the resolution I
formed to increase the number of your comforts at
home, and thus render them the less necessary. I
determined, then, to fit up a kitchen-garden."

Father. "This was well thought, my dear; but we
must not despise the trips to the vessel either. This
very day we discovered in her a handsome little pinnace, which may be of the greatest service to us."

Mother. "I cannot say that this discovery gives me
pleasure. I have no desire to trust myself again on the
sea. But should it at any time be necessary, I must

confess I should prefer a well-made, solid vessel to our raft composed of tubs."

Father. " Well, this you shall possess, if you will consent to my returning once more to the wreck. In the meanwhile let us have supper, and then we will retire to rest. And if my little workmen should be industriously inclined to-morrow, I shall reward them with the novelty of a new trade to be learnt."

This did not fail to excite the curiosity of all. But I kept my word, and made them wait till the following day for the explanation I had to give.

CHAPTER XX

THE BAKEHOUSE

I waked the boys very early, reminding them that I had promised to teach them a new trade.

" What is it? What is it?" exclaimed they all at once, springing suddenly out of bed and hurrying on their clothes.

Father. " It is the art of baking, my boys, which at present I am no more acquainted with than yourselves. But we will learn it together. Hand me those iron plates that we brought yesterday from the vessel, and the tobacco-graters also."

Mother. " I really cannot understand what tobacco-graters and iron plates can have to do with making bread. A good oven would afford me much better hopes."

Father. " These very iron plates you looked so disdainfully upon yesterday will serve the purpose. I cannot promise to produce light and handsome-looking bread; but I can answer that you shall have some excellent-tasted cakes, though they should be a little flat and heavy. Ernest, bring hither the roots found underground; but first, my dear, I must request you to make me a small bag of a piece of the strongest wrapper linen."

I spread a large piece of coarse linen on the ground, and assembled my young ones round me. I gave each of the boys a grater, and showed him how to rest it on the linen, and then to grate the roots of manioc, so that in a short time each had produced a considerable heap of a substance resembling pollard. The occupation proved infinitely amusing to them all, and they looked no further into the matter.

A very short time was sufficient for producing a considerable quantity of ground manioc. By this time my wife had completed the bag. I had it well filled with what we called our pollard, and she closed it effectually by sewing up the end. I was now to contrive a kind of press. I cut a long, straight, well-formed branch of considerable strength from a neighbouring tree, and stripped it of the bark. I then placed a plank across the table we had fixed between the arched roots of our tree, and which was exactly the right height for my purpose, and on this I laid the bag. I put other planks again upon the bag, and then covered all with the large branch, the thickest extremity of which I inserted under an arch, while to the other, which projected beyond the planks, I suspended all sorts of heavy substances, such as lead, our largest hammers, and bars of iron, which, acting with great force as a press on the bag of manioc, caused the sap it contained to issue in streams.

Mother. " But, pray tell me, are we to prepare the

whole of this manioc at once? If so, we have at least a whole day's work, and a great part must be spoiled at last."

Father. " Not so, my dear. When the pollard is dry it may be placed in casks, and it will keep for years; but you will see that the whole of this large heap will be so reduced in quantity by the operation we are going to apply of baking, that there will be no cause for your apprehension."

Fritz. " Father, it no longer runs a single drop. May we not now set about making the dough?"

Father. " I have no objections; but it would be prudent to make only a small cake at first which, as I said before, we will give to the monkey and the fowls, and wait to see the effect."

We now opened the bag, and took out a small quantity of the pollard, which already was sufficiently dry. We stirred the rest about with a stick, and then replaced it under the press. The next thing was to fix one of our iron plates, which was of a round form and rather convex, so as to rest upon two blocks of stone at a distance from each other. Under this we lighted a large fire, and when the iron plate was completely heated we placed a portion of the dough upon it with a wooden spade. As soon as the cake began to be brown underneath it was turned.

As soon as the cake was cold we broke some of it into crumbs, and gave it to two of the fowls, and a larger piece to the monkey, who nibbled it with a perfect relish.

" But what, I pray you, may there be in that boiling vessel yonder?" said I, turning to my wife.

" It is the penguin that Jack brought home," she replied.

To say the truth, the bird was of a strong and fishy

flavour. Jack, however, was of a different opinion, and he was left at full liberty to regale himself to his appetite's content.

The first thing we did after dinner was to visit our fowls. Those among them which had eaten the manioc were in excellent condition, and no less so the monkey.

" Now then, to the bakehouse, young ones!" said I.

The grated manioc was soon emptied out of the bag, a large fire was quickly lighted, and when it was sufficiently hot I placed the boys where a flat surface had been prepared for them, and gave to each a plate of iron and the quantity of a coco-nut shellfull for them to make a cake apiece, and they were to try who could succeed the best. They were ranged in a half-circle round the place where I stood myself, that they might the better be enabled to observe how I proceeded. The result was not discouraging, though we were now and then so unlucky as to burn a cake. My little rogues could not resist the pleasure of frequently tasting their cake, a little bit at a time, as they went on. At length the undertaking was complete. The cakes were put in a dish, and served in company with a handsome share of milk to each person. With this addition, they furnished us an excellent repast. What remained we distributed among our animals and fowls. I observed that the penguins which I had preserved alive accommodated themselves perfectly to this food, and that they began to lose their timid behaviour. I therefore ventured to disengage them from their comrades. This indulgence procured me the pleasure of seeing them in a state of newly-acquired content.

The rest of the day was employed in drawing to Tent House the remaining articles we had brought from the ship. When all this was done we retired to rest, having first made another meal on our cakes, and concluded all with pious thanks to God for the blessings His goodness thought fit to bestow upon us.

CHAPTER XXI

THE PINNACE AND THE CRACKER

From the time of discovering the pinnace, my desire of returning to the vessel grew every moment more irresistible. One thing I saw was absolutely necessary, which was to collect all my hands and go with sufficient strength to get her out from the situation where we had found her. I therefore thought of taking with me the three boys. I even wished that my wife should accompany us; but she assured me the very attempt would make her ill, and thus occasion her to be an additional trouble rather than of use. I had some difficulty to prevail upon her to let the children go.

After breakfast, then, we prepared for setting out. We took with us an ample provision of boiled potatoes and cassave, and, in addition, arms and weapons. We embarked and reached Safety Bay without the occurrence of any remarkable event. Here we thought it prudent to put on our cork-jackets. We then scattered some food for the geese and ducks which had taken up their abode there, and soon after stepped gaily into our tub-boat, at the same time fastening the new raft by a rope to her stern. We put out for the current, though not without fear of finding that the wreck had disappeared. We soon, however, perceived that she still remained. Having got on board, our first care was to load our craft with different stores, that we might not return without some acquisition of comfort. Then we repaired to that part of the vessel called the bulkhead, which contained the enviable prize, the pinnace. On further observation, it appeared to me that the plan we had formed was subject to at least two perhaps insurmountable difficulties. The one was the situation of the pinnace in the ship, and the other was the size and weight it would necessarily acquire when put together. The enclosure in which she lay in pieces was far back in the interior of the ship, and close upon the side which was in the water, immediately under the officers' cabin. Several inner timbers of prodigious bulk and weight separated this enclosure from the breach at which only we had been able to get on board, and in this part of the deck there was not sufficient space for us to work at putting the pinnace together, or to give her room should we succeed in completing our business. The breach also was too narrow and too irregular to admit of her being launched from this place, as we had done with our tub-raft. In short, the separate pieces of the pinnace were too heavy for the possibility of our removing them. What, therefore, was to be done? I stood on the spot absorbed in deep reflection, while the boys were conveying everything portable they could find, on board the raft.

The cabinet which contained the pinnace was lighted by several small fissures in the timbers, which, after standing in the place a few minutes to accustom the eye, enabled one to see sufficiently to distinguish objects. I discovered with pleasure that all the pieces of which she was composed were so accurately arranged and numbered, that I might flatter myself with the hope of being able to collect and put them together, if I could be allowed the necessary time and place. I therefore, in spite of every disadvantage, decided on the undertaking, and we immediately set about it. We proceeded, at first so slowly as to produce discouragement, if the desire of possessing a little vessel which might at some future day be the means of our deliverance, had not at every moment inspired us with new strength and ardour.

Evening, however, was fast approaching, and we had made but small progress when, with reluctance, we left our occupation and re-embarked. On reaching Safety Bay, we had the satisfaction of finding there our kind steward and little Francis. They had been during the day employed in some arrangements for our living at Tent House as long as we should have to continue the excursions to the vessel. This she did to shorten the length of the voyage, and that we might be always in sight of each other. This new proof of her attention affected me in a lively manner, and I could not sufficiently express the gratitude which I felt, particularly as I knew the dislike she had conceived to living in this spot. I made the best display I could of two casks of salted butter, three of flour, some small bags of millet seed and of rice, and a multitude of other articles of utility and comfort for our establishment. My wife rewarded me by the expression of her perfect satisfaction, and the whole was removed to our store-house at the rocks.

We passed an entire week in this arduous undertaking of the pinnace. I embarked regularly every morning with my three sons, and returned every evening, and never without some addition to our stores.

At length the pinnace was completed, and in a condition to be launched. The question now was, how to manage this remaining difficulty. She was an elegant little vessel, perfect in every part. She had a small neat deck; and her mast and sails were no less exact and perfect than those of a little brig. It was probable she would sail well from the lightness of her construction, and drawing comparatively little water. We had pitched and towed all the seams that she might be water-tight. We had even taken the superfluous pains of further embellishing by mounting her with two small cannon of about a pound weight, and, in imitation of larger vessels, had fastened them to the deck with chains. But in spite of the delight we felt in contemplating a commodious little vessel, yet the great difficulty still remained. The little vessel still stood fast, enclosed within four walls; nor could I conceive of a means of getting her out. To effect a passage through the outer side of the vessel by means of the utensils we had secured, seemed to present a prospect of exertions beyond our powers. We now examined if it might be practicable to cut away all intervening timbers to which, from the nature of the breach, we had easier access. But should we even succeed in this attempt, the upper timbers being, in consequence of the inclined position of the ship, on a level with the water, our labour would be unavailing; besides, we had neither strength nor time for such a proceeding. From one moment to another a storm might arise and engulf the ship—timber, pinnace, ourselves, and all. Despairing, then, of being able to find a means consistent with the sober rules of art, my impatient fancy inspired the thought of a project which must be attended with hazards.

I had found on board a strong iron mortar, such as is used in kitchens. I took a thick oak plank, and nailed to a certain part of it some large iron hooks: with a knife I cut a groove along the middle of the plank. I sent the boys to fetch some match-wood from the hold, and I cut a piece sufficiently long to continue burning at least two hours. I placed this train in the groove of my plank. I filled the mortar with gunpowder, and then laid the plank, thus furnished, upon it, having previously pitched the mortar all round; and, lastly, I made the whole fast to the spot with strong chains crossed by means of the hooks in every direction. Thus I accomplished a sort of cracker. I hung this infernally-contrived machine against the side of the bulkhead next the sea, having taken previous care to choose a spot in which its action could not affect the pinnace. When the whole was arranged I set fire to the match, the end of which projected far enough beyond the plank to allow us time to escape. I now hurried on board the raft, into which I had sent the boys before applying a light to the match. Though they had assisted in forming the cracker, they had no suspicion of the use for which it was intended.

On our arrival at Tent House, I immediately put the raft in a certain order, that she might be in readiness to return speedily to the wreck, when the noise produced by the cracker should have informed me that my scheme had taken effect. We set busily to work to empty her, when, during the occupation, our ears were assailed with the noise of an explosion of such violence, that my wife and the boys, who were ignorant of the cause, were dreadfully alarmed. "What can it be? What is the matter? What can have happened?" cried all at once.

Mother. "The sound appeared to come in the direction of the wreck; perhaps she has blown up. Were you careful of not leaving any light which could communicate with gunpowder?"

From the bottom of her heart she made this last

suggestion, for she desired nothing more earnestly than that the vessel should be annihilated, and thus an end be put to our repeated visits.

Father. " If this is the case," said I, " we had better return and convince ourselves of the fact. Who will be of the party?"

" I, I, I!" cried the boys; and the three young rogues lost not a moment in jumping into their tubs, whither I soon followed them, after having whispered a few words to my wife, somewhat tending to tranquillize her mind during the trip we had now to engage in.

We rowed out of the bay with more rapidity than on any former occasion. Curiosity gave strength to our arms. When the vessel was in sight, I observed with pleasure that no change had taken place in the part of her which faced Tent House, and that no sign of smoke appeared. We advanced, therefore, in excellent spirits. But instead of rowing as usual straight to the breach, we proceeded round to the side on the inside of which we had placed the cracker. The scene of devastation we had caused now broke upon our sight. The greater part of the ship's side was shivered to pieces; innumerable splinters covered the surface of the water. The whole exhibited a scene of destruction, in the midst of which presented itself our elegant pinnace entirely free from injury! I could not refrain from the liveliest exclamations of joy, which excited the surprise of the boys. They fixed their eyes upon me with the utmost astonishment. " Now then, she is ours!" cried I—" the elegant little pinnace is ours! for nothing is now more easy than to launch her. Come, boys, jump upon her deck, and let us see how quickly we can get her down upon the water."

Fritz. " Ah! now I understand you, Father. You

have yourself blown up the side of the ship with that machine you contrived in our last visit, that we might be able to get out the pinnace. But how does it happen that so much of the ship is blown away?"

Father. " I will explain all this to you, when I have convinced myself that the pinnace is not injured, and that there is no danger of any of the fire remaining on board. Let us well examine." We entered by the new breach, and had soon reason to be satisfied that the pinnace had escaped from injury, and that the fire was extinguished. The mortar, however, and pieces of the chain, had been driven forcibly into the opposite side of the enclosure.

I now perceived that it would be easy, with the help of the crowbar and the lever, to lower the pinnace into the water. In putting her together, I had used the precaution of placing the keel on rollers. Before letting her go, however, I fastened the end of a long thick rope to her head, and the other end to the most solid part of the wreck, for fear of her being carried out too far. We put our whole ingenuity and strength to this undertaking, and soon enjoyed the pleasure of seeing our pretty pinnace descend gracefully into the sea, the rope keeping her sufficiently near, and enabling us to draw her close to the spot where I was loading the tub-boat, and where for that purpose I had lodged a pulley on a projecting beam, from which I was enabled also to advance with the fixing of the masts and sails for our new barge. I endeavoured to recollect minutely all the information I had ever possessed on the art of equipping a vessel, and our pinnace was shortly in a condition to set sail.

On this occasion a spirit of military affairs was awakened in the minds of my young flock, which was never afterwards extinguished. We were masters of a vessel mounted with two cannon, and furnished amply with guns and pistols! This was at once to be invincible, and in a condition for resisting and destroying the largest fleet the savages could bring upon us! For my own part, I answered their young enthusiasm with pious prayers that we might ever escape such a calamity as being compelled to use our firearms against human beings. Night surprised us before we had finished our work, and we accordingly prepared for our return to Tent House, after drawing the pinnace close under the vessel's side. We arrived in safety, and took great care, as had been previously agreed on, not to mention our new and invaluable booty to the good mother, till we could surprise her with the sight of it in a state of entire completeness.

Two whole days more were spent in equipping and loading the little barge. When she was ready for sailing, I found it impossible to resist the earnest importunity of the boys, who, as a recompense for the industry and discretion they had employed, claimed my permission to salute their mother, on their approach to Tent house, with two discharges of cannon. These accordingly were loaded, and the two youngest placed themselves, with a lighted match in hand, close to the touch-holes, to be in readiness. Fritz stood at the mast to manage the ropes, while I took my station at the rudder. These matters being adjusted, we put off. The wind was favourable, and so fresh that we glided with the rapidity of a bird along the mirror of the waters.

Our old friend the tub-raft had been deeply loaded and fastened to the pinnace, and it now followed as an accompanying boat to a superior vessel. We took down our large sail as soon as we found ourselves at the entrance of the Bay of Safety, to have the greater command in directing the barge; and soon the smaller ones were lowered one by one. Thus, proceeding at a slower rate, we had greater facilities for managing the important affair of the discharge of the cannon. Arrived within a certain distance—" Fire!" cried commander Fritz. The rocks behind Tent House returned the sound. " Fire!" said Fritz again. Ernest and Jack obeyed, and the echoes again majestically replied. Fritz at the same moment had discharged his two pistols, and all joined instantly in three loud huzzas.

" Welcome, welcome, dear ones!" was the answer from the anxious mother, almost breathless with astonishment and joy. " Welcome!" cried also little Francis, as he stood clinging to her side, and not well knowing whether he was to be sad or merry! We now tried to push to shore with our oars, that we might have the protection of a projecting mass of rocks, and my wife and little Francis hastened to the spot to receive us.

" Ah, dear ones!" cried she, heartily embracing me, " what a fright have you and your cannon and your little ship thrown me into! I saw it advancing rapidly towards us, and was unable to conceive from whence it could come, or what it might have on board. I stole with Francis behind the rocks, and when I heard the firing, I was near sinking to the ground with terror. If I had not the moment after heard your voices, God knows where we should have run to—but come, the cruel moment is now over, and thanks to Heaven I have you once again in safety! But tell me where you got so unhoped-for a prize as this charming little vessel? In good truth it would really almost tempt me to venture once more on a sea-voyage, especially if she would promise to convey us back to our dear country! I foresee of what use she will be to us, and

for her sake I think that I must try to forgive the many
sins of absence you have committed against me."

Fritz now invited his mother to get on board, and
gave her his assistance. When they had all stepped
upon the deck, they entreated for permission to salute
by again discharging the cannon, and at the same
moment to confer on the pinnace the name of their
mother—*The Elizabeth.*

My wife was particularly gratified by these our late
adventures. " But do not," said she, " imagine that
I bestow so much commendation without the hope of
some return. On the contrary, it is now my turn to
claim from you, for myself and little Francis, the same
sort of agreeable recompense. For we have not, I
assure you, remained idle. No, not so; little Francis
and his mother found means to be doing something
also, though not at this moment prepared to furnish
such unquestionable proofs as you, by your salutations of cannon and pistols. But wait a little, and our
proofs shall hereafter be apparent in some dishes of
excellent vegetables. It depends, to say the truth, only
on yourselves to go with me and see what we have
done."

We did not hesitate to comply, and jumped briskly
out of the pinnace. Taking little Francis by the hand
she led the way, and we followed in the gayest mood.
She conducted us up an ascent of one of the rocks,
and stopping at the spot where the cascade is formed
from Jackal's River, she displayed a commodious
kitchen-garden, laid out in beds and walks, and, as she
told us, everywhere sowed with the seed of useful plants.

" This," said she, " is the pretty exploit we have
been engaged in, if you will kindly think so of it. In
this spot the earth is so light, that Francis and I had
no difficulty in working it, and then dividing it into

different beds—one for potatoes, one for manioc, and other smaller shares for lettuces of various kinds, not forgetting to leave a due proportion to receive some plants of the sugar-cane. You, dear husband, and Fritz will easily find means to conduct sufficient water hither from the cascade, by means of pipes of bamboo, to keep the whole in health and vigour, and we shall have a double source of pleasure from the general prosperity, for both the eyes and the palate will be gratified. But you have not yet seen all. There, on the slope of the rock, I have transplanted some plants of the ananas. Between these I have sowed some melon-seeds. Here is a plot allotted to pease and beans, and this other for all sorts of cabbage. Round each bed or plot I have sowed seeds of maize, to serve as a border, while on account of its tall and bushy form it will protect my young plants from the scorching heat of the sun."

I stood transported in the midst of so perfect an exhibition of such persevering industry. I could only exclaim that I should never have believed in the possibility of such a result in so short a time, and particularly with so much privacy as to leave me wholly unsuspicious of the existence of such a project.

Mother. "To confess the truth, I did not myself expect to succeed, for which reason I resolved to say nothing of the matter, that I might not be put to the blush for my presumption. But as I found my little calculations answer better than I expected, I was encouraged, and the hope of surprising you so agreeably gave me new strength. I had my suspicions that your visits to the wreck were connected with some great mystery, which at a certain time you would unfold. So, mystery for mystery, thought I, and thus it has turned out."

"I had almost forgotten though," said my wife after a short pause, " one little reproach I had to make you. Your trips to the vessel have made you neglect the bundle of fruit-saplings we laid together in mould at Falcon's Stream. I fear they by this time must be dying for want of being planted, though I took care to water and cover them with branches. Let us go and see about them."

I should have been no less grieved than my wife to see this charming acquisition perish for want of care. We had reason on many accounts to return quickly to Falcon's Stream, where different matters required our presence. We had now in possession the greater part of the cargo of the vessel, but almost the whole of these treasures were at present in the open air, and liable to injury.

My wife prepared with alertness for our walk, and the rather from the aversion she had ever entertained, on account of the intense heat, for Tent House. We hastened to unload the boat, and to place the cargo safely under shelter along with our other stores.

The pinnace was anchored on the shore, and fastened with a rope to a stake. When all our stores were thus disposed of, we began our journey to Falcon's Stream, but not empty-handed. We took with us everything absolutely wanted for comfort; and when brought together, it was really so much that both ourselves and our beasts of burden had no easy task to perform.

CHAPTER XXII

GYMNASTIC EXERCISES—VARIOUS DISCOVERIES— SINGULAR ANIMALS, ETC.

I had recommended to the boys to continue the exercise we began upon the first Sunday of our abode in these regions—the shooting of arrows; for I had an extreme solicitude about increasing their strength and agility. Nothing tends more to the extinction of courage than the consciousness of wanting that strength of limb, or that address, which may be necessary to aid us in defending ourselves or in escaping from dangers. I counselled them, therefore, to add the exercises of running, jumping, getting up trees, both by means of climbing by the trunk, or by a suspended rope, as sailors are obliged to do to get to the mast-head. We began at first by making knots in the rope at a foot distance from each other, then we reduced the number of knots, and before we left off we contrived to succeed without any. I next taught them an exercise of a different nature, which was to be effected by means of two balls made of lead, fastened one to each end of a string about a fathom in length. While I was preparing this all eyes were fixed upon me. " What can it be intended for?" " How can we use it?" " Will it soon be ready?"

Father. " Have patience, boys. This is nothing less than an imitation of the arm used by a valiant nation remarkable for their skill in the chase, and whom you have heard of. I mean the Patagonians, inhabitants of the most southern point of America. Every Patagonian is armed with this simple instrument. If they desire to kill or wound an enemy or an animal, they fling one of the ends of this cord at him, and draw it back by the other, which they keep carefully in their hand, to be ready for another throw if necessary. But if they wish to take an animal alive, and without hurting it, they possess the singular art of throwing it in such a way as to make it run several times round the neck of the prey, occasioning a perplexing tightness. They then throw the second stone, and with so certain an aim that they scarcely ever miss their object. The operation of the second is the so twisting itself about the animal as to impede his progress, even though he were at a full gallop. The stones continue turning, and carrying with them the cord. The poor animal is at length so entangled he falls a prey to the enemy."

This was heard with much interest by the boys, who now all entreated I would that instant try the effect of my own instrument upon a small tree. My throws entirely succeeded, and the string with the balls at the end so completely surrounded the tree that the skill of the Patagonian huntsmen required no further illustration. Each of the boys must then needs have a similar instrument, and in a short time Fritz became quite expert in the art, as indeed he was in every kind of exercise that required strength or address.

The next morning, as I was dressing, I remarked from my window in the tree that the sea was violently agitated, and the waves swelled with the wind. I rejoiced to find myself in safety in my home. Though such a wind was in reality quite harmless for skilful sailors, for us it might be truly dangerous, from our ignorance in these matters. I observed then to my wife that I should not leave her the whole day, and should therefore hold myself ready to execute any little concerns she found wanting in our domestic arrangement. We now fell to a more minute examination than I had hitherto had time for of all our possessions. She showed me many things she had herself found means to add to them during my repeated absences from home. Among these was a large barrel filled with small birds half-roasted and stowed away in butter to preserve them fresh. This she called her *game*, which she had found means to ensnare with bird-lime. Next she showed me a pair of young pigeons which had been lately hatched, and were already beginning to try their wings, while their mother was again sitting on her eggs. From these we passed to the fruit-trees we had laid in earth to be planted, and which were in real need of our assistance, being almost in a dying state. I immediately set myself to prevent so grievous a mishap. I had promised the boys the evening before to go all together to the wood of gourds, for the purpose of providing ourselves with vessels of different sizes. They were enchanted with the idea, but I bargained that they must first assist me to plant all the young trees.

When we had finished, a little disappointment, however, occurred. The evening seemed too far advanced for so long a walk, especially as my wife and little Francis were to be of the party. We accordingly postponed the excursion till the following day, when we made the necessary preparations for leaving Falcon's Stream very early in the morning. By sunrise all were on foot. The ass was harnessed to the sledge. In the journey out he carried our dinner, and some powder and shot. I took with me a double-barrelled gun, one barrel loaded with shot and one with ball.

Turning round Flamingo Marsh we soon reached the pleasant spot which before had so delighted us.

Fritz took a direction a little farther from the sea-shore, and sending Turk into the tall grass, he followed himself, and both disappeared. Soon, however, we heard Turk barking loud, a large bird sprang up, and almost at the same moment a shot from Fritz brought it down. But the bird, though wounded, was not killed; it raised itself and ran off with incredible swiftness. Turk pursued with eagerness. Fritz followed; and Ponto threw the monkey off his back and fell speedily into the same track. It was Ponto that seized the bird, and held it fast till Fritz came up. But now a different sort of scene succeeded from that which took place at the capture of the flamingo. The legs of that bird are long and weak, and it was able to make but a poor resistance. The present captive was large in size, and proportionately strong. It struck the dogs, or whoever came near, with its legs with so much force, that Fritz, who had received a blow or two, retired from the field of battle, and dared not again approach. Turk was also discouraged by some severities applied to his head by his sturdy combatant, and yielded the contest. The brave Ponto alone withstood the animal's attacks. He seized one of its wings, and did not let it go till I reached the spot, which I was long in doing on account of the height of the grass. When I was near enough to distinguish the bird as it lay on the ground, I was overjoyed to see that it was a female bustard of the largest size. I had long wished to possess and to tame for our poultry-yard a bird of this species, which closely resembles the turkey.

To effect the complete capture of the bird without injury, I took out my pocket-handkerchief and threw it over its head. It could not disengage itself, and its efforts only served to entangle it the more. As in this situation it could not see me, I got sufficiently near to pass a string with a running knot over its legs, which I then drew tight. I gently released the wing from Ponto, and tied that and its fellow close to the bird's body. The bustard was at length vanquished, though not till most of us had felt the powerful blows it was capable of inflicting.

We fixed the bustard on the sledge, and then pursued our way towards the wood where Fritz and I had seen such troops of monkeys. Fritz again recounted the adventure to his mother, and during this recital Ernest was wandering a little from us in every direction, in admiration of the height and beauty of the trees. He stopped in delight at the sight of one in particular which stood alone, gazing with wonder at the prodigious distance from the root to the nearest bunches of coco-nuts, which he saw hanging in clusters under their crown of leaves, and which excited an eager desire to possess some of them.

Father. " Yes, Ernest, they are indeed at a most unaccommodating height, and not a monkey in the way to throw them down to you. Even were I to set Knips at liberty, besides that he is not in the habit of giving away what he might keep for himself, he would perhaps take it into his head to stay in the tree. It is a pity, and I am sure you are of my opinion, that those fine coco-nuts cannot find a way to drop down into your mouth."

Scarcely had I ended my sentence when a nut fell down. Ernest stepped aside and looked up at the tree; another fell, and almost near enough to touch me, so that I was no less surprised than he. Not the smallest sign of a living creature appeared.

Ernest ventured to take up the nuts. We found them too unripe to be made use of, and were more than ever at a loss to account for their falling from the tree. In vain we strained our eyes; we saw nothing but now and then a slight motion of the leaves.

Fritz at this moment came up, and we told him what had passed. " I shall soon," said he, " see what it all means," raising his face to gaze at the tree. " If one would but fall at this moment, I would soon tell you who threw it."

At the very instant two nuts fell, and so near to the speaker as to bruise his lip and his chin. Ernest could not refrain from laughing heartily. " The magician is at least polite," said he; " he conducts his gift to your very mouth. It is no fault of his if your mouth is not quite large enough to receive it. But look, look! there are two more falling close to our mother and Francis! Let us quickly open one of them, and refresh ourselves with the liquor it contains in drinking to the health of our unknown friend."

We did this, and all called out together as they drank it, looking up at the tree, " Long life and thanks to the good magician!"

" Ah, ah! I see him! There he is!" exclaimed Jack suddenly. " What a hideous creature! What an ugly shape! He is as large as my hat, and has two monstrous pincer-claws!"

" Where is he then?" said I. " I do not see him."

" There, that is he, Father; crawling slowly down the tree. Do you see him now?"

It was a land-crab—an animal that, to say the truth, fully deserved Jack's description of him. The land-crab resembles the sea-crab, but is ten times more hideous. The one we now met with was of the kind called coco-crab, on account of its fondness for that fruit. It crawls up the trunk of the tree. When it has reached the clumps of leaves at the top, it falls to pinching off the bunches of coco-nuts at the stalks.

It separates the nuts in the bunch and then throws them down one by one, which often bruises them considerably. The crab then descends, and finds below a plentiful repast. It is said by some that their claws are strong enough to break the shell of the nut. But for myself, I doubt this. I expect the animal sucks the milk by means of the small hole found near the stalk. The land-crab is not dangerous unless you are within reach of its claws, or, which is rarely the case, when they are found together in great numbers. Little Francis on seeing the animal was terribly frightened, and hid himself behind his mother. Even Ernest drew back. Jack raised the butt of his gun, and all of us cast looks of curiosity as the creature slowly descended. The moment he was on the ground the intrepid Jack aimed a blow at him with his gun, which missed him. The crab, finding himself attacked, turned round and advanced with his claws stretched open towards his enemy. My little ruffian defended himself valiantly. He did not retreat a single step, but his attempts to strike entirely failed, for the crab was perfect in the art of evading every blow. I, however, determined not to interfere. I saw that there could be no danger to the boy, and that the scene would conclude by his subduing the animal, if he conducted the affair with address.

After some time, being tired out with so many fruitless attempts, and perhaps recollecting that the pinches he might get from the animal's claws would not be very agreeable, Jack suddenly gave him the slip and ran off. The other boys now burst into peals of laughter, bawling out, " So the magician has conquered you! He has made you run away! Poor Jack! But why did you engage with a magician, Jack?" On this, the lad, piqued by their jeers, stopped short, threw his gun and his game-bag on the ground, stripped off his coat, spread it before him, and made a stand at his adversary, who was making up to him with his claws stretched out. Jack quickly threw his coat upon the creature and wrapped him round in it. Then tapping on the outside upon his shell, " Wicked magician," cried he, " I have you at last! I will teach you to brandish your horns at me another time !"

I laughed so heartily at this scene that I had not the power to give him any assistance. I saw by the motion under the coat that the crab was still alert and angry. I therefore took my hatchet and applied two or three powerful blows with it on the coat, which I took for granted would finish the affair at once. I lifted up the coat, and, as I expected, the terrible animal was practically dead, but still preserved a menacing posture.

I put the animal along with the coco-nuts together on the sledge, and we resumed our march. As we advanced the wood became thicker and more difficult to pass. I was frequently obliged to use the hatchet to make a free passage for the ass. The heat also increased, and we were all complaining of thirst, when Ernest, whose discoveries were generally of a kind to be of use, made one at this moment. He has already been described as a great lover of natural history, and now he was continually gathering such plants as he met with. He found a kind of hollow stalk of a tolerable height, which grew at the foot of the trees, and frequently entangled our feet. He cut some of the plants with his knife, and was much surprised to see a drop of pure fresh water issue from them. He showed it to us, put it to his lips, and found it perfectly agreeable, and felt much regret that there was no more. I then fell to examining the phenomenon myself, and soon perceived that the want of air prevented a more considerable issue of water. I made some more incisions, and presently water flowed out as if from a small conduit. Ernest, and after him the other boys, refreshed themselves and quenched their thirst at this new fountain.

I tried the experiment of dividing the plants longways, and they soon gave out water enough to supply even the ass, the monkey, and the wounded bustard. We were still compelled to fight our way through thick bushes, till at length we arrived at the wood of gourds, and we were not long in finding the spot where Fritz and I had once before enjoyed so agreeable a repose. Our companions had not soon done wondering at the magnificence of the trees they now beheld, and the prodigious size of the fruit which grew in so singular a manner. Fritz performed the office of lecturer to the rest, as I before had done to him. I strolled about the wood, choosing among the gourds such as were suited for our necessities, and marking the places in my mind's eye.

I found Jack and Ernest actively employed in collecting dried branches, while their mother was attending to the poor bustard, which was not materially injured. She remarked to me that it was cruel to keep her any longer blinded and her legs tied together. To please her, I took off the covering and loosened the string, but still left it so as to be a guard against its running away or inflicting blows. I contented myself with tying her by a long string to a tree. She had by no means the savageness of manners I should have expected, excepting when the dogs went near her. She did not appear to have any dread of man; which confirmed my previous belief that the island had no human inhabitants but ourselves.

The boys now amused themselves with making a large fire, which they joyously surrounded. I took the liberty to laugh at them, and asked if they had become salamanders, or inhabitants of the planet Mercury, who, it is said, make fires to refresh themselves from the burning heat of the sun.

" The fire, Father, is to enable us to cook the magician."

" Ah, hah ! that is quite another thing," replied I. " It was for the same purpose, I suppose, that I saw you picking up shells. You mean no doubt to use them in the cooking, instead of the rind of the gourds, which would not bear sufficient heat."

They all agreed to my conclusion.

" I require also," said my wife, " some vessels to contain milk, and a large flat spoon to cut out my butter, and next some pretty plates for serving it at table."

Father. " You are perfectly reasonable in your demand, dear wife," said I, " and for me there must be manufactured some nests for pigeons, some baskets for eggs, and some hives for bees."

Jack. " But first, Father, let me make a dish for my crab. The heat would certainly make him unfit to be eaten by the evening. I should soon have finished if you will tell me how to divide one of the rinds with a string."

Father. " Well, well, it is but fair to allow you to enjoy the fruit of your victory. As to the cutting with a string, it was good for something when we had no saw. I will, however, show you how to do it, though I took care to bring here the instruments I thought we might want. Gather then a sufficient quantity of the gourds, of different sizes, and you shall see how soon we will cut them."

They all began to gather, and we were soon in possession of a sufficient number. We now began our work. Some had to cut; others to saw, scoop out, and model into agreeable forms. It was a real pleasure to witness the activity exhibited in this manufacture: each tried what he could present for the applause of his companions. For my own part, I made a pretty basket, large enough to carry eggs, with one of the gourds, leaving an arch at the top to serve as a cover. I likewise accomplished a certain number of vessels, also with covers, fit to hold our milk, and then some spoons to skim the cream. My next attempt was to execute some bottles large enough to contain a supply of fresh water, and these occasioned me more trouble than all the rest. It was necessary to empty the gourd through the small opening of the size of one's finger, which I had cut in it. I was obliged, after loosening the contents by means of a stick, to get them out by the friction of shot and water well shaken on the inside.

Lastly, to please my wife I undertook the labour of a set of plates. Fritz and Jack engaged to make the hives for the bees, and nests for the pigeons and hens. For this last object they took the largest gourds, and cut a hole in front, proportioned to the size of the animal for whose use it was intended. The pigeons' nests were intended to be tied to the branches of our tree; those for the hens, the geese, and the ducks were to be placed between its roots or on the sea-shore, and to represent a sort of hen-coop. When the most essential of the utensils were finished, I allowed the boys to add a dish to dress their crab in. This also was soon accomplished. But when the cooking was completed they discovered that they had no water. We found nothing on this spot like our providential *fountain* plants, as we had named them. The boys entreated me to go about with them in different directions and try to find water, as I would not allow them to venture farther into the woods alone.

I was therefore of necessity compelled to accompany them. Ernest had gone on a little ahead of us. It was not long before we heard him calling to us, and saw him returning in great alarm.

" Run quick, Father," said he, " here is an immense wild boar ! I heard him grunting, and then he scampered away to the woods, and I hear him at this very moment."

" Here, here !" I then called out to the boys. " Call the dogs quickly. Halloo here ! Turk ! Ponto !"

The dogs arrived full gallop. Ernest was our leader, and conducted us to the place where the boar had approached him. But he was gone, and we saw nothing but a plot of potatoes, which had the appearance of having been ransacked by the animal. The ardour for the chase had been somewhat checked in Jack and Ernest, when they considered for a moment that they had so formidable a creature as a boar to encounter. They stopped short and began to dig potatoes, and left it to Fritz and me to follow the traces of the dogs. We soon heard their cry, and advanced with caution to the spot, holding our guns in readiness to fire. Presently the spectacle of the two brave creatures attacking him on the right and left presented itself. Each held one of his ears between their teeth. But the beast was not a boar, as the account of Ernest had made me suppose, but a pig of the true common breed, which on our approach appeared rather to ask for our assistance than to have any inclination to attack us. Fritz and myself also suddenly lost the relish for the sport, for we immediately recognized in the supposed boar our own sow which had run away and had so long been lost. After the first surprise we could not resist a hearty laugh, and then we hastened to disencumber our old friend of the teeth of her two adversaries. Her frightful squalling resounded through the wood and drew the attention of our companions, who now ran to the place, where a warfare of banter and accusation went round. Fritz knew certain persons whose passion for the chase ended in digging potatoes! Jack and Ernest returned the sally by complimenting Fritz on the wild boar he had been so fortunate as to make captive!

The attention of all was attracted to what looked like a kind of small potato which we observed lying thick on the grass around us, and which had fallen from some trees loaded with the same production. Our sow devoured them greedily, thus consoling herself for the fright she had been put into, and the pain the dogs had occasioned her.

The fruit was of different colours, and extremely pleasing to the eye. Fritz expressed his apprehension that it was a pernicious kind of apple called the Mancenilla. But the sow ate them with so much eagerness, and the tree which bore them being neither so high, and having neither the form nor foliage ascribed by naturalists to the Mancenilla, made me doubt of the truth of his idea. I desired my sons to put some of the fruit in their pockets, to make an experiment with them upon the monkey. We now again, from extreme thirst, recollected our want of water, and determined to seek for some in every direction. Jack sprang off and sought among the rocks, hoping, and with reason, that he should discover some little stream; but scarcely had he left the wood, than he bawled to us that he had found a crocodile.

" A crocodile!" cried I, with a hearty laugh. " Whoever saw a crocodile on such scorching rocks as these, and with not a drop of water near? Now, Jack, you are surely dreaming."

" Not so much of a dream as you may think, Father," answered Jack, trying to speak in a low voice. " Fortunately he is asleep; he lies here on a stone at his full length; he is exactly like Mother."

Father. " This is excellent, upon my word! So then your mother is like a crocodile?"

Jack. " I meant, Father, that the crocodile is about as long as the height of Mother; I had not, I assure you, the least idea of a joke. It is certainly a crocodile, though perhaps only a young one. Do, Father, step here and look at it."

I knew not what to think. We stole softly to the place where the animal lay, but instead of a crocodile, I saw before me an individual of a large sort of lizard, named by naturalists *Yguana*, the flesh of which is considered in the West Indies as the greatest delicacy. I explained this to my sons, and tranquillized them as to the danger of approaching this animal, of a mild character, and excellent as food. All were then seized with the hope of seizing the lizard and presenting a prize to their mother. Fritz had his gun ready, and was taking aim, but I was in time to prevent him.

" Let us try another way, as he is asleep," I said. " We need not be in a hurry; only a little contrivance is necessary to have him safe in our power alive."

I cut a stout stick from a bush, to the extremity of which I tied a string with a running knot. I guarded my other hand simply with a little switch, and thus with cautious steps approached the sleeping animal. When I was very near to him I began to whistle a lively air, taking care to make the sounds low at first, and to increase in loudness till the lizard was awaked. The creature appeared entranced with pleasure as the sounds fell upon his ear. He raised his head to receive them still more distinctly, and looked round on all sides to discover from whence they came. I now advanced by a step at a time, without a moment's interval in the music, which fixed him like a statue to the place. At length I was near enough to reach him with my switch, with which I tickled him gently, still continuing to whistle. The lizard was bewildered by the music. He stretched himself at full length, made undulating motions with his long tail, threw his head about, raised it up, and by this sort of action disclosed the range of his sharp-pointed teeth. I quickly seized the moment of his raising his head to throw my noose over him. When this was accomplished the boys drew near also, and wanted to draw it tight and strangle him; but this I forbade. I had used the noose only to make sure of him in case it should happen that a milder mode of killing him, which I intended to try, failed of success. Continuing to whistle, I seized a favourable moment to plunge my switch into one of his nostrils. The blood flowed in abundance, and soon deprived him of life, without his exhibiting the least symptom of being in pain; on the contrary, to the last moment he seemed to be still listening to the music.

As soon as he was dead I allowed the boys to come quite near. My sons were delighted with the means I had used for killing him.

" Little praise is due to me," I replied, " for I have often read the description of the manner of destroying this animal, so well known in the West Indies. But now let us consider of the best way for transporting him to Falcon's Stream."

I perceived that I had better carry him across my shoulders. The figure I made with so singular an animal on my back, with his tail dragging on the ground, was not the least amusing circumstance of the adventure. Fritz and Jack presented themselves as pages, contending which should support my train, as they called the tail, which, independently of the good-humour inspired amongst us, considerably eased me of the weight, and gave me the air of an old Chinese emperor habited in a superb royal mantle of many colours, for those of the lizard shone like precious stones in the eyes of the sun.

We were already far advanced in our return, when we distinguished the voice of my wife calling upon my name in a tone which indicated great uneasiness, and in addition we heard loud sobs from little Francis. Our long absence had excited painful apprehensions concerning us. No sooner, however, did our cheerful notes in speaking reach their ear, than their fears were changed to joy, and we soon found ourselves assembled together under a large gourd-tree, where we related to our dear companions every particular of the excursion we had made, not forgetting Jack's fancy of finding a resemblance between his mother and the lizard. We had so many things to inform her of that we lost sight of the principal object which caused our separation. Till she reminded us with some regret at our ill success, we forgot that we had failed of procuring any water. My sons had taken out some of the unknown apples from their pockets, and they lay on the ground by our side. Knips soon scented them, and according to custom he came slily up and stole several, and fell to chewing them with great eagerness. I myself threw one or two to the bustard, who also ate them without hesitation. Being now convinced that the apples were not poisonous, I announced to the boys, who had looked on with envy all the time, that they also might now begin to eat them, and I myself set the example. We found them excellent, and I began to suspect that they might be the sort of fruit called *guava*. The tree which bears them is sometimes twenty feet in height; no doubt, therefore, those from which we procured the fruit were too young to have attained their full stature.

This feast of guavas had in some measure relieved our thirst. On the other hand, it had increased our hunger; and as we had not time for preparing a portion of the lizard, we were obliged to content ourselves with the cold provisions we had brought with us. But we contrived to have an excellent dessert of potatoes, which the boys had had the foresight to lay under the cinders of the fire they had made to cook their crab.

We had scarcely finished before my wife entreated that we might begin our journey home, to be sure of arriving before dark. In fact, it appeared to me, as the evening was so far advanced, that it would be prudent to return without the sledge, which was heavy laden, and the ass would have driven it but slowly. I was, besides, inclined to take a shorter road by a narrow path that divided a plantation of thick bushes, which would have been too difficult a passage for the ass burthened with the sledge. I therefore determined to leave it till the following day, when I could return for it, contenting myself with loading the ass for the present with the bags which contained our new sets of porcelain and the lizard. Francis, who began to complain of being tired, I also placed on the back of the ass. I took these arrangements upon myself, and left to my wife and Fritz the care of confining the bustard in such a manner that she could walk without danger of escaping.

On leaving the wood of gourds, we arrived at a spot where we found more of the guava-trees, and could not resist the temptation to secure a new supply. The course of our route lay next along a majestic wood of oaks, interspersed with fig-trees of luxuriant growth, and of the same species as those at Falcon's Stream. The ground in this place was absolutely covered with acorns. My young travellers, ever on the watch for something gratifying to the palate, could not refrain from tasting them.

I more than ever admired the magnificence of the trees which at this moment covered us with their shade. On considering, I recognized that they were a kind of oak which remains always green, and are a common production of the woods in Florida, and that the Indians of North America extract from its fruit an excellent kind of sweet oil, which they use in cooking their rice. Numerous kinds of birds subsist upon these acorns. This we were led to remark by the wild and discordant cries of several sorts of jays and parrots. The boys would have fired their guns, and I could only prevail upon them to desist by observing how late it was, and promising that we would return another time.

We arrived sooner than we expected at Falcon's Stream. The path we had taken had so considerably lessened the distance, that we were in time to employ ourselves in some trifling arrangements before it was completely dark. My wife had great pleasure in taking out her service of porcelain and using some of the articles, particularly the egg-basket and the vessels for the milk. Fritz was instructed to dig a place in the ground to serve for a cooler, the better to preserve the milk, and we covered it with boards and put heavy stones to keep them down. Jack took the pigeons' nests and scampered up the tree, where he nailed them to the branches. He next laid some dry moss within, and placed one of the female pigeons we had contrived to tame, and which at the time was brooding, upon it. He put the eggs carefully under the mother, who seemed to accept his services, and to coo with gratitude.

My own employment was to clean the lizard and prepare a piece for our supper. My wife having expressed an extreme repugnance to both the lizard and the crab, we added some potatoes and some acorns, and dressed them together, and thus suited every palate. Francis had the care of turning the spit, and liked his office all the better for its allowing of his being near his mother. We all drew near a clear brisk fire while the supper was in hand. We concluded the exertions of the day by contriving a comfortable bed for the bustard by the side of the flamingo, and then hastened to stretch our limbs upon the beds, rendered by fatigue luxurious, that waited for us in the giant tree.

CHAPTER XXIII

EXCURSION INTO UNKNOWN COUNTRIES

It is scarcely necessary to relate that my first thought the next morning was to fetch the sledge. I had a double motive for leaving it there, which I had refrained from explaining to my wife to avoid giving her uneasiness. I had formed a wish to penetrate a little farther into the soil, and ascertain whether anything useful would present itself beyond the wall of rocks. I was, besides, desirous to be better acquainted with our island. I wished Fritz only to accompany me. We took Turk with us. We set out very early in the morning, and drove the ass before us for the purpose of drawing home the sledge.

On reaching the wood of evergreen oaks, we found the sow feeding upon the acorns under the trees. We wished her a good appetite, and begged her to admit us to the honour of partaking her breakfast. Accordingly Fritz filled the pockets of his waistcoat with some of them. As we were quietly picking up the acorns, we observed some birds flying towards us. Some of them were clothed with a plumage of exquisite beauty, and for this once I could not refuse Fritz the pleasure of firing upon them, that we might in consequence obtain a nearer view, and inform ourselves respecting their species. He brought down three. I recognized one to be the great blue Virginia jay, and the other two were parrots. One of the two was a superb red parrot, the other was green and yellow.

We soon arrived at the guava-trees, and a little after at the spot where we had left the sledge, when we found our treasures in the best possible condition. As the morning was not far advanced, we entered upon our project of penetrating beyond the wall of rocks.

We pursued our way in a straight line at the foot of these massy productions of nature, every moment expecting to reach their extremity, or to find some turn, or breach, or passage through them, that should conduct us into the interior of the island, if, as I presumed, it was not terminated by these rocks. We walked on, continually looking about, that nothing worthy of notice might escape us, or to be enabled to anticipate and avoid such dangers as should threaten. Turk as usual took the lead, the ass followed with lazy steps, shaking his long ears, and Fritz and I brought up the rear. We met from time to time with some small streams, which afforded a most agreeable refreshment. We passed a wood of guava-trees, and fields of potatoes and manioc, the stalks of which perplexed our way; but we were recompensed by the fine views which everywhere presented themselves, and which the low stature of the plants enabled us to see in perfection. To the right, on the high grounds, we saw hares and agoutis amusing themselves in the morning sun. Fritz mistook them for marmots, but not one of them made the whistling kind of sound which is customary with these animals when they see a strange object.

We next entered a pretty little grove, the trees of which were unknown to us. Their branches were loaded with large quantities of berries of an extraordinary quality, being entirely covered with a wax which stuck to our fingers as we attempted to gather them. I knew of a sort of bush producing wax that grows in America, and named by botanists *Myrica cerifera*. I had no doubt that this was the plant, and the discovery gave me great pleasure. " Let us stop here," said I to Fritz, " for we cannot do better than collect a great quantity of these berries as a useful present to your mother."

A short time after another kind of object presented itself with equal claims to our attention. It was the singular behaviour of a kind of bird scarcely larger than a chaffinch, and clothed in feathers of a common brown colour. These birds appeared to exist as a republic, there being among them one common nest, inhabited at pleasure by all their tribes. We saw one of these nests in a tree in a somewhat retired situation. It was formed of platted straws and bulrushes intermixed. It appeared to us to enclose great numbers of inhabitants, and was constructed in an irregular form round the trunk of the tree where the branches sprout. It appeared to us to have a kind of roof formed of roots and bulrushes, but more carefully knit than the rest of the structure. In the sides, which were unequally formed, we observed a quantity of small apertures, seemingly intended as doors and windows to each particular cell. From a few of these apertures issued small branches, which served the birds as points of rest. The external appearance of the whole excited the image of an immensely large, open sponge. The birds which inhabited it were very numerous. They passed in and out continually, and I estimated that it might contain at least a million. The males were somewhat larger than the females, and there was a trifling difference in their plumage.

While we were examining this interesting little colony, we perceived a very small kind of parrot, not much larger than the birds themselves, hovering about the nest. Their gilded green wings and the variety of their colours produced a beautiful effect. They seemed to be perpetually disputing with the colonists, and not unfrequently endeavoured to prevent their entrance. They attacked them fiercely, and even endeavoured to peck at us if we but advanced our hand to the structure. Fritz, who was well trained in the art of climbing trees, was earnestly desirous to take a nearer view of such extraordinary beings, and to secure, if possible, a few individuals. He threw his bundles to the ground, and climbed till he reached the nest. He then tried to introduce his hand into one of the apertures, and to seize whatever living creature it should touch in that particular cell. What he most desired was to find a female brooding hen, and to carry both her and the eggs away. Several of the cells were empty, but by perseverance he found one in the situation he wished. But he did not pursue his plan without meeting with the punishment of his curiosity. He received so violent a stroke from the beak of an invisible bird, that his only care was now to withdraw his hand. But though punished he was not cured. No sooner had the pain subsided, than he ventured a second time to pass his hand into the nest, and succeeded in seizing his prey, which he laid hold of by the middle of the body, and in spite of the bird's resistance, its cries and wailings, he drew it through the aperture and squeezed it into his breast-pocket, and buttoning his coat securely, he slid down the tree and reached the ground in safety. The signals of distress sent forth by the prisoner collected a multitude of birds from their cells, who all surrounded him, uttering piteous cries and flying at him with their beaks, till he had made good his retreat. The birds pursued him till he was quite close to my side, when, by making a loud noise and waving my pocket-handkerchief, I succeeded in driving them away. Fritz now released the prisoner, and we discovered him to be a beautiful little green parrot, which Fritz entreated he might be allowed to preserve and make a present of to his brothers. I did not oppose his request, but thinking we had spent too much time upon this singular bird-colony, I bade him prepare for returning home. The birds were naturally the subject of our conversation on the road. It was the first time I had ever witnessed such a spectacle as a swarm of birds living together in one nest, and I was surprised at it. From the circumstance of so young a bird being nestled within the structure, it appeared probable

that the true right of property was in this species, and
that the brown-coloured birds we at first observed
were intruders endeavouring to deprive them of it.

We had proceeded a considerable way, and had
reached a wood, the trees of which were unknown to
us, though they in a small degree resembled the wild
fig-tree—at least the fruit they bore, like the fig, was
round in form, and contained a soft juicy substance full
of small grains. It had, however, a sharpness and sour-
ness in the taste. We took a nearer view of these trees,
so remarkable for their height. The bark of the trunk
was prickly or scaly, like the pine-apple, and wholly
bare of branches, except at the very top, where they
are loaded with them. The leaves of these trees, at
the extremity of the branches, are very thick. In substance tough, like leather, their upper and under sur-
faces presented different tints. But what surprised us
the most was a kind of gum, or bituminous matter,
which appeared to issue in a liquid state from the
trunk of the tree, and to become immediately hardened
by the air. This discovery awakened Fritz's whole
attention. In Europe he had often made use of the
gum produced by cherry-trees, either as a cement or
varnish, and the thought struck him that he could do
the same with what he now saw. He accordingly
collected with his knife a certain quantity.

As he continued walking he looked frequently at his
gum, which he tried to soften with his breath or with
the heat of his hand, as he had been accustomed to do
with that from the cherry-trees, but he found he could
not succeed. On the other hand, his endeavours
revealed a still more singular property in the substance
—that of stretching considerably on being pulled by
the two hands at its extremities, and, on letting go, of
reducing itself instantly by the power of an elastic

principle.   He was struck with surprise and sprang towards me, exclaiming, " Look, Father! if this is not the very kind of India rubber we formerly used to rub out the bad strokes in our drawings. See! I can stretch it, and it instantly shrinks back when I let go !"

" Ah! what do you tell me?" cried I with joy. " The best thanks of all will be due to you if you have discovered the true caoutchouc-tree which yields the Indian rubber.   Quick, hand it here that I may examine it."

Fritz. " Look, Father, how it will stretch! Can it be made to serve any other purpose than rubbing out a pencil-mark? Nor am I quite sure that it is the very same ingredient.   Why is it not black, like that we used in Europe?"

Father. " Caoutchouc is a milky sap which runs from certain trees. This liquid is received by those who collect it in vessels placed for the purpose.   It is afterwards made to take the form of dark-coloured bottles of different sizes, such as we have seen them, in the following manner. Before the liquid which runs out has time to coagulate, small earthen bottles are dipped into it a sufficient number of times to form the thickness required. These vessels are then hung over smoke, which dries them, and gives the dark colour you allude to. Before they are entirely dry a knife is drawn across them, which produces the lines or figures with which you have seen them marked. The concluding part of the operation is to break the bottle which has served for a mould, and to get out the pieces by the passage of the neck, when the ingredient remains in the complete form of a bottle, soft to the touch, firm in substance, yet flexible and convenient to carry about, from being not liable to break, and may be even used as a vessel to contain liquid if necessary.

Fritz. " The fabrication seems simple, so let us try to make some bottles of it."

Father. " Its quality is admirable, too, Fritz, for being made into shoes and boots without seams. There is, besides, another use for which this substance is both fit and excellent. It renders waterproof any kind of linen or woollen production to which it may be applied."

Well satisfied with the discovery we had made, we continued our way, endeavouring still farther to explore the wood. After passing through it, we rested ourselves with great pleasure for a few minutes, and were regaled with two coco-nuts, which Turk had forced from two little monkeys, which were playing on the ground like children. After this refreshment we resumed our route. We were determined to reach the farthest outlet of this great wood to examine the dimensions of our empire. In a short time we had taken some observations to ascertain this point, and, looking attentively, we recognized the great bay on the right, and on the left Cape Disappointment, which latter had been the farthest point of our earliest excursion.

In this spot alone, and mixed with a quantity of coco-trees, I discovered a tree of smaller growth, which I presumed must be the sago palm. One of these had been thrown down by the wind, so that I was able to examine it. I perceived that the trunk contained a quantity of a mealy substance; I therefore with my hatchet laid it open longways, and cleared it of the whole contents, and on tasting the ingredient I found it was exactly like the sago I had often eaten in Europe.

We began to consider how much farther we would go. The thick bushes of bamboo, through which it was impossible to pass, seemed to furnish a natural conclusion to our journey. We were therefore unable to ascertain whether we should have found a passage beyond the wall of rocks. We perceived, then, no better resource than to turn to the left towards Cape Disappointment, where the luxurious plantations of sugar-canes again drew our attention. That we might not return empty-handed to Falcon's Stream, we each took the pains to cut a large bundle of the canes, which we threw across the ass's back, not forgetting the ceremony of reserving one apiece to refresh ourselves. We soon reached the wood of gourds, where we found our sledge as we had left it the night before. We took the sugar-canes from the ass and fastened them to the sledge, and then we harnessed the ass, and the patient animal began to draw towards home.

We arrived at Falcon's Stream rather early in the evening. Each of the boys seized a sugar-cane and began to suck it, as did their mother also. Nothing could be more amusing than to hear Fritz relate the recent discoveries we had made. Then came the history of the colony of birds and their singular habitation, and of the green parrot, all of which was listened to with the delight excited by a fairy tale. Fritz showed them the handsome red parrot, dead, also the great blue jay, both of which they did not cease to admire. But when he took out of his pocket the little parrot all alive, there were no bounds to their ecstasy. At length the bird was fastened by the leg to one of the roots of the trees till a cage could be made, and was fed with acorns, which he appeared to relish. My wife was delighted with the prospect of the candles I assured her I was now able to furnish.

Fritz took a bit of the rubber from his pocket and drew it to its full length, and then let it suddenly go, to the great amusement of little Francis.

Soon after nightfall, after partaking of a hearty supper, we all mounted the ladder, and, having carefully drawn it up, we fell, exhausted, into sound and peaceful slumbers.

CHAPTER XXIV

USEFUL OCCUPATIONS AND LABOURS—EMBELLISH-
MENTS—A PAINFUL BUT NATURAL SENTIMENT

On the following day, neither my wife nor the boys left me a moment's tranquillity till I had put my manufactory of candles in some forwardness. I soon perceived that I should be at a loss for a little suet or mutton-fat to mix with the wax from the berries, for making the light burn clearer. But as I had neither of these articles, I was compelled to proceed without them. I put as many berries into a vessel as it would contain, and set it on a moderate fire. My wife in the meantime employed herself in making some wicks with the threads of sail-cloth. When we saw an oily matter of a pleasing smell and light-green colour rise to the top of the liquid, we skimmed it off and put it into a separate vessel, taking care to keep it warm. We continued this process till the berries had produced a considerable quantity of wax. We next dipped the wicks one by one into it while it remained liquid, and then hung them on the bushes. In a short time we dipped them again, and continued till the candles were increased to the proper size. They were then put in a place and kept till sufficiently hardened for use. We were all eager to judge of our success that very evening by burning one of the candles, and we had reason to be well satisfied. We should now be able to sit up later, and consequently spend less of our time in sleep. But independently of this advantage, the mere sight of a candle, which for so long a time we had been deprived of, caused ecstasies of joy to all.

Our success in this last enterprise encouraged us to think of another, the idea of which had long been cherished—it was the construction of a cart. I tried earnestly and long to accomplish my object, but for long did not succeed, and wasted both time and timber. I, however, at last produced what from courtesy we called a cart, but I would not advise my readers to take it for a model, though it answered the purpose.

While I was thus engaged, the boys and their mother were no less busy, and I now and then left my cart to assist them with my advice; though I must say they seldom stood in need of it. They undertook to transplant the greatest part of the European fruit-trees, to place them where they would be in a better situation for growth, according to the properties of each. They planted vineshoots round the roots of the magnificent tree we inhabited, and round the trunks of some other kinds of trees which grew near. We watched them, in the fond anticipation that they would in time ascend to a height capable of being formed into a sort of trellis, and help to cool us by their shade. In the climate we inhabited, the vine requires the protection of the larger trees against the rays of the sun. Lastly, we planted two parallel lines of saplings, consisting of chestnut, cherry, and the

common nut trees, to form an avenue from Family
Bridge to Falcon's Stream, which would hereafter
afford us a cool shade in our walks to Tent House.
This last undertaking was not to be effected without
labour and fatigue. The ground was to be cleared,
and a certain breadth covered with sand, left higher
in the middle than on the sides, for the sake of being
always dry. The boys fetched the sand from the sea-
shore in their wheelbarrows, and I nailed together
a few pieces of wood, in the form of a tub, which could
be harnessed to the ass to ease in some measure their
fatigue.

Our next concern was to introduce, if possible,
some shade and other improvements on the barren
site of Tent House, and to render our visits there more
secure. We began by planting all those sorts of trees
that thrive best in the sun, such as lemon, pistachio,
almond, mulberry, and lime trees; lastly, some of a
kind of orange-tree which attains to a prodigious
size, and bears a fruit as large as the head of a child,
and weighs not less than twelve or fourteen pounds.
The commoner sorts of nut-trees we placed along the
shore. The better to conceal and fortify our tent,
which enclosed all our stores, we formed on the accessible side a hedge of orange and lemon trees,
which produce an abundant prickly foliage. To add
to the agreeableness of their appearance, we introduced here and there the pomegranate. Nor did I
omit to make a little arbour of the guava-shrub, which
bears a small fruit rather pleasant to the taste. We
also took care to introduce at proper places a certain
number of the largest sorts of trees, which in time
would serve the purpose of shading annual plants,
and, with benches placed under them, be a kind of
private cabinet. Should any accident or alarm compel

us to retire to Tent House, a thing of the first importance would be to find there food for our cattle. For the greater security I formed a plantation of the thorny fig-tree, of sufficient breadth to occupy the space between our fortress and the river, thus rendering it difficult for an enemy to approach.

The curving form of the river having left some elevations of the soil within the enclosure, I found means to work them into slopes and angles so as to serve as bastions to our two cannon and our other firearms, should we ever be attacked. My concluding labour was to plant some cedars along the usual landing-places, to which we might fasten our vessels.

We employed many weeks in effecting what for the present it was possible to effect, of these arrangements. The exercise of mind and body they imposed contributed to the health of the boys, and to the support of cheerfulness in ourselves. The more we embellished our abode by the work of our own hands, the more it became dear to our hearts. The strict observance of the Sabbath-day afforded such an interval of rest as could not fail to restore our strength and inspire us with the desire of new exertions.

Our labours wore out our clothes so fast that another trip to the vessel was absolutely necessary. We had exhausted the stock we had brought away, and were now in rags. We feared we saw the time when we should be compelled to renounce European dress. I had also another reason for wishing to visit the ship. The cart I had just completed disclosed a defect which it was scarcely possible to endure. It was a violent creaking of the wheels at every turn, and in addition the wheels moved so imperfectly round the axle-tree, that the united strength of the ass and the cow could scarcely drag the machine along. It was in vain that, in spite of my wife's reproofs, I applied a little butter; in an hour or two the butter was dried, and the wheels remained the same.

These two circumstances compelled us, then, once more to have recourse to the vessel. We knew there remained on board five or six chests containing apparel, and we suspected there were also some tubs of pitch and grease for wheels in her hold. To these motives were added that of an earnest desire to take another look at her, and, if practicable, to bring away a few pieces of cannon which might be fixed on the new bastions at Tent House.

The first fine day I assembled my three eldest sons, and put my design into execution. We reached the wreck and found her still fixed between the rocks. We did not lose a moment in searching for the tubs of pitch, which, with the help of the pulley, we soon conveyed into the pinnace; we next secured the chests of clothes, and whatever remained of ammunition stores—powder, shot, and even such pieces of cannon as we could remove, while those that were too heavy we stripped of their wheels.

But to effect our purpose it was necessary to spend several days in visits to the vessel, returning constantly in the evening, enriched with everything of a portable nature which the wreck contained; doors, windows, locks, bolts, nothing escaped our grasp, so that the ship was now entirely emptied, with the exception of the heavy cannon and three or four immense copper caldrons, which were too heavy. We by degrees contrived to tie these heavy articles to two or three empty casks well pitched, which would effectually sustain themselves and the cannon above water. When these measures were taken, I came to the resolution of blowing up the wreck. I directed my views to that part of

the vessel which had been entirely stripped of everything; I supposed that the wind and tide would
convey the beams and timbers ashore, and thus with
little pains we should be possessed of materials for
erecting a building.

We accordingly prepared a cask of gunpowder,
which we left on board. We made a small opening in
its side, and at the moment of quitting the vessel we
inserted a piece of match-wood, which we lighted at
the last moment, as before. We then sailed with all
possible expedition for Safety Bay. We could not,
however, withdraw our thoughts from the wreck and
from the expected explosion. I had cut the match a
sufficient length for us to hope that she would not go
to pieces before dark. I proposed to my wife to have
our supper carried to a little point of land from whence
we had a view of her, and here we waited for the
moment of her destruction.

About the time of nightfall, a majestic rolling sound
like thunder, accompanied by a column of fire and
smoke, announced that the ship was that instant
annihilated, and withdrawn for ever from the face of
man! At this moment, love for the country that gave
us birth, that most powerful sentiment of the human
heart, sunk with a new force into ours. Could we hope
ever to behold that country more?

My wife was the only person who was sensible of
consolation. She was now relieved from all the fears
for our safety in our visits to the wreck. From this
moment she conceived a stronger partiality for our
island. A night's repose relieved the melancholy of
the preceding evening, and I went early in the morning with the boys to make further observations as to
the effects of this remarkable event. We perceived in
the water and along the shore abundant vestiges of

the departed wreck, and among the rest, at a certain distance, the empty casks, caldrons, and cannon, all tied together, and floating. We jumped instantly into the pinnace, with the tub-boat fastened to it, and made a way towards them, and in a little time reached the object of our search, which from its great weight moved slowly upon the waves. With this rich booty we returned to land.

We performed three more trips for the purpose of bringing away more cannon, caldrons, fragments of masts, &c., all of which we deposited in Safety Bay. And now began our most fatiguing operations, the removing such numerous and heavy stores from the boats to Tent House. We separated the cannon and the caldrons from the tub-raft and from each other, and left them in a place which was accessible for the sledge and the beasts of burden. With the help of the crowbar we succeeded in getting the caldrons upon the sledge, and in replacing the four wheels we had before taken from the cannon, which we found it easy to make the cow and the ass draw. We in the same manner conveyed away all the wood we wished to preserve dry, and what stores remained we tied with cords to stakes to protect them from the tide.

The largest of the boilers or copper caldrons, which had been intended as utensils for a manufactory of sugar, we now found of the most essential use. We brought out all our barrels of gunpowder, and placed them on their ends in three separate groups at a short distance from our tent; we dug a little ditch round the whole to draw off the moisture from the ground, and then put one of the caldrons turned upside down upon each group of barrels, which answered the purpose of an out-house. The cannon were covered with sail-cloth, and upon this we laid heavy branches of trees. The larger casks of gunpowder we removed under a projecting rock, where, should they even blow up, no mischief could arise to the inhabitants of Tent House.

My wife made the agreeable discovery that two of our ducks and one of the geese had been brooding under a large bush, and at the time were conducting their little families to the water. The news produced general rejoicings. Fritz and Ernest looked forward to some luxurious Sunday dinners, and Jack and Francis wondered what the young birds could think when they first saw human creatures! We in a short time found means to tame them by throwing them crumbs of manioc. This last employment, together with the gambols of the little creatures, so forcibly carried our thoughts to Falcon's Stream, that we all conceived the desire of returning to the society of the old friends we had left there. One sighed for his monkey, another for his flamingo; Francis for his parrot, and his mother for her poultry-yard, her various housewifery accommodations, and her comfortable bed. We therefore fixed the next day for our departure, and set about the necessary preparations.

CHAPTER XXV

A NEW EXCURSION—PALM-TREE WINE

On entering our new plantation of fruit-trees forming the avenue to Falcon's Stream, we observed that they inclined to droop. We therefore immediately resolved to support them with sticks, and I proposed a walk to the vicinity of Cape Disappointment for the purpose of cutting some bamboos. I had no sooner pronounced the words than the three eldest boys and their mother exclaimed at once that they would accompany me. Our provision of candles was nearly exhausted, and a new stock of berries must therefore be procured, for my wife now repaired our clothes by candle-light, while I employed myself in composing a journal of the events of every day; then, the sow had again deserted us, and nothing could be so probable as that we should find her in the acorn wood; Jack would fain gather some guavas for himself, and Francis must needs see the sugar-canes. In short, all would visit this land of Canaan.

We accordingly fixed the following morning, and set out in full procession. For myself, I had a great desire to explore this part of our island, and to reap some more substantial advantages from its produce. I therefore made some preparations for sleeping, should we find the day too short. I took the cart instead of the sledge, having fixed some planks across it for Francis and his mother to sit upon when they should be tired. I was careful to be provided with the different implements we might want; some rope machinery I had contrived for rendering the climbing of trees more easy; and lastly, provisions, consisting of a piece of the salted tortoise, water in a gourd-flask, and one bottle of wine. When all was placed in the cart, I for this occasion harnessed to it both the ass and the cow, as I expected the load would be increased on our return. We set out, taking the road of the potato and manioc plantations. Our first halt was at the tree of the colony of birds. Close upon the same spot were also the trees whose berries produced the wax, and intermixed with these some of the guava kind. On this second occasion of seeing the birds, I recollected to what species they belonged, which by naturalists is named *Loxia gregaria* (Sociable Grossbeak).

It was not without difficulty that we conducted the cart through the thick bushes. We succeeded tolerably well at last, and that the poor animals might have time to rest, we determined to pass several hours in this place. We began by gathering a bagful of the guavas, and after regaling ourselves put the remainder into the cart. We next examined anew the structure of the nest inhabited by the colony of birds, and concluded, contrary to the opinion I had formerly entertained, that the little green parrot was an invader, for numerous flocks of the brown-coloured birds now passed in and out, rested upon the bushes which produced the wax, and devoured large quantities of the berries, which explained the reason of their building their abode in this particular spot. We claimed the same privilege as the birds, and had soon filled another bag. Seeing them so greedily consumed by those little creatures, the boys desired to follow their example, and tasted them, but found them insipid.

We continued our way, and soon arrived at the caoutchouc or gum-elastic trees. I thought we could not do better than to halt here and collect a sufficient quantity of the sap to make the different kinds of utensils, and the impermeable boots and shoes, as I had before proposed. It was with this design that I had taken care to bring with me several gourd rinds. I made deep incisions in the trunks, and fixed some large leaves of trees, partly doubled together lengthways, to the place, to serve as a sort of channel to conduct the sap to the vessels. We had not long begun this process before we perceived the sap begin to run out as white as milk, and in large drops, so that we were not without hopes by the time of our return to find the vessels full.

We pursued our way to the wood of coco-trees. Thence we passed to the left, and stopped half-way between the bamboos and sugar-canes, to furnish ourselves with a provision of each. We aimed our course so that on clearing the skirts of the wood we found ourselves in an open plain, with the sugar-cane plantations on our left, and on our right those of bamboo interspersed with various kinds of palm-trees, and in front the magnificent bay formed by Cape Disappointment.

The prospect that now presented itself to our view was of such exquisite beauty that we determined to choose it for our resting-place, and to make it the central point of every future excursion. We were even more than half disposed to desert our pretty Falcon's Stream. A moment's reflection, however, betrayed the folly of quitting the thousand comforts we had assembled there.

Our next proceeding was to divide amongst us the different occupations which were the objects of our walk. Some scampered away to the right to cut bamboos, others to the left to secure the sugar-canes, of both of which a large bundle was collected. The exertions made by the boys again excited their desire to eat. They sucked some of the canes, but their hunger was not appeased. Their mother, however, refused to let them have the remainder of the provisions, and they therefore cast a longing eye to the tops of the trees, where they saw a great number of coco-nuts. After a short deliberation it was determined that two of them should venture on climbing to the top, a height of from sixty to eighty feet, and with the hatchet, which would be fastened to his waist, should beat them down. Fritz and Jack had no hesitation. They selected the trees for their attempt, and proceeded a considerable way. But the trunks were too thick to be easily grasped by their legs and arms, and they were obliged to come down again much quicker than they had ascended. It was now my part to suggest something. " I have something here," said I, " which may help. Here are some pieces of prepared shagreen, which must be tied round your legs. Then with this cord I shall fasten you by the body to the trunk of the tree, but so loosely that it will move up and down when you do. By sitting occasionally on this cord you will be enabled to rest when necessary, and so push on by little and little. This manner of climbing trees is practised by savages with success."

The boys had listened with entire attention. Excited by the description, they demanded to be equipped for the experiment, and their success exceeded our expectation. They with tolerable ease reached the top, where the thick-tufted foliage furnished a seat, whence they sent forth exulting salutations. They now set to work, when presently a shower of coco-nuts descended. The monkey took the fancy of imitating his masters, and springing into one of the trees, he with his teeth and his paws sent down as many nuts as the hatchet. He then came down with equal swiftness, and seating himself on the ground began to crack one of the nuts, making all the time such strange grimaces as to occasion us all much merriment.

Ernest was the only person who took no part in this animated scene. His brothers began to banter him on the old subject of his indolence. They gravely offered him some coco-nut, *to refresh him after so much fatigue.* He made no reply, and pushed the offering aside. He

then rose from his seat, and began to examine the trees
one by one with deep attention. He requested me to
saw off the top of a coco-nut for him, which he emptied,
and fastened round it cross-ways a string with a loop
to hang it to the button of his waistcoat. Not one of
us could imagine what he was going to do. He placed
a small hatchet in his girdle, and then advancing a
few paces out of the group we formed, he in a graceful
manner pronounced the following little address:

" I am sensible, my dear parents, that in our republic,
or rather in our kingdom, I am, I say, sensible that
here, as in Europe, he who has sufficient talent to raise
himself above the rest is held in high consideration and
esteem. For my own part, I must confess I had more
pleasure in remaining in tranquillity without endeavours to obtain distinction. I have but little ambition, and am fond of quiet, and therefore the greater
will be my desert if I, like the rest, resolve to contribute
to the general good of this our country, by executing,
as the other subjects have done, the task of climbing
trees, well satisfied if, like them, I should obtain the
applauses of my king and of my fellow-citizens ! To
the tree then, since climbing is the question !" said he,
saluting us with his hand as he sprang away to a high
palm-tree of the cabbage species.

I looked with extreme curiosity, but when I saw him
courageously grasp the trunk with his legs and arms,
and proceed to climb, I approached the tree and offered
him the shagreen and the cord. He accepted the first
but refused the cord. " I am naturally somewhat
awkward," observed he, " and to have to draw a cord
after me would only add to my difficulty; besides,
I think I have no occasion for it." In fact, he exerted
his limbs with so much spirit, that I was astonished
at the rapidity of his ascent, and conceived at every

remove the most alarm, since the farther from the ground the more danger would attend him should any slip or other accident occasion him to fall. When Ernest now showed himself at the very top of the tree, Fritz and Jack burst into an immoderate fit of laughter. " Pains enough for nothing, Master Ernest!" bawled they as loud as they could. " In your wisdom you have chosen a tree which has no fruit upon it. Not a single coco-nut will you bring down, your most devoted fellow-subjects can truly assure you!"

" Not a coco-nut, certainly," replied Ernest in his loudest voice; " but, brothers, you shall receive a crown instead!" and at the same instant he with his hatchet cut off the tufted summit of the palm-tree, and a large mass of tender leaves fell at our feet.

" Mischievous boy!" cried his mother. " Disappointed of his coco-nuts, see if he has not cut off the head of this magnificent palm-tree, and it will perish in consequence!"

" I am happy, Mother, to be able to correct your mistake!" cried Ernest from his stately column, where he stood erect and looked like a statue. " What I have done was from a desire to procure you one of the finest kinds of food this country affords. The tree is the cabbage palm-tree, and, believe me, you will find it a more valuable acquisition than even our coco-nuts!"

" A cabbage!" exclaimed Fritz. " Ah, ah, Master Ernest, so you would make us believe that cabbages grow on palm-trees!"

" Examine this production, to which the name of palm-cabbage has been given by naturalists," said I. " It has not the shape of our European cabbage, but, as Ernest tells you, it is a most delicious food. He has also had the merit of distinguishing this tree from others. And let me seize the present occasion, young ones, to reprove you for the taunting spirit in which you viewed your brother's proceedings, who, though less enterprising and less alert than you, so far surpasses any one of you in observation and reflection. To him we are indebted for the most useful of the discoveries which have been made—the potatoes and the manioc."

We now looked up to invite Ernest to come down. We beheld him in a fixed erect position in the very centre of the palm-tree which he had stripped of its crown, as motionless as if he had become a cabbage. The effect of this spectacle was irresistibly ludicrous; and accordingly the boys, in spite of the lecture I had that moment concluded, burst into a fit of laughter.

I now called out to Ernest. "Do you mean," said I, "to stay all night in your tree, or are you afraid to come down?"

"Far from it, Father," answered he, "but I am engaged in preparing you here some good sauce for the cabbage, and the operation takes a longer time than I imagined."

"What can he mean?" asked little Francis. "Do you know, Papa, I have been thinking that this must be an enchanted forest, like those I have read about. Perhaps some of these trees are all the time princes and princesses. Do you think it very likely, Fritz?" said the young innocent, with so real and fearful a persuasion that we all laughed heartily as we answered his question.

By this time Ernest had finished his work, and was descending cautiously from the tree. When he reached the ground he released the coco-shell from his button, held it delicately in one hand, while with the other he drew from his pocket a small bottle, and pulling out the cork he emptied the contents into the shell and presented it to his mother, saying:

" Most gracious sovereign, permit your devoted cup-bearer to present you with a specimen of a new and choice beverage; may it be pleasing to your royal taste. It is called palm-wine, and your slave waits but your commands to obtain a larger supply !"

The other boys looked on in astonishment. I was myself less surprised, having read accounts of this production in different books.

" It is excellent, my boy," said my wife, smiling at her son's quaint address, " and we shall unite in drinking to your health."

I now made some inquiries of Ernest as to his previous knowledge of the tree and its properties.

" I knew," continued he, " that there was a sort of palm which bore a cabbage at the top; I thought that the tree which had no coco-nuts was most likely to be the sort; and you see I was lucky in my guess." He then related his expectation of finding some of our famous palm-wine also. " When I had cut off the cabbage," said he, " a quantity of juice issued from the place, which I tasted and found first-rate. You know the rest, Father," added he, " and I have only to regret that I had not a larger bottle to receive it; but now that we know the means, we can obtain the liquor when we please."

" A small quantity at a time," observed I, " will always be best; for the juice, though so like to champagne in flavour, and which would, perhaps, affect our heads as soon if we were to use it freely, would by tomorrow be quite sour. As there are abundance of the trees, we can, as you say, procure the liquor at pleasure, only taking care to be moderate; for if the cabbage at the top is cut off the tree dies. There are other sorts of palm-trees besides those we have noticed; one in particular, which yields a kind of oil which burns

whatever it is applied to. In the meantime let us
render thanks to Providence for the benefits He has
bestowed."

It was now past noon. As we had determined to
pass the night in this enchanting spot, we began to
think of forming some large branches into a sort of
hut. I accordingly set to work. I had brought a piece
of sail-cloth with me from Falcon's Stream, and I
drove some stakes into the ground, and covered them
with it, filling the opening in the front with branches.
While we were engaged in our work, which was
nearly completed, we were suddenly roused by the
loud braying of the ass, which we had left to graze at
a distance. As we approached, we saw him throwing
his head in the air and kicking and prancing about in
a most extraordinary manner; and while we were
thinking what could be the matter, he set off on a
full gallop. Unfortunately, Turk and Ponto, whom
we sent after him, took the fancy of entering the
plantation of the sugar-canes, while the ass had preferred the direction of the bamboos. In a little time the
dogs returned, and showed no signs, by scenting the
ground or otherwise, of any pursuit. I made a turn
round the hut to see that all was well, and then sallied
forth with Fritz and the two dogs in the direction the
ass had taken, hoping the latter might be enabled to
trace him. But the dogs could not be made to understand our meaning. As night was coming on, I gave
up the pursuit and returned to my companions.

Fatigued, and vexed with the loss of the ass, I
entered the hut, which I found complete with branches
strewed on the ground for sleeping, and with some
reeds for making a fire. After supper we were glad to
enjoy the blessing of sleep. When all was safe, I watched
and replenished the fire till midnight, rather from

habit than the fear of wild beasts, and then took possession of the little corner assigned me.

CHAPTER XXVI

A NEW COUNTRY DISCOVERED—THE TROOP OF BUFFALOES—A PRECIOUS ACQUISITION

The following morning found us all in good health, and thankful for the Divine protection we had enjoyed. We breakfasted on milk, boiled potatoes, and a portion of Dutch cheese, and formed during our meal the plan of the business for the day. It was decided that one of the boys and myself, attended by the two dogs, should seek the ass in every direction. As I was to take both the dogs, I left the two eldest boys to protect little Francis and his mother, and took for my own escort the agile Jack.

We took our hatchets, firearms, a saw for coconuts, and began our course with the dawn. We soon reached the bamboo plantation, and found means to force ourselves along its intricate entanglements. After the most exhausting fatigue, and when we were on the point of relinquishing all hope, we discovered the print of the ass's hoofs, which inspired us with new ardour. After spending a whole hour in further endeavours, we at length, on reaching the skirts of the plantation, perceived the sea, and soon after found ourselves in an open space which bounded the great bay. A considerable river flowed into the bay, and we perceived that the ridge of rocks which we had invariably observed to the right extended to the shore, terminating in a precipice, leaving only a narrow passage, which during every flux of the tide must necessarily be under water, but which at that moment was dry and passable. The probability that the ass would prefer passing by this narrow way to the hazard of the water, determined us to follow in the same path. We had also some curiosity to ascertain what might be found on the other side of the rocks, for as yet we were ignorant whether they formed a boundary to our island or divided it into two portions. We continued to advance, and at length reached a stream which issued foaming from a large mass of rock and fell in a cascade into the river. The bed of this stream was so deep, and its course so rapid, that we were a long time finding a place to cross. When we had got to the other side, we found the soil again sandy and mixed with a fertile kind of earth. In this place we no longer saw naked rock, and here we again discovered the print of the ass's hoof.

We beheld with astonishment that there were the prints of the feet of other animals also, that they were somewhat different from those of the ass, and much larger. Our curiosity was so strongly excited that we resolved to follow the tracks. They conducted us to a plain at a great distance, which presented to our eyes the image of a terrestrial paradise. We ascended a hill which partly concealed from our view this scene, and then with the glass looked down upon a range of country exhibiting every rural beauty that the mind could conceive. To our right appeared the majestic wall of rocks, some of which appeared to touch the heavens, while mists partially concealed their tops. To the left a chain of gently rising hills stretched as far as the eye could discern, and were interspersed with little woods of palm-trees of every kind. The river we had crossed flowed in a serpentine course through this exquisite valley. I could with difficulty take my eyes from this enchanting spectacle, and seated myself on the ground to enjoy it at 'leisure. Neither on the plain nor on the hills was there the smallest trace of man.

By straining our eyes, however, we perceived at a great distance some specks that seemed to be in motion. We hastened towards the spot, and as we drew nearer, to our surprise discovered a group of animals, which presented something like the outline of a troop of horses or of cows. I observed them sometimes run up to each other, and then suddenly stoop to graze. Though we had not lately met with traces of the ass, I was not without hope of finding him among this group. We accordingly drew near by a path we found in a plantation of reeds, that we might not give notice of our approach, being ignorant of the kind of animal we were about to meet. We had not gone far when the soil became so marshy, and the reeds entangled to such a degree, that we were obliged to get out of the plantation and wind along on the outside. We were soon near the animals, which we perceived consisted of rather a numerous troop of wild buffaloes. This animal is formed at first sight to inspire the beholder with terror. It is endowed with extraordinary strength, and two or three of them were capable of destroying us in a moment. My alarm was so great that I remained for a few moments fixed to the spot like a statue. By good luck the dogs were far behind us, and the buffaloes, having never beheld the face of man, gave no sign of fear or of displeasure at our approach. They stood perfectly still, with their large round eyes fixed upon us in astonishment. Those which were lying down got up slowly, but not one seemed to have any hostile disposition towards us. We drew back quietly, and prepared our firearms. It was not, however, my intention to make use of them but for defence. I therefore thought only of retreating, and with Jack, for whom I was more alarmed than for myself, was proceeding in this way, when unfortunately Turk and Ponto ran up to us, and we could see were noticed by the buffaloes. The animals instantly and altogether set up such a roar as to make our nerves tremble with the shock of so terrible a noise. They struck their horns and their hoofs upon the ground, which they tore up and scattered in the air. I with horror foresaw the moment when, confounding us with the dogs, which no doubt they mistook for jackals, they would rush upon us and trample us. Our brave Turk and Ponto, fearless of danger, ran among the troop in spite of all our efforts to detain them, and, according to their manner of attacking, laid hold of the ears of a young buffalo which happened to be standing a few paces nearer to us than the rest. Although the creature began a tremendous roar and motion with his hoofs, they held him fast, and were dragging him towards us. Thus hostilities had commenced, and unless we could resolve to abandon our valiant defenders, we were now forced upon the measure of open war, which, considering the strength and number of the enemy, wore a face of the most pressing and inevitable danger. Our every hope seemed now to be in the chance of the terror the buffaloes would feel at the noise of our musketry. With a palpitating heart and trembling hands, we fired both at the same moment. The buffaloes, terrified by the sound and by the smoke, remained for an instant motionless, and then one and all betook themselves to flight with such rapidity that they were soon beyond our sight. We heard their loud roaring from a considerable distance, which by degrees subsided into silence, and we were left with only one of their terrific species near us. This one, a cow, was no doubt the mother of the young buffalo which the dogs still kept a prisoner. She had drawn near on hearing its cries, and had been wounded by our guns, but not killed. The creature was in a furious state. After a moment's pause she took aim at the dogs, and with her head down was advancing in her rage, and would have gored them to death, if I had not prevented her by firing upon her with my double-barrelled gun, and thus putting an end to her existence.

We now began to breathe. We might now hope that danger was over. I was enchanted with the behaviour of Jack, who had stood in a firm posture by my side, and had fired with a steady aim. I bestowed on him the commendation he deserved, but I had not time for a long discourse. The young buffalo still remained a prisoner, with his ears in the mouths of the dogs, and I was fearful he might do them some injury. I therefore determined to give them what assistance I might find practicable. I scarcely knew in what way to effect this. The buffalo, though young, was strong enough to revenge himself if I were to give the dogs a sign to let go his ears. I had the power of killing him with a pistol, but I had a great desire to preserve him alive and to tame him, that he might be a substitute for the ass. I found myself altogether in a state of indecision, when Jack unexpectedly interposed a most effective means for accomplishing my wishes. He had his string with balls in his pocket. He drew it out, and making a few steps backward, threw it so skilfully as to entangle the buffalo completely, and throw him down. As I could then approach him safely, I tied his

legs together with a very strong cord. The dogs released his ears, and we considered the buffalo as our
own. Jack was almost mad with joy. " What a magnificent creature! How much better than the ass he
will look harnessed to the cart! How my mother and
the boys will be surprised and stare at him as we
draw near!" cried he.

Father. " Ah, ha! What, already you have harnessed
him to the loaded cart, while for my part I have not
yet been able to conceive a means for even removing
him from this place! Will you carry him upon your
back?"

Jack. " If I were Samson or Hercules I would most
willingly; but, Father, he will be able to walk if we
untie his legs."

Father. " And if we bid him do so, you think he will
obey us?"

Jack. " The dogs would make him get on."

Father. " And the buffalo might kill the dogs, Jack.
On reflection, the best way, I think, will be to tie his
two fore-legs together, so tight that he cannot run,
and loose enough for him to walk. I will assist the
scheme by trying a method which is practised in Italy
for subduing the buffalo. You will think it cruel, but
success is probable. It shall afterwards be our study
to make him amends by the kindest treatment. Hold
you the cord which confines his legs with all your
strength."

I then called Turk and Ponto, and made each again
take hold of the ears of the animal, who was now
keeping his head quite still. I took my knife, and held
a piece of string in my hand. I placed myself before
the buffalo, and taking hold of his snout I made a
hole in his nostril, into which I quickly inserted the
string, which I immediately tied so closely to a tree

that the animal was prevented from the least motion of the head, which might have increased his pain. I drew off the dogs the moment the operation was performed. The first attempt I made to pull the cord found him docile, and I perceived that we might now begin our march. I left him for a short time to make some other preparations.

I was unwilling to leave so fine a prey as the dead buffalo. I therefore, after considering what was to be done, began by cutting out the tongue, which I sprinkled with some of the salt we had in our provision-bag. I next took off the skin from the four feet, taking care not to tear it in the operation. I remembered that the Americans use these skins, which are of a soft and flexible quality, as boots and shoes. I lastly cut some of the flesh of the animal with the skin on, and salted it.

We now seated ourselves under the shade of a large tree, and as we ate we amused ourselves with a review of the scene which had been passing.

As we were not disposed to leave the spot in a hurry, I desired Jack to take the saw and cut down a small quantity of reeds, which, from their size, might be of use to us. We set to work, but I observed that he took pains to choose the smallest."

" What shall we do," said I, " with these small-sized reeds? You were thinking, I presume, of providing a bagpipe to announce a triumphal arrival to our companions !"

" You are mistaken, Father," answered Jack; " I am thinking rather of some candlesticks to present to Mother."

" This is a good thought, my boy," said I. " I am well pleased both with the kindness and the readiness of your invention, and I will give you my assistance in trying to empty the reeds without breaking them."

I now helped him, and soon after we set out on our return.

We had so many heavy articles to remove, that I did not hesitate to dismiss, for that day, all thoughts of looking further for the ass, that we might return the sooner to our companions. I began now to think of untying the young buffalo, and on approaching him perceived with pleasure that he was asleep, a proof that his wound was not extremely painful. When I awoke him he gave a start as I began to pull him gently with the string. But he seemed to forget his pain, and followed me without resistance. I fastened another string to his horns, and led him on by drawing both together, and he performed the journey with little inconvenience, and with so unexpected a docility, that to ease ourselves of a part of the heavy burdens we had to carry, we even ventured on fastening the bundles of reeds upon his back, and upon these we laid the salted buffalo meat. The creature did not seem aware that he was carrying a load. He followed as before, and thus on the first day of our acquaintance he rendered an essential service.

In a short time we found ourselves once more at the narrow passage between the torrent and the precipice which I have already mentioned. Near this spot we met with a large jackal, who on perceiving us slunk away, but was stoutly pursued by our dogs, who overtook him at the entrance of a cavern, and forced him to give battle. The fight, however, was unequal; the dogs were two to one, besides being protected by their pointed collars. When we got up to them the jackal was already killed. On examining our prey we found it was a female, and we concluded that she probably had her young in the cavern. Jack would instantly have entered to search, but I prevented him, from the apprehension that the male jackal might also be there. I accordingly used the precaution of shooting off my piece into the cavern, when, finding all quiet, I gave Jack leave to enter.

For some moments after entering the cavern the complete darkness prevented Jack from seeing anything, but when his eyes had become accustomed to it, he discerned in a corner a litter of young jackals. The dogs had discovered them by the smell. They flew upon the creatures, and with the exception of one, which Jack found means to preserve, put an end to their existence. He came out of the cavern with the young jackal in his arms, asking if he might have leave to rear it as Fritz had done the monkey. To this I made no objection, as I felt disposed to make an experiment on the effects of training on the wild creature. At all events it seemed worth while to try. Jack therefore promised to bestow upon him so faultless an education that he should become the gentlest little creature in the world.

We now left the cavern. I had fastened the young buffalo to a tree, without remarking of what species it might be. When I went to release him, I saw that it was a kind of small palm-tree, and on looking about me I observed also some other kinds of the palm which I had not before met with. One of the kinds was from ten to twelve feet in height. Its leaves were armed with thorns, and it bore a fruit resembling a small cucumber, but which was immature, so that we could not taste it. The second, smaller, was also thorny. It was now in blossom, and had no fruit. I suspected that the first of these was the *little royal palm*, sometimes called *awiva* or *Adam's needle*, and the other the *dwarf* palm. I resolved to avail myself of both for further fortifying my enclosure at Tent House, and also to protect the outer side of the narrow pass over the torrent of the cascade. I determined to return and plant a line of them there.

We repassed the river and regained the hazardous and narrow pass at the turn of the rocks. We proceeded with caution, and finding ourselves safe on the other side, thought of quickening our pace to arrive the sooner at the hut. We accordingly had the happiness to rejoin our friends before evening; and though we were somewhat fatigued, yet were well satisfied with the success of our undertakings. We were received with demonstrations of joy, and, as usual, a thousand questions.

CHAPTER XXVII

THE SAGO MANUFACTORY

My wife the next morning began the conversation. She told me the children had been good and diligent, and had ascended Cape Disappointment together; that they had gathered wood and made some torches for the night, and had ventured to fell an immense palm-tree. During labours a somewhat unfortunate visit took place. A numerous group of monkeys had found their way to the hut. Every drop of the palm-wine these intrusive gentry contrived to swallow. They had upset and thrown about all the potatoes, stolen the coco-nuts, and almost wholly demolished the order of the branches and other contrivances we had recourse to for our hut, so that my children on their return were employed a full hour in repairing the damage.

When we had all finished our narratives, my wife began her usual lamentations upon the subject of so many animals being brought, which she said must, from the food they required, become burthensome to us. I consoled her by observing that the buffalo would be a good substitute for the ass, and I established as an invariable law, that he who wished to have a useful animal in his service should also have the care of it.

I next had a fire lighted and a quantity of green wood put on it, for raising a thick smoke, over which I meant to hang the buffalo meat, to preserve it. The young buffalo was beginning to browse, but the cow's milk was still given it. Jack succeeded also in making his little jackal drink some. We added to the buffalo's meal, whose appetite we found to be enormous, a heap of sliced potatoes, the whole of which he devoured, which led us to conclude that the pain from his nose was subsided, and that he would soon become tame.

Supper-time now arrived, and we did not fail to acquit ourselves at it, as well, to say the least, as our cattle, seasoning our repast with affectionate conversation. The combat with the buffaloes excited much raillery, which we saw was none the less intended for compliment. The candle-moulds, too, came in for a share in these playful attacks upon what they called the wonderful feats we had performed. Jack persisted in defending himself, and this he did so cleverly as to point the laughter at the adversary. The arrangements for this night were much the same as for the preceding. We tied the young buffalo by the side of the cow, and were pleased to see them agree and bid fair to live in peace together. The dogs were set upon the watch. The time of repose elapsed so calmly that none of us awoke to keep in the torch-lights. Directly after breakfast I chanted the summons for our setting out, but my young ones had some projects in their heads, and neither they nor their mother were just then in the humour to obey me.

" Let us reflect a little first," said my wife. " As we had so much difficulty in felling the palm-tree, would it not be a pity to lose our labour by leaving it in this place? It is the one from which Ernest cut the famous cabbage. Ernest assures me it is a sago-tree. If so, the pith would be an excellent ingredient for our soups. I hope you will see if we can turn it to account."

I found Ernest was right; the tree was a sago-palm. To extract the sago would employ fully a day, since to open the trunk sixty feet long was not a trivial task. I assented, however, with some readiness, as, apart from the pith, I could, by emptying the halves of the trunk, obtain two troughs for the conveyance of water from Jackal's River to my wife's kitchen-garden at Tent House, and to my plantations of trees.

Fritz. " One of the halves, Father, will answer that purpose, and the other will serve as a conduit for our little stream from Falcon's Nest into my pretty basin lined with tortoise-shell. We shall then be constantly regaled with the agreeable view of a fountain."

" And I, for my part," said Ernest, " long for a sight of the sago formed into small grains as I have seen it in Europe. Can you, Father, make it up into that sort of composition."

" With your help I think I could. But let us first make the sago-paste. Have we one of our manioc-graters at hand?"

" Yes, certainly," replied Ernest. " We were even thinking of making some graters here for our amusement, but we found we were not likely to want employment." He accordingly scampered off to fetch the grater to me, while the rest crowded round.

"Patience, children, patience!" exclaimed I. "We are not yet in readiness to use the grater. Many other matters are previously requisite. In the first place, you must first assist me to raise this palm-tree from the ground, and it must be done by fixing at each end two small cross-pieces or props to support it. To split it open as it lies would be a work of too much labour. This done, I shall want several wooden wedges to keep the cleft open while I am sawing it, and afterwards a sufficient quantity of water."

"There is the difficulty," said my wife. "Our Falcon's Stream is too far off."

Ernest. "That is of no consequence, Mother. I have seen hereabouts so great an abundance of the plants which contain water that we need not be at a loss. They will fully supply us, if I could only contrive to get vessels enough to hold the water."

We now produced the enormous reeds we had brought home, which would answer the purpose of vessels for water; and as some time was required to draw off the water from such small tubes, Ernest and Francis set to work. They cut a number of the plants, which they placed slantingly over the brim of a vessel, and whilst that was filling they were preparing another. The rest of us, with our united strength, soon succeeded in raising the heavy trunk, and the top of it was then sawed off. We next began to split it through the whole length, and this the softness of the wood enabled us to effect with little trouble. We soon reached the pith that fills up the middle of the trunk. When divided, we laid one half on the ground, and we pressed the pith together with our hands so as to make temporary room for the pith of the other half of the trunk, which rested still on the props. We wished to empty it entirely, that we might employ it as a kneading trough, leaving merely enough of the pith at both ends to prevent it running out. We then proceeded to form our paste. We had fastened the grater at one end, for the purpose of squeezing the paste through the small holes as soon as it was made.

My young manufacturers, with stripped arms, joyfully fell to work, and really surpassed my expectation. They brought water in succession and poured it gradually into the trough, whilst we mixed it with the flour. In a short time the paste appeared sufficiently fermented. I then made an aperture at the bottom of the grater on its outside, and pressed the paste strongly with my hand. The farinaceous parts passed with ease through the small holes of the grater, and the fibrous parts were thrown aside in a heap. My boys were in readiness to receive in the reed vessels what fell from the grater, and conveyed it directly to their mother, whose business was to spread out the small grains in the sun upon sail-cloth for the purpose of drying them. The subsequent process was the making of vermicelli, by working up the paste into a thicker consistence and pressing it more forcibly against the perforations of the grater. It passed through in slender rolls of different lengths, which were quickly dried by means of a gentle fire. To reward our toil my wife promised to dress us a dish of this new manufacture, with some Dutch cheese. Thus we procured a good supply of a wholesome and pleasant food, and should have had a larger stock had we not been restricted as to time. But the privilege of renewing the process at pleasure, by felling a sago-tree, added to impatience to take home our two pretty conduits and employ them as proposed, prompted us to expedite the business.

We employed ourselves the remainder of the evening in loading the cart with our tools and two halves of the tree. Night coming on, we retired to our hut, where we enjoyed our usual repose, and next morning were ready to return to Falcon's Stream. Our buffalo now commenced his service yoked with the cow. He was very tractable. It is true I led him by the cord which passed through his nose, and thus I restrained him within the bounds of his duty.

We returned the same way as we came, in order to load the cart with a provision of berries, wax, and elastic gum. I sent forward Fritz and Jack with one of the dogs. They were to cut a commodious road through the bushes. My sons well performed their task, and we reached without any serious accident the wax and gum-trees, where we halted to place our sacks filled with berries in the cart. The elastic gum had not yielded as much as I expected, from the too rapid thickening caused by an ardent sun, and an incrustation formed over the incision. We obtained. however, about a quart.

We set out again, still preceded by our pioneers, who cleared the way for us through the little wood of guavas. Suddenly we heard a dreadful noise which came from our vanguard, and beheld Fritz and Jack hastening towards us. I began now to fear a tiger or panther was near at hand, or had perhaps attacked them. Turk began to bark so frightfully, and Ponto, running up to him, joined in so hideous a yell, that I prepared myself, not without terror, for a bloody conflict. I advanced at the head of my troop, who expressed their determination to follow me, and my high-mettled dogs ran furiously up to a thicket, where they stopped and, with their noses to the ground, strove to enter. I had no doubt some terrible animal was lurking there, and Fritz, who had seen it through the leaves, confirmed my suspicion. He said it was about the size of the young buffalo, and that its hair was black and shaggy. I was going to fire, when Jack, who had thrown himself on his face on the ground to have a better view of the animal, got up in a fit of laughter. " It is only," exclaimed he, " dame pig that has played us another trick—our old sow." He had hardly spoken when the grunting of the monster justified the assertion. Half-vexed, half-laughing, we broke into the midst of the thicket, where we found our sow stretched on the earth, but by no means in a state of dreary solitude; the good matron had round her seven little creatures, which had been littered a few days. This discovery gave us considerable satisfaction, and we all greeted the creature, who seemed to welcome us with a sociable kind of grunting. We rewarded her docility with potatoes, sweet acorns, and manioc bread; for the boys readily consented to go without. A general consultation took place. Should this swinish family be left where we found it or conveyed to Falcon's Stream? Fritz voted for their being all left to run at large like the wild boars in Europe, that he might have the sport of hunting them. My wife proposed that two of them at least should be domesticated for breeding; and as to the old sow, as she was always running away, we could kill her later on, and she would afford a large provision of salt-meat. We decided upon this course. For the moment they were suffered to keep quiet possession of their retreat.

We then, so many adventures ended, pursued our road to Falcon's Stream, and arrived there in safety and content.

We all passed an excellent night in our green castle and in our good beds, which we returned to with abundant satisfaction.

CHAPTER XXVIII

ORIGIN OF SOME EUROPEAN FRUIT-TREES—BEES

We commenced the next day a business which we had long determined to engage in, to plant bamboos close to all the young trees, to support them. We quitted our tree with great alertness, having our cart loaded with canes and a large pointed iron to dig holes in the ground. We left my wife with only her little Francis, requesting them to prepare a plentiful dinner, and to include the palm-tree cabbage and the sago-macaroni mixed with some Dutch cheese. In addition, they volunteered the melting some of the wax berries for candles.

We did not take the buffalo with us, as I wished to give it a day's rest for its nose to heal up, and the cow was sufficient for drawing the load of light bamboo canes. Before setting out we gave the buffalo a few handfuls of salt to ingratiate ourselves with our horned companion.

We began our work at the entrance of the avenue which we had formed, and nearest to Falcon's Stream. The walnut, chestnut, and cherry trees we had planted in a regular line and at equal distances we found disposed to bend considerably. I took upon myself the task of making holes which I easily performed, taking care to go deep enough to fix the stake firmly. In the meantime the boys selected the bamboos, cut them of equal lengths, and pointed the ends to go into the ground. When they were all fixed we threw up the earth compactly about them, and fastened the saplings to them with some long tendrils of a plant.

In the midst of our exertions we entered into a conversation respecting the culture of trees.

After much arduous labour we got to the end of our alley of trees, which looked all the better. This accomplished, we crossed Family Bridge on our way to the southern plantation of trees, in order to raise and prop them also. We were delighted with the view of beautiful orange, citron, and pomegranate trees, that were thriving to our satisfaction, as well as the pistachio and mulberry trees.

We quickly set to work and towards noon a keen appetite hastened our return to Falcon's Stream, where we found an excellent and plentiful dinner prepared by our good and patient steward, of which the palm-tree cabbage was the chief dish. Ernest, who had procured it, received the thanks of all the table.

When the sharpness of hunger was appeased, a new subject was introduced which I and my wife had been seriously revolving for some time. She found it difficult and even dangerous to ascend and descend our tree by the rope-ladder. We never went there but on going to bed, and each time felt an apprehension that one of the children might make a false step. Bad weather might come on and compel us for a long time together to seek an asylum in our aerial apartment, and consequently to ascend and descend oftener.

A staircase on the outside was not to be thought of; the considerable height of the tree rendered that impracticable, as I had nothing to rest it on, and should be at a loss to find beams to sustain it. But I had for some time formed the idea of constructing winding stairs within the immense trunk of the tree, if it should happen to be hollow, or I could contrive to make it so. Francis had excited this idea in speaking of the bees.

"Did you not tell me, dear wife," said I, "that there is a hole in this tree of ours, in which a swarm of bees is lodged?"

"Without doubt," answered she. "It was there little Francis was stung in attempting to thrust in a stick."

"Then," replied I, "we have only to examine how far this excavation goes, whether it extends to the roots, and what the circumference of it is."

All my children seized the idea with ardour. They sprang up, and prepared themselves to climb the tops of the roots like squirrels, to succeed in striking at the trunk with axes, and to judge from the sound how far it was hollow. But they soon paid dearly for their attempt. The whole swarm of bees, alarmed at the noise, issued forth, buzzing with fury, attacked the little disturbers, began to sting them, stuck to their hair and clothes, and soon put them to flight. My wife and I had some trouble to stop the course of this uproar, and cover the stings with fresh earth to allay the smart. Jack had struck exactly upon the bees' nest, and was more severely attacked by them than the rest. It was necessary, so serious was the injury, to cover the whole of his face with linen. The less active Ernest got up the last, and was the first to run off when he saw the consequences, and thus avoided any further injury than a sting or two. But some hours elapsed before the other boys could open their eyes or be relieved from the pain. When they grew a little better, the desire of being avenged of the insects had the ascendant in their minds. They teased me to hasten the measures for getting everything in readiness for obtaining possession of their honey. The bees in the meantime were still buzzing furiously round the tree. I prepared tobacco, a pipe, some clay, chisels,

hammers, &c. I took the large gourd long intended
for a hive, and I fitted a place for it by nailing a
piece of board on a branch of the tree. I made a
straw roof for the top to screen it from the sun and
rain. As all this took up more time than I was aware
of, we deferred the attack on the fortress to the following day, and got ready for a sound sleep, which completed the cure of the wounded patients.

———————

CHAPTER XXIX

VICTORY OVER THE BEES——WINDING STAIRCASE
——TRAINING OF VARIOUS ANIMALS——DIVERS
MANUFACTURES——FOUNTAIN, ETC.

Next morning, almost before dawn, all were up and
in motion. The bees had returned to their cells, and
I stopped the passages with clay, leaving only a sufficient aperture for the tube of my pipe. I then smoked
as much as was requisite to stupefy the little warlike
creatures. At first a humming was heard in the hollow
of the tree, and a noise like a gathering tempest, which
died away by degrees. All was calm, and I withdrew
my tube without the appearance of a single bee. Fritz
had got up by me. We then began with a chisel and a
small axe to cut out of the tree, under the bees' entrance,
a piece three feet square. Before it was entirely separated I repeated the fumigation, lest the stupefaction
produced by the first smoking should have ceased, or the
noise we had been just making revived the bees. As soon
as I supposed them lulled again, I separated from the
trunk the piece I had cut out, producing as it were the

aspect of a window, through which the inside of the tree was laid entirely open to view, and we were filled with astonishment on beholding the wonderful work of this colony of insects. There was a stock of wax and honey that we feared our vessels would be insufficient to contain. The whole interior of the tree was lined with honeycombs. I cut them off with care, and put them in the gourds the boys constantly supplied me with. When I had somewhat cleared the cavity, I put the upper combs, in which the bees had assembled in clusters and swarms, into the gourd which was to serve as a hive, and placed it on the plank I had raised. I came down, bringing with me the rest of the honeycombs, with which I filled a small cask, previously well washed in the stream. Some I kept out for a treat at dinner, and had the barrel carefully covered with cloths and planks, that the bees might be unable to get at it. We then sat round the table, and regaled ourselves with the delicious honey. Having finished our meal, my wife put by the remainder, and I proposed to my sons to go back to the tree, to prevent the bees from swarming again there on being roused from their stupor, as they would not have failed to do but for the precaution I took of passing a board at the aperture and burning a few handfuls of tobacco on it, the smell and smoke of which drove them back from their old abode whenever they attempted to return to it. At length they became reconciled to their new residence, where their queen, no doubt, had settled herself.

I resolved to take full possession next day. The cask of honey was emptied into a kettle, except a few prime combs, which we kept for daily consumption. The remainder, mixed with a little water, was set over a gentle fire and reduced to a liquid consistence, strained and squeezed through a bag, and afterwards poured back into the cask, which was left upright and uncovered all night to cool. In the morning the wax was entirely separated, and had risen to the surface in a compact and solid cake that was easily removed; beneath was the purest, most beautiful, and delicate honey. The cask was then carefully headed again, and put into cool ground near our wine vessels. This task accomplished, I mounted to revisit the hive, and found the bees going forth in swarms and returning loaded, from which I judged they were forming fresh edifices in their new dwelling-place. I was surprised to see the numbers that had occupied the trunk of the tree find room in the gourd, but on looking round me I perceived a part of them collected in a cluster upon a branch, and I then concluded a young queen was amongst them. On perceiving this I procured another gourd, into which I shook them, and placed it by the former; thus I had the satisfaction of obtaining at an easy rate two fine hives of bees in activity.

We soon after these operations proceeded to examine the inside of the tree. I sounded it with a pole from the opening I had made, and a stone fastened to a string served us to sound the bottom. To my surprise, the pole penetrated to the branches on which our dwelling rested, and the stone descended to the roots. The trunk, it appeared, had wholly lost its pith, and most of its wood internally; nothing, therefore, was more practicable than to fix winding stairs in this capacious hollow. I determined to begin our construction that very day. The undertaking appeared at first beyond our powers, but patience, time, and a firm resolution vanquished all obstacles. We were not disposed to relax in any of these requisites; and I was pleased to find opportunities to keep my sons in continual action.

We began to cut into the side of the tree towards the sea a doorway equal in dimensions to the door of the captain's cabin, which we had removed with all its framework and windows. We next cleared away from the cavity all the rotten wood, and rendered the interior even and smooth, leaving sufficient thickness for cutting out resting-places for the winding stairs. I then fixed in the centre the trunk of a tree ten or twelve feet high and a foot thick, completely stripped of its branches, in order to carry my winding staircase round it. On the outside of this trunk, and the inside of the cavity of our own tree, we formed grooves, so calculated as to correspond with the distances at which the boards were to be placed to form the stairs. These were continued till I had got to the height of the trunk round which they turned. The window I had opened at the top to take out the honey gave light enough. I made a second aperture below, and a third above it, and thus completely lighted the whole ascent. I also effected an opening near our room, that I might more conveniently finish the upper part. A second trunk was fixed upon the first, and firmly sustained with screws and transverse beams. It was surrounded, like the other, with stairs cut slopingly. Thus we eventually effected the undertaking of conducting a staircase to our bed-chamber. To render it more solid I closed the spaces between the steps with boards. I then fastened two strong ropes, the one descending the length of the little tree, the other along the side of the large one, to assist in case of slipping. I fixed the sash-windows taken from the captain's cabin in the apertures we had made to give light to the stairs. When the whole was complete, it was so pretty, solid, and convenient that we were never tired of going up and coming down it.

A few days after the commencement of our staircase, the two she-goats gave us two kids, and our ewes five lambs, so that we now saw ourselves in possession of a pretty flock. But lest the domestic animals should follow the example of the ass, and run away from us, I tied a bell to the neck of each. We had found a sufficient number of bells in the vessel, which had been shipped for trading with the savages, it being one of the articles they most value. We could now immediately trace a deserter by the sound.

Next to the winding stairs my chief occupation was the young buffalo, whose nose was quite healed, so that I could lead it at will with a cord or stick passed through the orifice. I preferred the latter method, which answered the purpose of a bit, and I resolved to break in this spirited beast for riding as well as drawing. It was already used to the shafts, and very tractable in them. But I had more trouble in inuring him to the rider and to wear a girth, I having made one out of the old buffalo's hide. I formed a sort of saddle with sail-cloth, and tacked it to the girth. Upon this I fixed a burthen, which I increased progressively. I was indefatigable in the training of the animal, and soon brought it to carry, without fear or repugnance, large bags full of potatoes, salt, and other articles. The monkey was his first rider, who stuck so close to the saddle, that in spite of the plunging and kicking of the buffalo it was not thrown. Francis was then tried, as the lightest of the family. Throughout his excursion I led the beast with a halter. Jack now showed some impatience to mount the animal. Some restraint was requisite. I passed a piece of wood through the buffalo's nose, and tied strong packthread at each end of the stick, bringing the threads together over the neck of the animal. I then put this new-fashioned bridle into the hands of the young rider, directing him how to use it. For a time the lad kept his saddle, notwithstanding the repeated jumps of the horned steed; but at length a side jolt threw him on the sand, without his receiving much injury. Ernest, Fritz, and lastly myself got on successively, with more or less effect. His trotting shook us badly, the rapidity of his gallop turned us giddy, and our lessons in horsemanship were reiterated many days before the animal could be ridden with either safety or pleasure. At last, however, we succeeded without any serious accident. The strength and swiftness of our buffalo were prodigious; it seemed to sport with the heaviest loads. My three eldest boys mounted it together now and then, and it ran with them with the swiftness of lightning. By continued attentions it at length became extremely docile. It was not in the least apt to start, and I really felt satisfaction in being thus enabled to make my sons expert riders, so that if they should ever have horses, they might ride without fear. Fritz and Jack, with my instructions, amused themselves in training the animal as horses are exercised in a riding-house, and by means of the little stick through the nose they were able to do what they pleased with him.

Our whole company, including even Ernest, was infected with the passion of becoming instructors. Ernest tried his talents with the monkey. It was no poor specimen of the ludicrous to see the lad; he whose movements were habitually slow and studied, now constrained to skip, jump, and play a thousand antics with his pupil during training hours, and all the time deeply interested in carrying forward the lesson the grotesque mimic was condemned to learn, of carrying small loads, climbing the coco-trees, and to

find and fetch the nuts. He and Jack made a little
hamper of rushes, very light. They put three straps
to it, two of which passed under the fore, and one
between the hind legs of the animal, and were then
fastened to a belt in front to keep the hamper steady.
This apparatus was at first intolerable to poor Knips.
He gnashed his teeth, rolled on the ground, jumping
like a mad creature, and did everything to get rid of
it; but all in vain, and he soon found he must submit.
The hamper was left on day and night; his sole food
was what was thrown into it, and in a short time Knips
was so much accustomed to the burden, that he began
to spit and growl whenever we attempted to take it
off. Knips became at length a useful member of our
society. But he would only obey Ernest. Jack was
less successful with his little jackal, which he had
named *Hunter*, hoping that its qualities would justify
the name. He made continual attempts to induce the
animal to go after game, but for the first six months
he advanced no further in the lesson than teaching
him to bring what was thrown to him; and when it
was dead game, Hunter was sure to devour it on the
way, and to bring home the skin alone. But it was
nevertheless so pretty and tractable a creature, that I
entreated the boy not to relinquish a task that would
prove so beneficial to us, and he persevered with
considerable zeal.

These different occupations filled up several hours of
the day, and after working at our stairs, we assembled
in the evening round our never-failing constant friend,
the good mother, to rest ourselves. Forming a little
circle, every individual of which was affectionate and
cheerful, it was her turn to give us some agreeable and
less fatiguing occupation; such, for example, as
endeavouring to improve our candle-manufactory, by

blending the berry and the bees'-wax and employing the reed-moulds invented by Jack. Having found some difficulty in taking out the candles when cold, I adopted the plan of dividing the moulds, cleaning the inside, and rubbing it over with butter to prevent the wax from adhering. I rejoined both halves with a band that could be loosened at pleasure to facilitate the extraction of the candles. The wicks gave us most trouble, as we had no cotton. We tried with moderate success the fibrous threads of the karata, and those of the algava or flame-wood, but each had the inconvenience of becoming a sort of cinder. The substance which gave us the most satisfaction was the pith of a species of elder. It did not, however, lessen our desire to discover the only really appropriate substance, namely, the cotton-tree.

We had also been engaged in the construction of our fountain, which afforded a perpetual source of pleasure. In the upper part of the stream we built with stakes and stones a kind of dam, that raised the water sufficiently to convey it into the palm-tree troughs, and afterwards, by means of a gentle slope, to our habitation, where it fell into the tortoise-shell basin. It was so contrived that the surplus water passed off through a cane-pipe fitted to it. I placed two sticks athwart each other for the gourds, that served as pails, to rest on. We thus produced, close to our abode, an agreeable fountain, delighting with its rill, and supplying us with a pure crystal fluid. The only inconvenience was, that the water flowing in this open state was heated, and not refreshing when it reached us. I resolved to obviate this inconvenience by employing instead of the uncovered conduits, large bamboo-canes fixed deep enough in the ground to keep the water cool.

CHAPTER XXX

THE WILD ASS—DIFFICULTY IN BREAKING IT— PREPARING WINTER QUARTERS

We were scarcely up one morning, and had got to work in putting the last hand to our staircase, when we heard at a distance two strange voices that resembled the howlings of wild beasts, mixed with hissings and sounds of some creature at its last gasp, which I was at a loss to explain. Our dogs, too, pricked up their ears, and seemed to whet their teeth.

We loaded our guns and pistols, placed them together within our castle in the tree, and prepared to repel vigorously any hostile attack. The howlings having ceased an instant, I descended from our citadel, and put on our two faithful guardians their spiked collars and side-guards. I assembled our cattle about the tree to have them in sight, and reascended to look around for the enemy's approach.

At this instant the howlings were renewed quite close to us. Fritz got as near as he could, listened attentively, then threw down his gun and burst into laughter, exclaiming: " Father, it is our ass—the deserter comes back to us, chanting the hymn of return! Listen! do you not hear his melodious braying?" We lent an ear; our doubts ceased, and we felt somewhat mortified at our preparations of defence against such an ignoble foe.

I was, however, soon reconciled to the offence against our pride, since it also insured our safety. And a fresh roar, in sounds unquestionable, raised loud peals of laughter among us. Then followed the usual train of jests and mutual banter at the alarm we had all betrayed. Shortly after, we had the satisfaction of seeing among the trees our old friend Grizzle, moving towards us leisurely, and stopping now and then to browse. But to our great joy we perceived in his train one of the same species of very superior beauty, and when it was nearer I knew it to be a fine onagra or wild ass, which I conceived a strong desire to possess. Without delay I descended the ladder with Fritz, desiring his brothers to keep still. I consulted my privy-councillor on the means of taking the stranger captive. I got ready a long cord with a running knot, one end of which I tied fast to the root of a tree. The noose was kept open with a little stick slightly fixed in the opening so as to fall of itself on the cord being thrown round the neck of the animal, whose efforts to escape would draw the knot closer. I also prepared a piece of bamboo about two feet long, which I split at the bottom, and tied fast at the top to serve as nippers. Fritz attentively examined my contrivance, without seeing the use of it. Prompted by the impatience of youth, he took the ball-sling and proposed aiming at the wild ass with it. I declined adopting this Patagonian method, fearing the attempt might fail, and the beautiful creature avail itself of its natural speed to evade us beyond recovery. I told him my project of catching it by the noose, which I gave him to manage, as being nimbler and more expert than myself. The two asses drew nearer and nearer to us. Fritz, holding in his hand the open noose, moved softly on from behind the tree where we were concealed, and advanced as far as the length of the rope allowed him. The onagra was extremely startled on perceiving a human figure; it sprung some paces backward, then stopped as if to examine the unknown form. As Fritz now remained quite still, the animal resumed its composure and continued to browse. Soon after Fritz approached the old ass, hoping that the confidence that would be shown by it would raise a similar feeling in the stranger. He held out a handful of oats mixed with salt; our ass instantly ran up to take its favourite food; this was quickly perceived by the other. It drew near, raised his head, breathed strongly and came up so close, that Fritz succeeded in throwing the rope round its neck. The motion and stroke so affrighted the beast that it instantly sprang off, but was checked by the cord. It could go no farther, and after many exhausting efforts, it sank panting for breath upon the ground. I hastened to loosen the cord and prevent its being strangled. I then quickly threw our ass's halter over its head. I fixed the nose in my split cane, which I secured at the bottom with packthread. I wholly removed the noose that seemed to bring the creature into a dangerous situation. I fastened the halter with two long ropes to two roots near us, on the right and left, and let the animal recover itself, noticing its actions, and devising the best way to tame it in the completest manner.

The rest of my family had by this time come down from the tree, and beheld the fine creature with admiration, its graceful shape and well-turned limbs, which placed it so much above our ass, and nearly raised it to the noble structure of the horse. In a few moments the onagra got up, kicked out furiously, and seemed resolved to free itself from its bonds. But the pain of its nose, which was grasped and violently squeezed in the bamboo, forced it to lie down again. My eldest son and I now gently undid the cords, and half-led, half-dragged it between two adjoining roots, to which we fastened it afresh. We also guarded against Master Grizzle playing truant again, and tied him fast with a new halter, confining his fore-legs with a rope. I then fastened him and the wild ass side by side, and put before both plenty of good provender.

We had now the additional occupation of training the onagra for our service or our pleasure. My boys exulted in the idea of riding it. I did not conceal that we should have many difficulties in taming it. I let the nippers remain on its nose, which appeared to distress it, though we could plainly perceive the good effect in subduing the creature, for without them no one could have ventured to approach it. I took them off, however, at times when I gave it food, to render eating easier; and I began, as with the buffalo, by placing a bundle of sail-cloth on its back to inure it to carry. When it was accustomed to the load, I strove to render the beast still more docile by hunger and thirst, and I observed that when it had fasted a little, and I supplied it with food, its actions were less wild. I also compelled the animal to keep erect on its four legs, by drawing the cords closer that fastened it to the roots, in order to subdue by fatigue its natural ferocity. The children came in turns to play with it and scratch its ears gently, which were remarkably tender, and it was on these I resolved to make my last trial if all other endeavours failed. For a long time we despaired of success. The onagra made furious starts and leaps when any of us went near it, kicked with its hind-feet, and even attempted to bite those who touched it. This obliged me to have recourse to a muzzle, which I managed with rushes, and put on when it was not feeding. To avoid being struck by its hind-feet, I partially confined them by fastening them to the fore-feet with cords, which, however, I left moderately loose, that we might not encroach too much upon the motion necessary for its health. It was at length familiarized to this discipline, and was no longer in a rage when we approached, but bore to be handled and stroked.

At last we ventured to free it by degrees from its restraints, and to ride it as we had done with the buffalo, still keeping the fore-feet tied. But notwithstanding this precaution it proved as unruly as ever for the moment. The monkey, who was first put on its back, held on pretty well by clinging to its mane, from which it was suspended as often as the onagra furiously reared and plunged. It was therefore for the present impracticable for either of my sons to get upon it. The perverse beast baffled all our efforts, and the perilous task of breaking it was still to be persevered in with apprehension. In the stable it seemed tolerably quiet, but the moment it was in any degree unshackled, it became wholly unmanageable.

I was at length reduced to my last expedient, but not without much regret, as I resolved, if it did not answer, to restore the animal to full liberty. I tried to mount the onagra, and just as in the act of rearing up violently to prevent me, I seized with my teeth one of the long ears of the enraged creature, and bit it till it bled. Instantly it stood almost erect on its hind-feet, motionless. It soon lowered itself by degrees, while I still held its ear between my teeth. Fritz seized the moment and sprang on its back. Jack, with the help of his mother, did the same, holding by his brother, who on his part clung to the girth. When both assured me they were firmly seated, I let go the ear. The onagra made a few springs less violent than the former, and, checked by the cords on its feet, gradually submitted, began to trot up and down more quietly, and ultimately grew so tractable that riding it became one of our chief pleasures. My lads were soon expert horsemen, and their horse, though rather long-eared, was very handsome and well broken-in.

" Wherever," said my wife to me, " did you learn this strange notion of biting the animal's ear?"

" I learned it," replied I, " from a horse-breaker. He had lived long in America, and employed half-tamed horses of the southern provinces. They are at first unruly and resist burthens, but as soon as the hunter bites one of their ears they become submissive."

In a few weeks the onagra was so tamed that we all could mount it without fear. I still, however, kept his two fore-legs confined together with the cord, to moderate the extreme swiftness of its running. In the room of a bit I contrived a curb, and with this and a good bite applied as wanted to the ear, it went to right or left at the will of the rider.

During the training of the wild ass, which we named *Lightfoot*, a triple brood of our hens had given us a crowd of little feathered beings. Forty of these at least were chirping and hopping about us, to the great satisfaction of my wife.

" Here," she said, " are animals of real utility in a family, far beyond your monkeys and jackals, that do nothing but eat, and are unfit to be eaten." The buffalo was not found fault with, because it brought her the provisions; nor the onagra, on which she liked to see her sons gallop. From the time we had trained it to this, the rough-paced buffalo that shook us to pieces was no longer used for riding, but kept entirely for drawing.

This increase of our poultry reminded us of the necessity of an undertaking we had long thought of, and was not in prudence to be deferred any longer. This was the building between the roots of our great tree covered sheds for all our bipeds and quadrupeds.

The rainy season, which is the winter of these countries, was drawing near, and it was requisite to provide shelter.

We began by forming a roof above the arched roots of our tree, and employed bamboo canes for the purpose. The longest and strongest supported the roofing in the place of columns, the smaller composed the roof. I filled up the interstices with moss and clay, and I spread over the whole a thick coat of tar. I then made a railing round it, which gave the appearance of a pretty balcony, under which, between the roots, were various stalls that could be easily shut and separated from each other by means of planks nailed upon the roots. Part of them were to serve as a stable and yard, part as an eating-room, a store-room, &c., and as a hay-loft.

This work was soon completed. But afterwards it was necessary to fill these places with stores of every kind.

One evening, on our return from digging up potatoes, as our cart, loaded with bags, drawn by the buffalo, ass, and cow, was gently rolling along, seeing still a vacant place in the vehicle, I advised my wife to go home with the two youngest boys whilst I went round by the wood of oaks with Ernest and Fritz to gather sweet acorns. We had still some empty sacks. Ernest was accompanied by the monkey, who seldom left him, and Fritz was on the onagra. Notwithstanding the onagra was so well broken-in for riding, it continued to be very mettlesome and restive in the shafts, to which we could not inure it. Occasionally it submitted to our putting a loaded sack or two on its back, but we could seldom prevail even in this without Fritz being seated in front.

When we reached the oaks, Lightfoot was tied to a

bush, and we set actively to work to gather the acorns that had dropped from the trees. And now Ernest came forward, driving the monkey before him, and carrying his hat with the utmost care. He had stuck his girdle full of narrow sharp-pointed leaves, which reminded me of the production named sword-grass.

"I am going to take them home, they will please Francis," said he. "They are like swords, and will be the very thing he will like."

I applauded Ernest's idea, and encouraged him and Fritz to be thus ever considerate for the absent. It was now time to think of moving homeward. My two sons filled the bags with acorns and put them on Lightfoot. Fritz mounted, and we proceeded to Falcon's Stream, followed by our train-wagon. Fritz could not refrain from trotting on briskly, but he went rather faster than he intended. He had taken a handful of the pointed leaves with him, which he whisked before the eyes of the onagra till the animal was frightened, lost all restraint, and darting forward, hurried away at such a rate that we soon lost sight of them. Anxious for his safety, we followed as fast as possible, but on our arrival at Falcon's Stream we had the satisfaction of finding him there in perfect safety. His mother, indeed, had been somewhat alarmed in seeing him dash in like a thunderbolt, but firmly seated betwixt the bags on Master Lightfoot, who stopped short with wonderful precision at his stable door.

CHAPTER XXXI

FLAX, AND THE RAINY SEASON

Francis for a short time was highly amused with his sword-leaves, and then grew weary of them, and they were thrown aside. Fritz picked up some of them that were quite soft and withered. He held up one which was pliable as a riband.

" My little fellow," said he to his brother, " you can make whips of your sword-grass. Take the leaves and keep them, they will be of use in driving your goats and sheep." It had been decided that it should be the business of Francis to lead these to pasture.

" Well then, help me to make them," said the child.

They sat down together. Francis divided the leaves into long slips, and Fritz platted them into whip-cords. As they were working, I saw the flexibility and strength of the bands. I examined them closely, and found they were composed of fibres. This discovery led me to surmise that this might be the flax-plant of New Zealand. This was a valuable discovery in our situation. I knew how much my wife wished for the production, and that it was the article she felt most the want of. I therefore hastened to communicate the intelligence to her, upon hearing which she expressed the liveliest joy.

" This," said she, " is the most useful thing you have found. I entreat you lose not a moment in searching for more of these leaves. I will make you stockings, shirts, clothes, thread, ropes. . . . In short, give me flax, looms, and frames, and I shall be at no loss in the employment of it."

I could not help smiling at the scope she gave to her imagination on the mention of flax, though so much was to be done between the gathering the leaves and having the cloth she was already sewing in idea. Fritz whispered a word in Jack's ear. Both went to the stable, and without asking my leave, one mounted Lightfoot, the other the buffalo, and galloped off towards the wood. They were already out of sight. Their eagerness to oblige their mother in this instance pleaded their forgiveness, and I suffered them to go on without following them, purposing to proceed and bring them back if they did not soon return.

In waiting for them I conversed with my wife, who pointed out to me the various machinery I must contrive for spinning and weaving her flax for the manufactory of cloths, with which she said she should be able to equip us from head to foot, in speaking of which her eyes sparkled with the love of doing good, the purest kind of joy, and I promised her all she desired of me.

In a quarter of an hour our deserters came back on a full trot. Like true hussars they had foraged the woods and heavily loaded their cattle with the precious plant, which they threw at their mother's feet with joyful shouts. Jack made us laugh in recounting with his accustomed vivacity and drollery at what a rate he had trotted his buffalo to keep up with Lightfoot, and how his great horned horse had thrown him by a side leap.

Fritz. " How is flax prepared, Father, and what is meant by steeping it?"

Father. " Steeping flax or hemp is exposing it in the open air, by spreading it on the ground to receive the rain, the wind, and the dew in order in a certain degree to liquefy the plant. By this means the ligneous parts of the flax are separated with more ease from the fibrous; a kind of vegetable glue that binds them is dissolved, and it can then be perfectly cleaned with great facility, and the parts selected which are fit for spinning."

My wife suggested that we should soak the flax in Flamingo Marsh, and begin by making up the leaves in bundles, as they do hemp in Europe. We joined in this previous and necessary preparation of the flax during the rest of the day.

Next morning the ass was put to the small light car, loaded with bundles of leaves. Francis and the monkey sat on them, and the remainder of the family gaily followed with shovels and pick-axes. We stopped at the marsh, divided our large bundles into smaller ones, which we placed in the water, pressing them down with stones and leaving them in this state.

A fortnight after my wife told us the flax was sufficiently steeped. We then took it out of the water and spread it on the grass in the sun, where it dried so well and rapidly that we were able to load it on our cart the same evening, and carry it to Falcon's Stream, where it was put by till we had time to attend further to it, and make beetles, wheels, reels, carding-combs, &c., as required. It was thought best to reserve this task for the rainy season, and to get ready what would be then necessary during our confinement within doors. Uninformed as we were as to the duration of this season, it was highly important to lay in a competent stock of provisions. Occasional slight showers, the harbingers of winter, had already come on. The temperature, which hitherto had been warm and serene, became gloomy and variable. The sky was often darkened by clouds, the stormy winds were heard, and warned us to avail ourselves of the favourable moment.

Our first care was to dig up a full supply of potatoes and yams, for bread, with plenty of coco-nuts and some bags of sweet acorns. It occurred to us while digging, that the ground being thus opened and manured with the leaves of plants, we might sow in it to advantage the remainder of our European corn. Notwithstanding all the delicacies this stranger land afforded us, the force of habit still caused us to long for the bread we had been fed with from childhood. We had not yet laid ourselves out for regular tillage, and I was inclined to attempt the construction of a plough of some sort as soon as we had a sufficient stock of corn for sowing. For this time, therefore, we committed it to the earth with little preparation. The season, however, was proper for sowing and planting, as the ensuing rain would moisten and swell the embryo grain. We accordingly expedited the planting of the various palm-trees we had discovered in our excursions, at Tent House, carefully selecting the smallest and the youngest. In the environs we formed a large handsome plantation of sugar-canes.

These different occupations kept us several weeks. Our cart was incessantly in motion, conveying home our winter stock. Time was so precious that we could not even make regular meals, and limited ourselves to bread, cheese, and fruits.

Unfortunately the weather changed sooner than we had expected. Before we had completed our winter establishment, the rain fell in such heavy torrents that little Francis, trembling, asked me whether Father Noah's deluge was coming on again. And I could not myself refrain from painful apprehension in surmising how we should resist such a body of water, that seemed to change the whole face of the country into a perfect lake.

The first thing to be done was to remove our aerial abode, and to fix our residence at the bottom of the tree, between the roots and under the tarred roof I had erected; for it was no longer possible to remain above, on account of the furious winds that threatened to bear us away, and deluged our beds with rain through the large opening in front. Most fortunate did we deem ourselves in having made the winding stairs, which sheltered us during the operation of the removal. The stairs served afterwards for a kind of lumber-room. We kept in it all we could dispense with, and most of our culinary vessels, which my wife fetched as she happened to want them. Our little sheds between the roots, constructed for the poultry and the cattle, could scarcely contain us all, and the first days we passed in this manner were painfully embarrassing, crowded all together, and hardly able to move in these almost dark recesses, which the fœtid smell from the close-adjoining animals rendered almost insupportable. In addition, we were half stifled with smoke whenever we kindled a fire, and drenched with rain when we opened the doors. For the first time since our disaster we sighed for the comfortable houses of our dear country. But what was to be done? I strove to raise the spirits of my companions and obviate some of the inconveniences. The now doubly-precious winding stair was, as I have said, every way useful to us. The upper part of it was filled with numerous articles that gave us room below. As it was lighted and sheltered by windows, my wife often worked there, seated on a stair, with her little Francis at her feet. We confined our live stock to a smaller number, and gave them a freer current of air, dismissing from the stalls those animals that would be at no loss in providing for themselves. That we might not lose them altogether, we tied bells round their necks. Fritz and I sought and drove them in every evening that they did not spontaneously return. We generally got wet to the skin and chilled with cold during the employment, which induced my wife to contrive for us a kind of clothing more suitable to the occasion. She took two seamen's shirts from the chest we had recovered from the wreck, and, with some pieces of old coats, she made us a kind of cloth hoods joined together at the back, and well formed for covering the head entirely. We melted some elastic gum, which we spread over the shirts and hoods. The articles thus prepared answered every purpose of waterproof overalls. Our young rogues were ready with their derision the first time they saw us in them, but afterwards they would have been rejoiced to have had the same. This, however, the reduced state of our gum did not allow of, and we contented ourselves with wearing them in turn.

As to the smoke, our only remedy was to open the door when we made a fire. And we did without as much as we could, living on milk and cheese, and never making a fire but to bake our cakes. We then availed ourselves of the opportunity to boil a quantity of potatoes and salt meat enough to last us a number of days. Our dry wood was also nearly expended, and we thanked Heaven the weather was not very cold. A more serious concern was our not having provided sufficient hay and leaves for our European cattle, which we necessarily kept housed to avoid losing them. The cow, the ass, the sheep, and the goats, the two last of which were increased in number, required a large quantity of provender, so that we were ere long forced to give them our potatoes and sweet acorns. Milking, cleaning the animals, and preparing their food occupied us most of the morning, after which we were usually employed in making flour of the manioc root, with which we filled the large gourds, which were previously placed in rows. The gloom of the atmosphere and our low windowless habitation sensibly abridged our daylight. Fortunately we had laid in a huge store of candles. When darkness obliged us to light up, we got round the table, when a large taper fixed on a gourd gave us an excellent light, which enabled my wife to pursue her occupation with the needle; while I, on my part, was writing a journal, and recording what the reader has perused of our shipwreck and residence in this island, assisted from time to time by my sons and my wife, who did not cease to remind me of various incidents. To Ernest, who wrote a fine hand, was entrusted the care of writing off my pages. Our kind and faithful steward often surprised us agreeably on our return from looking after the cattle, by lighting up a faggot of dried bamboo, and quickly roasting a chicken, pigeon, duck, or penguin from our poultry-yard, or some of the thrushes we had preserved in butter, which were excellent, and welcomed as a treat. Every four or five days she made us new fresh butter in the gourd churn. This, with some deliciously fragrant honey on our manioc cakes, formed a collation that would have raised the envy of European epicures.

The fragments of our meals belonged to our domestic animals. We had the two dogs, the young jackal, and the monkey to feed. They relied on the kindness of their masters, who certainly would have deprived themselves to supply their helpless dependants. If the buffalo, the onagra, and pig had not found sustenance abroad, they must have been killed or starved, and that would have given us much pain. In the course of these discomforts it was unanimously resolved on that we would not pass another rainy season exposed to the same evils. Even my beloved consort, who felt such a predilection for the abode at Falcon's Stream, was frequently a little ruffled and out of temper with our inconvenient situation, and insisted on the propriety of building a more spacious winter residence. She wished, however, to return to our castle in the tree every summer, and we all joined with her in that desire. The choice of a fresh abode now engrossed our attention, and Fritz in the midst of consultation came forward triumphantly with a book he had found in the bottom of our clothes-chest. "Here," said he, "is our best counsellor and model, *Robinson Crusoe*. Since Heaven has destined us to a similar fate," said he, "whom better can we consult? As far as I remember, he cut himself an habitation out of the solid rock. Let us see how he proceeded. We will do the same, and with greater ease, for he was alone. We are six in number, and four of us able to work."

We assembled, and read the famous history with an ardent interest. It seemed, though so familiar, quite new to us. We entered earnestly into every detail and derived considerable information from it, and never failed to feel lively gratitude towards God, who had rescued us all together, and not permitted one of us to be cast, a solitary being, on the island.

Francis repeated his wish to have a Man Friday; Fritz thought it better to be without such a companion, and to have no savages to contend with. Jack was for the savages, warfare and encounters. The final result of our deliberations was to go and survey the rocks round Tent House, and to examine whether any of them could be excavated for our purpose.

Our last job for the winter, undertaken at my wife's

solicitation, was a beetle for her flax and some carding-combs. I filed large nails till they were even, round, and pointed. I fixed them at equal distances in a sheet of tin, and raised the sides of it like a box. I then poured melted lead between the nails and the sides, to give firmness to their points, which came out four inches. I nailed this tin on a board, and the contrivance was fit for work. My wife was impatient to use it, and the drying, peeling, and spinning her flax became a source of delight.

CHAPTER XXXII

SPRING—SPINNING—SALT-MINE

I can hardly describe our joy when, after gloomy weeks of rain, the sky began to brighten, the sun to dart its rays on the earth, the winds to be lulled, and the state of the air became mild and serene. We issued from our hovels with joyful shouts, and walked round our habitation breathing the balmy air, while our eyes were regaled with the verdure beginning to shoot forth on every side. Reviving nature opened her arms, every creature seemed reanimated, and we felt the genial influence of that luminary which had been so long concealed, now returning like a friend who has been absent, to bring us back blessings and delight. We forgot the embarrassments and weary hours of the wet season, and with hopeful hearts looked forward to the toils of summer as amusements.

The vegetation of our trees was rapidly advancing. The seed we had thrown into the ground was sprouting in slender blades that waved luxuriantly, a pleasing tender foliage adorned the trees, the earth was ena-melled with an infinite variety of flowers. Odorous exhalations were diffused through the atmosphere. The song of birds was heard around; they were seen between the leaves joyfully fluttering from branch to branch; their various forms and brilliant plumage heightened this delightful picture of spring, and we were at once struck with gratitude towards the Creator of so many beauties.

Our summer occupations commenced by arranging and thoroughly cleaning Falcon's Nest, the order and neatness of which the rain and dead leaves blown by the wind had disturbed. In other respects, however, it was not injured, and in a few days we rendered it fit for our reception. The stairs were cleared, the rooms between the roots reoccupied, and we were left with leisure to proceed to other employments. My wife lost not a moment in resuming the process of her flax industry. Our sons hastened to lead the cattle to the fresh pastures; whilst it was my task to carry the bundles of flax into the open air, where, by heaping stones together, I contrived an oven sufficiently com-modious to dry it well. The same evening we all set to work to peel, and afterwards to beat it and strip off the bark, and lastly to comb it with my carding-machine. I took this laborious task on myself, and drew out such distaffsful of long soft flax ready for spinning, that my enraptured wife ran to embrace me, requesting me to make her a wheel without delay, that she might enter upon her favourite work.

At an earlier period of my life I had practised turnery for my amusement; now, however, I was unfortunately destitute of the requisite utensils. But as I had not forgotten the arrangement and component parts of a spinning-wheel and reel, I by repeated endeavours found means to accomplish those two machines to my wife's satisfaction, and she fell so eagerly to spinning as to allow herself no leisure even for a walk, and scarcely time to dress our dinners. Nothing so much delighted her as to be left with her little boy, whom she employed to reel as fast as she could spin, and sometimes the other three were also engaged in turns at the wheel to forward her business while she was occupied in culinary offices. Not one of them was found so tractable as the cool-tempered, quiet Ernest, who preferred this to more laborious exertions. Our first visit was to Tent House, as we were anxious to ascertain the ravages of winter there, and we found them much more considerable than at Falcon's Stream. The tempest and rain had beaten down the tent, carried away a part of the sail-cloth, and made such havoc amongst our provisions, that by far the largest portion of them was spotted with mildew, and the remainder could be saved only by drying them instantly. Luckily, our handsome pinnace had been spared, but our tub-boat was in too shattered a state to be of any further service.

In looking over the stores we were grieved to find the gunpowder most damaged, of which I had left three barrels in the tent. The contents of two were rendered wholly useless. I thought myself fortunate on finding the remaining one in tolerable condition, and derived from this great and irreparable loss a cogent motive to fix upon winter quarters where our stores and wealth would not be exposed.

Notwithstanding the gigantic plan suggested by the enterprising characters of Fritz and Jack, I had little hope of being able to effect the excavation of a dwelling in the rock. Robinson Crusoe found a spacious cavern

that merely required enlarging and arrangement; no
such cavity was apparent in our rock, which was of
extreme hardness, so that it seemed that three or four
summers would scarcely have sufficed to execute the
design. Still, the earnest desire of a more substantial
habitation perplexed me incessantly, and I resolved
to make at least the attempt of cutting out a recess
that should contain the gunpowder, the most valuable
of all our treasures. With this resolution I set off one
day, accompanied by my two valiant workmen, Fritz
and Jack, leaving their mother at her spinning with
her assistants, Ernest and Francis. We took with us
pickaxes, chisels, hammers, and iron levers. I chose a
part of the rock nearly perpendicular, and much better
situated than our tent. The view from it was enchanting, for it embraced the whole range of Safety Bay,
and the banks of Jackal River and Family Bridge.
I marked out with charcoal the circumference of the
opening we wished to make, and we began the heavy
toil of piercing the quarry. We made so little progress
the first day, that in spite of all our courage we were
tempted to relinquish our undertaking. We persevered, however, and my hope was somewhat revived
as I perceived the stone was of a softer texture as we
penetrated deeper. We concluded from this, that the
ardent rays of the sun striking upon the rock had
hardened the external layer, and that the stone would
increase in softness as we advanced. This proved to
be the case, and when I had cut about a foot in depth
we could loosen the rock with the spade. This determined me to proceed with double ardour, and my
boys assisted me with a zeal beyond their years.

After a few days of labour we measured the opening,
and found we had already advanced seven feet. Fritz
removed the fragments in a barrow, and discharged

them before the place to form a sort of terrace.   I
applied my own labour to the upper part to enlarge
the aperture; Jack, the smallest of the three, was
able to get in and cut away below.   Jack worked a
long iron bar sharpened at the end.   When he was
driving this in with a hammer, to loosen a particularly
large piece of rock, he suddenly bawled out:

"It is pierced through, Father!"

"Ha, ha! Master Jack! What have you pierced
Is it the mountain? Not your hand or foot, is it, Jack?"
cried I.

Jack. "No, no, it is the mountain! Huzza, huzza!
I have pierced the mountain!"

Fritz now ran to him.

"Come, let us see," cried he.   "You should have
pushed on your tool boldly till you reached Europe,
which they say is under our feet.   I should have been
glad to peep into that hole."

Jack. "Well then, peep you may; but I hardly
know what you will see.   Now, come and look how
far the iron is gone in, and tell me if it is all my boast-
ing.   If there were not a hollow space behind, how
could it penetrate the rock so easily?"

"Come here, Father," said Fritz.   "This is really
extraordinary.   His iron bar seems to have got to a
hollow place."

I approached, thinking the incident worth attention.   I took hold of the bar, which was still in the
rock, and pressing it forcibly from one side to another,
I made a sufficient aperture for one of my sons to pass.
I observed that in reality the rubbish fell within the
cavity.   My two lads offered to go in together to examine it.   This, however, I firmly opposed.   I even
made them remove themselves from the opening, as
I smelled the bad air that issued abundantly from it,

and began myself to feel giddiness in consequence of having gone too near; indeed I was compelled to withdraw quickly, and inhale a purer air.

"Beware, my dear children," said I in terror, "of entering such a perilous cavern. Life might be suddenly extinguished there. I fear it is full with noxious vapours that would suffocate."

Jack. "Then all to be done is to be off quickly when one feels a stoppage of breath."

Father. "This is the natural course, when it can be taken; but the suffocation in such air usually begins by a dizziness of the head, so violent as to intercept motion, which is followed by an insurmountable oppression; efforts are made to breathe, fainting follows, and without speedy help death takes place. But there is a test of bad air of the kind I believe this to be: fire does not burn in it. We must try to light a fire in this hole."

The boys now hastened to gather some dry moss, which they made into bundles. They then struck a light, and set fire to them, and then threw the moss blazing into the opening; the fire was extinguished at the very entrance. We then made a very large fire near the opening, which we hoped would set up a draught, and gradually draw out the bad and admit good air. We were the more confident of this taking place, as we already observed a current of air outwards at the bottom of our hole. We kept the fire burning for some hours. Then we again threw in some lighted straw into the cavern, and found, to our great satisfaction, the bundles were entirely consumed. We could accordingly hope nothing was to be feared from the air. There still remained the danger of plunging into some abyss, or of meeting with a body of water. From these considerations I thought it more prudent to defer our entrance into this unknown recess till **we** had lights. I dispatched Jack on the buffalo to Falcon's Stream, to impart our discovery to his mother and two brothers, directing him to return with them, and bring all the tapers that were left. My intention was to fasten them together on a stick to form a large torch, and thus illuminated proceed with our whole troop to examine the interior of this grotto. I had not sent Jack on his embassy without a meaning; the boy possessed from nature a lively and poetical imagination. I knew he would tell his mother such wonders of the grotto, that in spite of the charms of her spinning-wheel he would induce her to accompany him, and bring us lights to penetrate the obscure sanctuary.

Overjoyed at his commission, Jack sprang on the buffalo, which he had nearly appropriated to himself, cracked his whip, and set off boldly. The intrepid boy was unencumbered by fear, and made a race-horse of his horned steed.

In waiting his return I proposed to Fritz to widen the entrance to the grotto, and make a way for his mother to pass in. After labouring three or four hours we saw them coming up in our car of state—the one I had equipped for the potatoes, and which was now drawn by the cow and the ass, and conducted by Ernest. Francis, too, played his part in the cavalcade, and contended with his brother for the ropes that served as reins. Jack, mounted on his buffalo, came prancing before them, blew through his closed hand in imitation of a French horn, and now and then whipped the ass and cow to quicken their motion. When they had crossed Family Bridge he came forward on the gallop, and when he got up to us, jumped off the beast, shook himself, took a spring or two from the ground, and thus refreshed ran up to the car to hand his mother out like a true and gallant knight.

I immediately lighted the torches, but instead of tying them together, as I had intended, I preferred that each should take one in his right hand, an implement in his left in case of accident, a taper in his pocket, and flint and steel. Thus we entered the rock in procession. I took the lead, my sons followed me, and their beloved mother, with the youngest, brought up the rear. We had scarcely advanced four paces within the grotto when all was changed to more than admiration and surprise. The most beautiful and magnificent spectacle presented itself. The sides of the cavern sparkled like diamonds, the light from our six tapers was reflected from all parts, and had the effect of a grand illumination. Innumerable crystals of every length and shape hung from the top of the vault, which, uniting with those of the sides, formed pillars, altars, entablatures, and a variety of other figures, constituting the most splendid masses. We might have fancied ourselves in the palace of a fairy, or in an illumined temple. In some places all the colours of a prism were emitted from the angles of the crystals, and gave them the appearance of precious stones. The waving of the lights, their bright coruscations, dark points here and there occurring, the dazzling lustre of others—the whole, in short, enchanted the sight and the fancy.

The astonishment of my family was so great as to be almost ludicrous. They were all in a kind of stupor, half-imagining it was a dream. I had seen stalactites, and read the description of the famous grotto of Antiparos, far more considerable than this, which, however, gave an idea of it. The bottom was level, covered with white, fine sand, so dry that I could not see the least mark of humidity. All this led me to hope the spot would be eligible for our residence. I now formed a conjecture as to the nature of the crystallizations, namely, that I was in a grotto of rock-salt. The discovery of this fact pleased us all exceedingly. The shape of the crystals, their little solidity, and finally their saline taste, were decisive evidences.

How highly advantageous to us and our cattle was this superabundance of salt, pure and ready to be shovelled out for use!

As we advanced, remarkable figures formed by the saline matter everywhere presented themselves. Columns reaching from the bottom to the top of the vault appeared to sustain it, and some even had cornices and capitals; here and there undulating masses which at certain distances resembled the sea. From the whimsical forms we beheld, fancy might make a thousand creations at its pleasure; windows, large open cupboards, benches, church ornaments, grotesque figures of men and animals, some like polished crystals or diamonds, others like blocks of alabaster.

We viewed with unwearied curiosity this repository of wonders, and we had all lighted our second taper, when I observed on the ground in some places a number of crystal fragments that seemed to have fallen off from the upper part. Such a separation might recur at any moment, and therefore I thought it prudent to retire, as other loosened pieces might fall on us. I directed my wife and three of the children to place themselves in the entrance, while Fritz and I examined every part that threatened danger. We loaded our guns with ball and fired them in the centre of the cavern; one or two fell, the rest remained immovable, though we went round with long poles and struck all we could reach. We at length felt confident that there was nothing to fear, and that we might proceed to fit

up our new habitation without dread. Many schemes
were formed for converting this beautiful grotto into
a mansion for our abode. All the force of our imagination was centred in that point. The greatest
difficulty was removed; we had possession of the most
eligible premises; the sole business now was to turn
them to the best account, and how to effect this was
our unceasing theme. Some voted for our immediate
establishment there, but they were opposed by more
sagacious counsel, and it was resolved that Falcon's
Stream should continue to be our headquarters till
the end of the year.

CHAPTER XXXIII

HOUSE IN THE SALT-ROCK

The lucky discovery of a cavern in the rock had, as
must be supposed, considerably lessened our labour.
Excavation was no longer requisite. To render it
habitable was the present object. The upper bed of
the rock in front of the cavern, through which my
little Jack had dug so easily, was of a soft nature, and
to be woiked with moderate effort. I hoped also that,
being now exposed, it would become by degrees as
hard as the first layer. From this consideration I began,
while it retained its soft state, to make openings for the
door and windows. This I regulated by the measure-
ment of those I had fixed in my winding staircase,
which I had removed for the purpose of placing them
in our winter tenement. Intending Falcon's Nest as
a retreat for the hottest days, the windows became
unnecessary. As to the door, I preferred making one

of bark similar to that of the tree itself, as it would conceal our abode the better. The doors and windows were therefore taken to Tent House, and afterwards properly fixed. I had previously marked out the openings to be cut for the frames, which were received into grooves. I took care not to break up the stone taken from the apertures, or at least to preserve it in large pieces, and these I cut into oblongs an inch and a half in thickness to serve as tiles. I laid them in the sun, and was gratified in seeing they hardened quickly.

When I could enter the cavern freely through a good doorway, and it was sufficiently lighted by the windows, I erected a partition for the distribution of our apartments and other conveniences. I was cautious to injure as little as possible the natural embellishments of this new mansion. But I could not avoid demolishing them in the division allotted to the stables. Cattle are fond of salt, and would not have failed to eat away these ornaments. However, I preserved the finest of the pillars and the most beautiful pieces to decorate our saloon. The large ones served us as chairs and tables, and the brilliant pilasters at once enlivened and adorned the apartment, and at night multiplied the reflection of the lights. I laid out the interior in the following manner. A very considerable space was first partitioned off in two divisions; the one on the right was appropriated to our residence, that on the left was to contain the kitchen, stables, and workroom. At the end of the second division, where windows could not be placed, the cellar and storeroom were to be formed; the whole separated by partition boards, with doors of communication, so as to give us a comfortable abode.

The side we designed to lodge in was divided into three chambers; the first, next the door, was the bedroom for my wife and me, the second a dining-parlour, and the last a bed-chamber for the boys. As we had only three windows, we put one in each sleeping-room; the third was fixed in the kitchen. A grating for the present fell to the lot of our dining-room, which, when too cold, was to be exchanged for one of the other apartments. I contrived a good fireplace in the kitchen near the window; I pierced the rock a little above, and four planks nailed together and passed through this opening answered the purpose of a chimney. We made the workroom near the kitchen of sufficient dimensions for the performance of undertakings of some magnitude; it served also to keep our cart and sledge in. Lastly, the stables, which were formed into four compartments to separate the different species of animals, occupied all the bottom of the cavern on this side; on the other were the cellar and magazine.

The long stay we made at Tent House during these employments furnished us an opportunity of perceiving several advantages we had not reckoned upon, and which we did not defer availing ourselves of. Immense turtles were very often seen on the shore, where they deposited their eggs in the sand, and they regaled us with a rich treat. But, extending our wishes, we thought of getting possession of the turtles themselves for live stock, and of feasting on them whenever we pleased. As soon as we saw one on the sands, one of my boys was dispatched to cut off its retreat. Meanwhile we approached the animal, turned it on its back, passed a long cord through the shell, and tied the end of it to a stake which we fixed close to the edge of the water. This done, we set the prisoner on his legs again. It hastened into the sea, but could not go beyond the length of the cord. Apparently it was quite happy, finding plenty of food alongshore, and we enjoyed the idea of being able to take it when wanted. I say nothing of sea-lobsters, oysters, and many other small fishes which we could catch in any number.

At this time I likewise made some improvements in our sledge. I raised it on two beams or axle-trees, at the extremities of which I put on the four gun-carriage wheels I had taken off the cannon from the vessel. By this alteration I obtained a light and very convenient vehicle, of moderate height, on which boxes and casks could be placed. Pleased with the operations of the week, we set out all together with cheerful hearts for Falcon's Stream, to pass our Sunday there, and once more offer our pious thanks to the Almighty for all the benefits He had bestowed upon His defenceless creatures.

———

CHAPTER XXXIV

NEW FISHERY—NEW EXPERIMENTS AND CHASE —NEW DISCOVERIES AND HOUSE

The arrangement of our grotto went on according to the importance of other concerns, and our progress was such as to afford the hope of our being securely established within it by the time of the rainy season.

I had made the fortunate discovery of a bed of gypsum in the neighbourhood of our grotto. I foresaw the great advantages I should derive from it, and tried to find a place in the continuation of the rock which I might be able to blow up. I had soon the good fortune to meet with a narrow slip between the rocks which I could easily convert into a passage that should terminate in our work-room. I found also a quantity of fragments of gypsum, and removed a number of them to the kitchen, where we did not fail to bake a few of the pieces at a time when we made a fire for cooking, which, thus calcined, rubbed into a powder when cold. We obtained a considerable quantity of it which I put carefully into casks for use when the time should come for finishing the interior of our dwelling. My notion was to form the walls for separating the apartments of squares of stone, and to unite them together with a cement of gypsum, which would be the means both of sparing our timber and increasing the beauty and solidity of the work.

About two months after the discovery of our grotto, we observed Safety Bay to be filled with large fishes, which seemed eager to push to the shore for the purpose of depositing their eggs. Jack was the first to discover this circumstance. He told me he had seen a number of whales swimming about in Jackal River. I replied that I could not conceive of a regiment of whales arriving in our diminutive rivulet.

It, however, appeared to me worth while to go and convince myself on the spot respecting these new-comers. Jack and I walked to the mouth of Jackal River, and perceived immense quantities of a large fish moving slowly towards the banks, and some of them from four to eight feet in length. By the pointed snout I supposed them to be sturgeons. " What say you, now, Father?" said Jack. " A single fish of this troop would fill a tub!"

" No doubt," answered I; and with great gravity I added, " Pr'ythee, Jack, step into the river, and fling them to me."

He looked at me for a moment with a sort of vacant

doubt, then seizing suddenly a new idea, " Wait a moment, Father," cried he, " and I will do so !" and he sprang off towards the cavern, from whence he returned with a bow and arrows, the bladders of some fish, and a ball of string. I looked on with interest to mark what was next to happen. He tied the bladders round at certain distances with a long piece of string, to the end of which he fastened an arrow and a small iron hook. He placed the large ball of string in a hole in the ground, at a sufficient distance from the water's edge, and then he shot off his arrow, which the next instant stuck in one of the largest fishes. My young sportsman uttered a shout of joy. At the same moment Fritz joined us, and witnessed this unexpected feat without the least symptom of jealousy. " Well done, brother Jack !" cried he; " but let me too have my turn." Saying this he ran back and fetched the harpoon and the windlass, and returned to us accompanied by Ernest, who also desired to show his prowess in a contest with our newly-discovered mariners. We were well pleased with their arrival, for the fish Jack had pierced struggled so fiercely that we dreaded at every jerk to see it escape. By degrees, however, its strength was exhausted, and aided by Fritz and Ernest we succeeded in drawing it to a bank.

This fortunate beginning of a plan for a fishery inspired us all with hope and emulation. Fritz eagerly seized his harpoon and windlass. I, for my part, like Neptune, wielded a trident. Ernest prepared the large fishing-rod, and Jack his arrow, with the same apparatus as before, not forgetting the bladders, which were effectual in preventing the fish from sinking when struck. Such numbers of fishes presented themselves that we had only to choose. Accordingly we were soon loaded to our heart's content. Jack's arrow, after missing twice, struck the third time a large sturgeon, which was so untractable that we had great difficulty in securing him. I had caught two, and had been obliged to go up to the middle in the water to manage my booty. Ernest, with his rod and line and a hook, had also taken two fish. Fritz with his harpoon had struck a sturgeon at least eight feet in length, and the skill and strength of our whole company were found necessary to conduct him to shore.

Our first concern was to clean our fish thoroughly. I took care of the bladders, thinking it might be possible to make a glue from them. I advised my wife to boil some of the smaller fish in oil, similar to the manner of preparing tunny fish in the Mediterranean, and while she was engaged in this process I was at work upon the glue. For the first, I washed the berries in several waters, and then pressed them closely in gourd-rinds in which a certain number of holes had been bored. When the water had run off, the berries were taken out in a substance like cheese, which was then conveyed to the hut to be dried and smoked. For the second, we cut the bladders into strips, which we fastened firmly by one end to a stake, and taking hold of the other with a pair of pincers, we turned them round and round till the strip was reduced to a kind of knot, and these were then placed in the sun to harden, this being the simple and only preparation necessary for obtaining glue from the ingredient. When thoroughly dry, a small quantity is put on a slow fire to melt. We succeeded so well, and our glue was of so transparent a quality, that I could not help feeling the desire to manufacture some pieces large enough for panes to a window-frame.

When these various concerns were complete, we began to meditate a plan for constructing a small boat as a substitute for the tub raft. I had a great desire to make it as the savages do, of the rind of a tree; but the difficulty was to fix on one of sufficient bulk, for, though many were to be found, each was on some account or other of too much value to be spared. We therefore resolved to make a little excursion in pursuit of a tree of capacious dimensions, and in a situation where it was not likely to yield us fruit, to refresh us with its shade, or to adorn the landscape round our dwelling.

In this expedition we as usual aimed at more than one object. Eager as we were for new discoveries, we yet allowed ourselves the time to visit our different plantations and stores at Falcon's Stream. We were also desirous to secure a new supply of the wax berry, of gourds, and of elastic gum. Our kitchen-garden at Tent House was in a flourishing condition; nothing could exceed the luxuriance of the vegetation, and we had excellent roots and plants in abundance, which came in succession, and promised a rich supply of peas, beans, lettuces, &c. We had, besides, melons and cucumbers in great plenty, which, during the hottest weather, we valued more than all the rest. We reaped a considerable quantity of Turkey wheat from the seed we had sown, and some of the ears were a foot in length. Our sugar-canes were also in the most prosperous condition, and one plantation of pine-apples on the high ground was also in progress to reward our labour with delicious fruit.

This state of prosperity at Tent House gave us flattering expectations from our nurseries at Falcon's Stream. Full of these hopes, we one day set out for our former abode.

We arrived at Falcon's Stream, where we intended to pass the night. We visited the ground my wife had so plentifully sowed with grain, which had sprung up with an almost incredible rapidity and luxuriance, and was nearly ready for reaping. We cut down what was fairly ripe, bound it together in bundles, and conveyed it to a place where it would be secure from the attacks of more expert grain consumers than ourselves, of which thousands hovered round the booty. We reaped barley, wheat, rye, oats, peas, millet, lentils—only a small quantity of each, it is true, but sufficient to enable us to sow again plentifully at the proper season. The plant that had yielded the most was maize, a proof that it best loved the soil and climate. The moment we drew near, a dozen, at least, of large bustards sprang up with a loud rustling noise, which awakened the attention of the dogs. They plunged into the thickest parts, and routed numerous flocks of birds of all kinds and sizes. Among the fugitives were some quails, who escaped by running, and lastly some kangaroos, whose prodigious leaps enabled them to elude the pursuit of the dogs.

We were so overcome by the surprise such an assemblage occasioned as to forget the resource we had in our guns.

Jack alone thought of how to repair the error, and also the giving us a specimen of the happy effects of the education he had bestowed on the young jackal. He let him loose, and he slipped slily away after the birds we supposed were quails. The jackal soon overtook them, seized one of them by the wing, and brought it to his master. In the same manner he carried him at least a dozen.

At the conclusion of this adventure we hastened forward to Falcon's Stream. I threw a few more bundles of maize into the cart, and without further delay we arrived at our tree, one and all sinking with faintness from hunger, thirst, and fatigue. It was on such occasions that my wife evinced the superior fortitude and generosity of her temper. Though more a sufferer than any, her first thought was what she could administer to relieve us. She contrived to bruise some of the maize between two large stones, and then put it in a linen cloth, and with all her strength squeezed out the sap. She then added some juice from the sugar-canes, and in a few minutes presented us with a draught of a cool refreshing liquid, beautifully white in appearance and agreeable to the taste.

Jack had been able to preserve alive only two of the quails. All the others were put on the spit for supper. The rest of the day was employed in picking the grains of the different sorts of corn from the stalks. We put what we wished to keep for sowing into gourd shells, and the Turkey wheat was laid aside in sheaves till we should have time to beat and separate it. Fritz observed that we should also want to grind it, and I reminded him of the hand-mill we had secured from the wrecked vessel.

Fritz. " But, Father, the hand-mill is so small, and so subject to be put out of order. Why should we not contrive a water-mill? We have surely rapid streams of water in abundance."

Father. " This is true, but such a mechanism is more difficult than you imagine. In the meantime, let us be thinking, boy, of our proposed excursion for to-morrow, for we should set out at latest by sunrise."

We began our preparations accordingly. My wife chose some hens and two fine cocks, with the intention of taking them with us and leaving them at large to produce a colony of their species. I, with the same view, visited our stable, and selected four young pigs, four sheep, two kids, and one male of each species, our numbers having so much increased that we could afford to spare these.

The next morning, after loading the cart with all things necessary, not forgetting the rope-ladder and the tent, we quitted Falcon's Stream. The animals, with their legs tied, were all stationed in the vehicle. We left abundance of food for those that remained behind. The cow, the ass, and the buffalo were harnessed to the cart. Fritz, mounted on his favourite, the onagra, pranced along before us to ascertain the best and smoothest path.

We took this time a new direction, which was straight forward between the rocks and the shore, that we might make ourselves acquainted with everything contained in the island. In effect, the line proceeding from Falcon's Stream to the Great Bay might be said to be the extent of our dominions, for, though Jack and I had discovered the adjacent exquisite country of the buffaloes, yet the passage to it by the end of the rocks was so dangerous, and at so great a distance, that we could not hope to settle ourselves upon its soil. We found, as usual, much difficulty in pushing through the tall tough grass, and alternately through the thick prickly bushes. We were often obliged to turn aside while I cut a passage with my hatchet. But these accidents seldom failed to reward my toil by the discovery of additions to our comfort: among others, some roots of trees curved by nature to serve both for saddles and yokes for our beasts of burden.

When we had spent about an hour in getting forward, a most singular phenomenon presented itself to our view: a small plain, or rather a grove of small bushes, to appearance almost covered with flakes of

snow, lay before us. Little Francis was the first to
call our attention to it, he being seated in the cart.

" Look, Father," cried he, " here is a place quite
full of snow !"

Though sure that what we saw could not be snow,
yet I was at a loss to explain the nature of what bore
so near a resemblance to it. Suddenly, however, a
suspicion crossed my mind, and was confirmed by
Fritz, who had darted forward and now returned with
one hand filled with tufts of cotton, so that the whole
surface of low bushes was in reality a plantation of
that article. The pods had burst from ripeness, and
the winds had scattered around their flaky contents,
so that the ground was strewed with them. They had
gathered in tufts on the bushes, and the air was full
of the gently-floating down.

The joy of this discovery was almost too great for
utterance. We collected as much cotton as our bags
would hold, and my wife filled her pockets with the
seed to raise it in our garden.

It was now time to proceed. We took a direction
towards a point of land which skirted the wood of
gourds, and, being high, commanded a view of the
adjacent country. I conceived a wish to remove our
establishment to the vicinity of the cotton plantation
and the gourd wood, which furnished so many of our
utensils. I pleased myself in idea with the view of the
different colonies of animals I had imagined, both
winged and quadruped; and in this elevation of my
fancy I even thought it might be practicable to erect
a sort of farmhouse on the soil, which we might visit
occasionally, and be welcomed by the agreeable
sounds of the cackling of our feathered subjects.

We accordingly soon reached the high ground, which
I found in all respects favourable to my design.

My plan for a building was approved, and we lost no time in pitching our tent. When we had refreshed ourselves with a meal, we each took up some useful occupation. My wife and the boys went to work with the cotton, which they thoroughly cleaned, and which was then put into the bags and served at night for bolsters and mattresses. I for my part resolved to look about in all directions, that I might completely understand what we should have to depend upon in this place. I had also to find a tree that would suit for the construction of a boat; and lastly, to meet with a group of trees at such fit distances from each other as would assist me in erecting my farmhouse. I was fortunate enough to find in this last respect exactly what I wanted. But I was not equally successful as regards the boat, the trees in the vicinity being of too small a bulk. I returned to my companions, whom I found employed in preparing beds of the cotton, upon which at an earlier hour than usual we all retired to rest.

CHAPTER XXXV

COMPLETION OF TWO FARMHOUSES—A LAKE

The trees that I had chosen for the construction of my farm were all about one foot in diameter; their growth was regular, and they formed a rough parallelogram with the longer side to the sea, the length being twenty-four feet and the breadth sixteen. I cut little hollow places or mortises in the trunks, at the distance of ten feet, one above the other, to form two stories.

The upper one I made a few inches shorter before than behind, that the roof might be in some degree shelving. I then inserted beams five inches in diameter in the mortises, and thus formed the skeleton of my building. We next nailed some laths from tree to tree at equal distances to form the roof, and placed on them a covering of pieces of bark cut into the shape of tiles, and in a sloping position for the rain to run off. As we had no great provision of nails, we used for the purpose the thorn of the acacia, which we had discovered the day before. The tree is known by the name of *Acacia with three thorns*, and exhibits, growing all together, three strong sharp-pointed thorns. We cut down a quantity of them and laid them in the sun, when they became as hard as iron, and of essential service.

On this occasion we made another agreeable discovery. My wife took up the remaining chips of the bark for lighting a fire, and we were surprised by a delicious aromatic odour which perfumed the air. On examining the half-consumed substance, we found some of the pieces to contain turpentine and others gum-mastich. It was less with a view to the gratifying our sense of smell, than with the hope of being able to secure a sort of pitch to complete our meditated boat, that we indulged our earnestness in the pursuit. The instinct of our goats, or the acuteness of their smell, discovered for us another acquisition. We observed with surprise that they ran from a considerable distance to throw themselves about on some particular chip of bark, and to chew it greedily. Jack seized a piece also, to find out what could be the reason of so marked a preference.

" Oh, it is indeed excellent," exclaimed he. " Only try this bit, brother Fritz, and tell us if it is not like cinnamon?"

Fritz was of Jack's opinion. My wife and I then followed and were convinced that it was cinnamon, though not so fine as that from Ceylon.

During our next meal we amused ourselves with a retrospect of the different discoveries we had made that day. I had to relate what I knew on the subject of the nature of these new productions: the turpentine, the mastich, and the cinnamon.

When our meal and the lecture were both ended, we resumed with ardour our undertaking of the farm.

We formed the walls of our building with matted reeds, interwoven with pliant laths to the height of six feet. The remaining space to the roof was enclosed with only a simple grating, that the air and light might be admitted. A door was placed in the front. We next arranged the interior, with as much convenience as the shortness of the time and our reluctance to use all our timber would allow. We divided it halfway up by a partition wall, into two equal parts. The largest was intended for the sheep and goats, and the smallest for ourselves. At the farther end of the stable we fixed a house for the fowls, and above it a sort of hay-loft for the forage. Before the door of entrance we placed two benches, contrived as well as we could of laths and odd pieces of wood, that we might rest under the shade of the trees and enjoy the exquisite prospect. Our own apartment was provided with a couple of the best bedsteads we could make of branches of trees, raised upon four legs and these were destined to receive our cotton mattresses. Our aim was to content ourselves for the present with these slight hints of a dwelling, and to consider hereafter what additions could be made. All we were now anxious about was to provide a shelter for our animal colonists, which should encourage them in the habit of assembling every evening in one place. For several days at first we took care to fill their troughs with their favourite food mixed with salt, and we agreed that we would return frequently to repeat this mode of invitation till they should be fixed in their expectation of finding it.

I had imagined we could accomplish what we wished at the farm in three or four days. But we found that a whole week was necessary, and our victuals fell short before our work was done. I therefore decided that on this trying occasion I would invest Fritz and Jack with an important mission. They were accordingly dispatched to Falcon's Stream and to Tent House to fetch new supplies for our subsistence, and also to distribute food to the animals.

During the absence of our purveyors, I rambled with Ernest about the neighbouring soil, to make what new discoveries I could.

We followed the winding of a river we had remarked, and which conducted towards the centre of the wall of rocks. Our course was here interrupted by an extensive marsh which bordered a small lake, the aspect of which was enchantingly picturesque. I perceived with joyful surprise that the whole surface of this swampy soil was covered with a kind of wild rice, ripe on the stalk, which attracted large flocks of birds. As we approached a loud rustling was heard, and we distinguished on the wing bustards and great numbers of smaller birds. We succeeded in bringing down five or six of them, and I was pleased to remark in Ernest a justness of aim that promised well for the future. The habits of his mind discovered themselves on this as on many previous occasions. He betrayed no ardour, he did everything with a deliberation that almost seemed to imply sluggishness; yet the coolness and constancy he applied to every attempt he had to engage in, so effectually assisted his judgment, that he was sure to arrive at a more perfect execution than the other boys. He had practised but little in the study of how to fire a gun; but Ernest was a silent observer, and accordingly his first essays were generally crowned with success. In this affair, however, of the birds, his skill would have proved fruitless if Jack's young jackal, which had followed us, had not plunged into the swamp and brought out the birds as they fell.

At a small distance was also Knips, who had taken his post on Ponto's back. Presently we saw him jump off and smell along the ground among some thick-growing plants, then pluck off something and eat of it voraciously. We ran to the spot to see what it could be, when, to the relief of our parched palates, we found he had discovered there the largest kind of strawberry.

After pursuing our way farther along the marsh, we reached the lake which was situated in a deep and abrupt valley. No traveller who is not a native of Switzerland can conceive the emotion which trembled at my heart as I contemplated this limpid, azure, undulating body of water, the faithful miniature of so many grand originals, which I had probably lost sight of for ever! My eyes swam with tears! " How glad I am to see a lake! I could almost think myself in Switzerland, Father!" said Ernest.

Alas, a single glance upon the surrounding pictures, the different characters of the trees, the vast ocean in the distance, destroyed the momentary illusion, and brought back our ideas to the painful reality that we were strangers in a desert island!

Another sort of object now presented itself to confirm the certainty that we were no longer inhabitants of Europe. It was the appearance of a quantity of swans which glided over the lake; their colour was a jetty black; and their plumage had so high a gloss as to produce, reflected in the water, the most astonishing effect. The six large feathers of the wing of this bird are white, exhibiting a singular contrast to the rest of the body. In other respects these creatures were remarkably like those of Europe.

We now began to look for the shortest path for rejoining our companions at the farm, which we reached at the same time with Fritz and Jack, who had well performed the object of their journey. We produced our strawberries and our specimen of rice, which were welcomed with pleasure and surprise.

The following day we took a silent leave of our animals and directed our course towards Cape Disappointment. On entering Monkey Wood, innumerable animals of the species from which it derives its name began to scamper away. We pursued our way, and arrived shortly after at the eminence we were in pursuit of in the vicinity of Cape Disappointment. We ascended it, and found it in every respect adapted to our wishes. From this eminence we had a view over the country which surrounded Falcon's Stream in one direction, and in others of a landscape comprehending sea, land, and rocks. When we had paused for a short time upon the beauties of the scene, we agreed that it should be on this spot we would build our second cottage. A spring of the clearest water issued from the soil near the summit, forming in its rapid course agreeable cascades. " Let us build here," exclaimed I, " and call the spot *Arcadia*!" to which my wife and all agreed.

We lost no time in again setting to work upon this undertaking. Our experience enabled us to proceed with rapidity, and our success was in every respect complete. The building contained a dining-room, two bed-chambers, two stables, and a store-room. We formed the roof square, with four sloping sides, and the whole had really the appearance of a European cottage, and was finished in the short space of six days.

CHAPTER XXXVI

THE BOAT—PROGRESS IN THE ABODE OF ROCKS

Our Arcadia being entirely completed, what remained to be done was to fix on a tree fit for a boat. After much search, I at length found one in most respects suitable to my views.

It was, however, no very encouraging prospect I had before me, being nothing less than the stripping off a piece of the bark that should be eighteen feet in length and five in diameter. I now found my rope-ladder of signal service. We cut quite round the trunk in two places, and then took a perpendicular slip from the whole length between the circles. By this means we could introduce the proper utensils for raising the rest till it was entirely separated. We toiled with increasing anxiety, dreading that we should not be able to preserve it from breaking. When we had loosened about half, we supported it by means of cords and pulleys, and when all was at length detached we let it down gently, and with joy beheld it lying safe on the grass. Our business was next to mould it to our purpose while the substance continued moist and flexible.

The boys observed that we had now nothing more to do than to nail a plank at each end, and our boat would be complete.   But I could not be contented with a mere roll of bark for a boat, and when I reminded them of the paltry figure it would make following the pinnace, they asked eagerly for my instructions. I made them assist me to saw the bark in the middle, the length of several feet from the ends.   These two parts I folded over till they ended in a point, naturally raised.   I kept them in this form by the help of the strong fish-glue, and pieces of wood nailed fast over the whole.   This operation tended to widen the boat in the middle, and thus render it of too flat a form. This we counteracted by straining a cord all round, which again reduced it to the due proportion, and in this state we put it to the sun to harden and fix.   Many things were still wanting to the completion of my undertaking, but I had not with me proper utensils. I therefore dispatched the boys to Tent House to fetch the sledge, and convey the boat there for our better convenience in finishing.

Before our departure for Tent House we collected several new plants.   We also made another trip to the narrow strait at the end of the wall of rocks, resolved to plant there a sort of fortification of trees, which should produce the double effect of discouraging the invasion of savages and of allowing us to keep our pigs on the other side, and thus secure our different plantations from injury.   We accomplished this to our satisfaction, and in addition we placed a slight drawbridge across the river beyond the narrow pass, which we could let down or take up at pleasure.   We now hastened our return to Arcadia, and after a night's repose loaded the sledge with the boat and other things, and returned to Tent House.

As soon as possible we resumed the completion of the boat.   In two days she had received a keel, a lining of wood, a flat floor, benches, a mast and triangular sail, a rudder, and a thick coat of pitch on the outside, so that the first time we saw her in the water we were all delighted at the appearance she made.

Our cow in the meantime had brought forth a bull calf. I pierced its nostrils, as I had so successfully practised with the buffalo, and the animal gave promise of future docility.

We had still two months before the rainy season, and we employed them in completing our grotto. We made the internal divisions of planks, and that which separated us from the stables of stone, to protect us from the smell of the animals. We took care to collect or manufacture a sufficient quantity of all sorts of materials, such as beams and planks, reeds and twigs for matting, pieces of gypsum for plaster, &c. At length the time of the rainy season was near at hand, and this time we thought of it with pleasure, as the period that would put us in possession of the enjoyments we had procured by unremitting industry and fatigue. We had an inexpressible longing to find ourselves domiciled and at leisure.

We plastered over the walls of the principal apartments with the greatest care, finishing them by pressure with a flat board. This work amused us all so much, that we began to think we might venture a step further in luxury, and agreed that we would make carpets with the hair of our goats. To this purpose we smoothed the ground in the rooms. We then spread over it some sail-cloth, which my wife had joined in breadths, and fitted exactly. We next strewed the goats' hair, mixed with wool from the sheep, over the whole. On this surface we threw hot water, in which cement had been dissolved. The whole was then rolled up, and beaten for a considerable time with hard sticks. The sail-cloth was now unrolled, and the inside again sprinkled, rolled, and beaten as before. This process was continued till the substance had become a sort of felt, which could be separated from the sail-cloth. We put it in the sun to harden, and found we had produced a very tolerable substitute for a European carpet. We completed two of them, one for our parlour and the other for our drawing-room, as we jocosely named them, both of which were completely fit for our reception by the time the rains had set in.

All we had suffered during the preceding rainy season doubled the value of the comforts with which we were now surrounded. In the morning our first care was to feed the cattle and give them drink. After this we assembled in the parlour, where prayers were read, and breakfast immediately served. We then adjourned to the common room, where all sorts of industry went forward. After dinner our work was resumed till night, when we lighted candles, which, as they cost no more than our own trouble, we did not refuse ourselves the pleasure of using. We had formed a portion of our dwelling into a small chapel, in which we left the crystals as produced by nature, and they exhibited a truly enchanting spectacle. Divine service was performed in it regularly every Sunday. I had raised a sort of pulpit, from which I pronounced such discourses as I had framed for the instruction of my affectionate group of auditors.

Jack and Francis had a natural inclination for music. I did the most I could in making a flageolet apiece for them of two reeds, on which they attained a tolerable proficiency. They accompanied their mother, who had a sweet-toned voice, the volume of which was doubled by the echoes of the grottos, and they produced together a very pleasing little concert.

Thus, we had made the first steps towards civilization. Separated from society, condemned perhaps to pass the remainder of life in this desert island, we yet possessed the means of happiness. We had abundance of necessaries, and many comforts. We had fixed habits of industry; we were in ourselves contented; our health and strength increased from day to day; the sentiment of tender attachment was perfect in every heart; and we every day acquired some new channel for the exertion of our physical and moral faculties.

Nearly two years had elapsed without our perceiving the smallest trace of civilized or savage man, without the appearance of a vessel upon the vast sea by which we are surrounded. Ought we then to indulge a hope that we shall once again behold the face of a fellow-creature? We encourage serenity and thankfulness in each other, and wait with resignation!

POSTSCRIPT BY THE EDITOR

I have presented the public, and in particular the sons of families, with the part I had in my possession of the journal of the Swiss pastor, who, with his family, were shipwrecked on a desert island. It cannot escape the observation of the parents who will read the work, that it exhibits a lively picture of the happiness which does not fail to result from the practice of moral virtues. Thus, in a situation that seemed calculated to produce despair, we see piety, affection, industry, and a generous concern for fellow-sufferers, capable of forming the basis of an unexpected state of happiness. We also see the advantage of including in the education of boys such a knowledge of the natural productions of the earth, of the various combinations by which they may be rendered serviceable, and of the use of tools, as may qualify them to assist others or preserve themselves under every possible occurrence. It now remains for me to inform the reader by what means the journal of the Swiss pastor came into my possession.

Three or four years subsequent to the occurrence of the shipwreck of the pastor and his family, an English transport was driven by the violence of a tempest upon the same shore. The name of the vessel was the *Adventurer*, Captain Johnson. It was on a voyage from New Zealand to the eastern coast of North America, by Otaheite, in the South Seas, to fetch a cargo of skins and furs for China, and to proceed from Canton to England. A violent tempest drove it from its track. The vessel beat about in unknown seas for many days, and was now so injured by the weather that the best hope of the captain and his company was to get into some port. They at length discovered a rocky coast, and as the wind had somewhat abated they made with all speed for the shore. When within a short distance they cast their anchor, and put out a boat to examine the coast and find a place for landing. They rowed backward and forward for some time without success, on account of the rocky nature of the coast. At length they turned a promontory, and perceived a bay whose calm water seemed to invite their approach. This was the *Safety Bay* of the wrecked islanders. The boat put on shore, and the officers beheld the traces of the abode of man. A handsome well-conditioned pinnace and a small boat were at anchor. Near the strand, under a rock, was a tent, and farther on in the rock a housedoor and windows announced European comforts and workmanship. The officers advanced towards the spot, and were met half-way by a man of middle age, dressed like a European and armed with a gun. The stranger accosted them with friendly tones and gestures. He spoke first German, and then some words in English. Lieutenant Bell, one of the English officers, who spoke German, answered. A mutual confidence immediately ensued. We need not add that the stranger was the father of the family whose adventures are narrated in the previous pages. His wife and children happened at the moment to be at Falcon's Stream. He had discovered the English ship with his glass, and, unwilling to alarm his family, had come, perceiving she bore that way, alone to the coast.

After an interchange of cordial greetings, and a hospitable reception of the officers at the grotto, the Swiss pastor put his journal into the hands of Lieutenant Bell, to be conveyed to Captain Johnson, that he also might become acquainted with the story of the islanders. After an hour's conversation the newly-made friends separated, in the expectation of meeting again on the following day. But Heaven had otherwise ordained.

During the night the tempest revived. The *Adventurer* dragged her anchor, and was obliged to steer to the bosom of the ocean. As there was no change of weather for several days, the vessel was driven so far from the coast of Safety Bay as to leave no possibility of returning, and Captain Johnson was compelled to renounce the gratification of seeing this most interesting family, or of proposing to convey them all to Europe.

Captain Johnson brought the journal of the Swiss pastor to England, from whence it was transmitted to a friend in Switzerland, who has deemed its contents an instructive lesson to the world.

At a later time the Pastor and his family were again heard of. Their island became a regular place of call for trading ships; and as prosperity increased, the Pastor was able to let his son Ernest proceed to Europe to pursue a course of professional study at one of the universities, where he attained distinction. The other sons married and remained with their parents as prosperous planters on their loved island home, to which Ernest also ultimately returned, bringing with him as wife his cousin Henrietta.

A word should be said about the title by which this entrancing record is known. Those who were responsible for publishing it, and giving the story to the world, could not but be struck by the many points of similarity between the adventures of the Swiss Pastor's family and those of the famous Robinson Crusoe. They therefore named the book *The Swiss Family Robinson Crusoe*, which in course of time became contracted to the title by which the book is now known, *The Swiss Family Robinson*.